1

THE CAROLINE QUEST

The electrifying new romance from the author of The Cornish Legacy

When her domineering but beloved mother dies, Holly Crozier is alone in the world. Her only hope of finding someone she might be able to call family is to trace her brother Jim's girlfriend, Caroline, and the baby she was carrying at the time of his death.

But when Holly reaches London, she discovers that Caroline may not want to be found...

THE CAROLINE QUEST

THE
CAROLINE QUEST

Barbara Whitnell

Severn House Large Print
London & New York

This first large print edition published in Great Britain 2002 by
SEVERN HOUSE LARGE PRINT BOOKS LTD of
9-15, High Street, Sutton, Surrey, SM1 1DF.
First world regular print edition published 2001 by
Severn House Publishers, London and New York.
This first large print edition published in the USA 2002 by
SEVERN HOUSE PUBLISHERS INC., of
595 Madison Avenue, New York, NY 10022

British Library Cataloguing in Publication Data

Whitnell, Barbara
    The Caroline quest. - Large print ed.
    1. Romantic suspense novels
    2. Large type books
    I. Title
    823.9'14 [F]

LINCOLNSHIRE
COUNTY COUNCIL

    ISBN 0-7278-7138-2

Except where actual historical events and characters are being
described for the storyline of this novel, all situations in this publication
are fictitious and any resemblance to living persons is purely
coincidental.

Printed and bound in Great Britain by
MPG Books Ltd, Bodmin, Cornwall.

One

Until the age of fifteen, I hated the British. Why? Because my mother told me to, that's why. If that makes me sound a dope, then I'm sorry – it really is necessary to have known my mother to understand. I've seen sixty-a-day men quit smoking, confirmed alcoholics turn from the demon drink, overweight actresses cut down to three lettuce leaves and a raw carrot per meal, all because she said so.

Why she harboured such negative emotions about our cousins across the pond I never knew. Not then. But there was no doubt whatsoever about what happened to make me change my mind. When I was just fifteen I met a cute sixteen-year-old English boy called Jeremy who was spending the summer in a house next to ours on Cape Cod. It's all of eight years since those hot, magical days in Corey Cove when we swam and sailed and laughed and kissed in the moonlight, but I've never forgotten him and still go a little weak at the knees when I think of him.

Naturally, I hardly expected Mom to feel the same way as I did about Jeremy, but I couldn't understand her resolute refusal to socialise with his folks or to see any good in him at all. She turned deaf ears to my assurances that the British were just *people* – some good, some bad, some boring, some fascinating.

'Their voices grate on me,' she grated. An actor once said her vocal chords sounded as if they were made of heavy-duty barbed wire wreathed in smoke, and I knew exactly what he meant. 'They're forged by centuries of arrogance and imperialism. And besides,' she added, 'what kind of a name is "Jeremy"?'

I ignored this irrelevance, forbearing to say that when it came to arrogance, Mom surely was the champion. If there'd been an international award, she would have beaten all comers. But as I grew older and understood her a little better, I recognised that this was simply a disguise it had been necessary for her to adopt, something she'd needed to make possible her hard climb to the top.

The white, clapboard house on Cape Cod was our vacation place, and although Jeremy was only there for the one summer that his dad was working in the States and I never saw him again after we returned to our New York apartment, it was sufficient to open my eyes and to prove to me that my mother could be both wrong and infuriating, although undoubtedly she was an admirable woman in many ways.

She had been left a widow when my brother Jim was eleven and I was just a baby. My father had died, leaving her with no assets but a sharp brain, an iron will, a kind of instinct about other people's talent and an endless capacity for work. I don't much remember the days when we were broke, but I know they happened. By the time I was aware of my surroundings, however, she had clawed her way up in the world of the theatre and was a highly respected theatrical agent with her own business: the Martha Crozier Theatrical Agency, Inc. We moved from a walk-up apartment via several intermediary addresses to a very swank place indeed overlooking Central Park, furnished with no expense spared. As well as going to Cape Cod pretty regularly, we vacationed in Acapulco, Bermuda, the Bahamas and even the continent of Europe; but we never, ever went to Britain.

As Jim got older, he became less and less at home in her world, and he was only with us in the new apartment for a short time. He was a rebel and argued endlessly with Mom about such things as the ethics of capitalism, the need for conservation, the validity of modern art and the sheer absurdity of our country's gun laws, to name but a few of the issues about which they held diametrically opposing views. He was convinced that America, the great consumer society, was hell-bent on self-destruction. I guess he was a little pompous and opinionated in those days, but though he changed a lot as the years went by, taking life and himself a lot less seriously, he never changed his basic belief that somehow things were managed much better in Britain.

Mom blamed everything on a school trip to London that he took when he was fifteen.

'You gathered all this in two short weeks?' she asked derisively. He had been telling us, at great length, about his impressions.

'No, of course not!' He shrugged helplessly. 'It's hard to explain. There's just so much history there. The place is soaked with it. You can feel the wisdom of the ages—'

'Oh, phooey!' Mom had heard enough and, flipping a dismissive hand in his direction, she swept from the room.

Though he was interested in all manner of current issues, art was Jim's first and most important love. He majored in History of Art in college, haunted galleries, collected paintings and had still more rows with Mom, who wanted him to forget what she described as 'all this nonsense' and join her in the Agency, demonstrating that for all their arguments, she had a healthy respect for his intelligence and acumen. And of course, she loved him; I knew that – knew, always, that he was the favourite. There was a time when I was resentful, jealous of the fact that she always gave him the best cut of meat, the biggest slice of pie. Jealous, even that he had a middle name. Can you beat that? He was called James Fenton Crozier and I was just Holly, which seemed to me in those days a nasty, prickly kind of name.

I got over it, of course. He never asked for any preferential treatment. He was just a nice, good-looking, upstanding sort of guy, and it was only natural that she should be proud of him.

But he wouldn't join the Agency, he told me. No way. She'd own him body and soul if he did, and for his own salvation he had to get away.

I, aged eleven and his devoted admirer, was the first one to learn that via some useful contacts in the art world he had secured a job in London in the fine art department of Lovells, the international auctioneers.

'Holly,' he said to me, coming into my room one day, his eyes bright with excitement, 'you're going to have to fasten your safety belt.'

'I sure am,' I breathed, after he had told me why. 'Mom's going to go ape.'

11

'I know.' I could tell, young as I was, that there was a touch of fear mixed in with the excitement. He crossed the room and sat down on the window seat, staring out at the park. It was fall, I remember, and all the trees were turning gold.

'She'll stop you,' I said. But when he turned to face me I could see by his expression that she wouldn't. Couldn't.

'I don't like to hurt her, but I've got to go,' he said. 'It's an incredible opportunity. I just hope she understands.'

'She won't.' I was only a kid, but I knew that much. 'Oh, Jim, I'll miss you terribly.'

He turned and held out his hand towards me, inviting me to curl up next to him on the window seat, and I thought, obeying his summons, what a great big brother he was. I'd long got over my childish resentment and now thought him far nicer and far better looking than any of the actors that frequented the house. And funny, too, in spite of his strong opinions. I felt hollow inside at the thought of losing him.

'I'll miss you, too,' he said, putting his arm round me and pulling me closer. 'When I'm settled you must come and stay and we'll do the grand tour.'

But we never did. When I finally saw the Tower of London and Buckingham Palace and Stratford-on-Avon, it was on a school trip. The day I waved goodbye to him at

Kennedy (Mom wouldn't come; it was the housekeeper who took me) was the last time I saw him, for almost three years later, before I was able to get to see him, he was killed by a hit-and-run driver.

It didn't make Mom like the British any better. You'd think, to hear her talk at the time, that no one had ever exceeded the speed limit in the good old US of A. The fact that the monster who had knocked Jim down and left him to die by the roadside was never caught hardly helped. Slow, inefficient, bumbling – she couldn't think of anything bad enough to say about the British police. It was only by degrees that I came to see that the anger was directed at herself as much as anyone else. Knowing she had let Jim go off without a kind word just about finished her.

She worked with an even greater frenzy and made a lot more money, particularly when, breaking the rule of a lifetime, she personally backed the proposed musical *Cherokee*, which, as the whole world now knows, broke all records on Broadway and then proceeded to do the same in London's West End. Even now, a day never passes without it being staged somewhere in the world.

For eight more years she was up at the crack of dawn, having probably been out at the theatre or dining at a nightclub until the small hours. No one ever saw her with a hair out of place or her nail varnish chipped; but then, suddenly, the heart seemed to go out of her and she decided to sell out to her partner. She felt like taking it easy for a change, she said, and wanted to spend her time checking the Dow Jones index and reading all the books she'd never had time for.

I was working in LA by this time, having landed a part in a soap opera that went out three times a week and kept me pretty busy, so I could only talk to her on the telephone. She was tired of it all, she assured me – all the hassles and the business lunches and the bruised egos and the megalomania. I never dreamt that the tiredness had another cause – never for one moment guessed, that night she called me to give me long-distance hell for my performance in that day's episode of *Bower Street*, that she was giving me hell for the last time.

I had just finished shooting for the day and was leaving the set when I was called to the phone. It was Frank Wheeler, Mom's long-time friend and attorney. Mom was dead, he told me. She had suffered a massive heart attack some time during the small hours and had been found that morning by the maid when she had taken in her morning coffee. It was a few days before Easter, when we were all due to take a short break, so flying back to New York immediately presented no problems for me.

'You mustn't take it so hard, Holly,' Frank said. He and Lilian, his wife, had come back to the apartment with me after the funeral. 'It was over so quickly. Martha would have hated to linger on, getting more and more dependent on others.

'Damn it, she was only sixty, Frank, and seemed even younger,' I said. 'Hardly at the dependent stage! She could have expected a lot more life yet.'

'I know, I know.' Poor guy, his little face was all furrowed, like a distressed hamster. Lilian looked much the same and suddenly, shockingly, I wanted to giggle hysterically, they looked so much alike in their misery.

'You shouldn't be on your own over the Easter holiday,' Lilian said to me. 'Isn't there anyone—?'

'No one,' I said, and it was true. I had friends, men and women, but there was no one I wanted near to me at that moment.

'What about the guy you're dating?'

Rick Mansfield, she meant; the man who played the part of the doctor in *Bower Street*. On screen he was warm, understanding, idealistic, witty, and very, very handsome. Half the teenagers of America were head over heels in love with him and he attracted twice as much fan mail as any other member of the cast.

Off screen, however – though still very, very handsome, which had fooled me for a while – he was hopelessly egocentric, with as much understanding and idealism as a rattlesnake, as well as being totally devoid of wit.

'I'm not dating him any more,' I said.

'Well, what about your friend – you know the one I mean! The one you went on vacation with. Kelly, isn't it? You and she were always close.'

'She married an engineer and went to live in New Mexico.'

Lilian bit her lip and gazed at me in an anguished kind of way.

'Such a tragedy there's no family.'

I said nothing to this. What was there to say? There'd been no one but Mom ever since Jim died. She'd had no siblings and neither had the long-dead father I'd never known, so there were no aunts or uncles or cousins.

In *Bower Street* I played the part of Mary Lou McAllister, youngest daughter of an Episcopalian minister, a ditzy blonde with a heart of gold, the one that did stupid things and said, 'Oh gee, I've done it *again!* I never meant *that* to happen!' when everything fell about her ears, as it invariably did. In the show I had three sisters and two brothers, devoted parents and a dear white-haired old grandma, who sat rocking on the stoop

16

shaking her head over my doings and uttering such things as 'born to trouble as the sparks fly upwards'. Strange that in real life my situation was so diametrically different.

Frank, it seemed, was thinking along the same lines. He reached out and patted my shoulder in an avuncular way.

'Well, you have your screen family,' he said.

I smiled as if in agreement, but the truth was that *Bower Street* was going down, down, down in the ratings and we all knew it would be axed very shortly. Its particular down-home charm was of the kind that had been out of date for years. It hurt me to admit it, but it was undoubtedly Rick Mansfield's association with the show that had kept it on screen for this long; now he wanted to be written out and it meant the end for all of us. Somehow the family spirit, if ever it existed, was disintegrating rapidly as everyone cast round for the next opportunity.

'I'll be all right,' I said, hoping to comfort Frank. 'I have to go back to LA when Easter's over, but I'm going up to Cape Cod first.'

The old, clapboard house at Corey Cove had always been a bolt hole for me; a haven in good times and bad. Somehow I felt I would come to terms with my mother's death and my aloneness up there. Convince myself that it didn't matter that I hadn't been able to tell either Jim or Mom goodbye before they were taken from me.

Both Frank and Lilian urged me to change my mind.

'Come and stay with us,' they said. 'You shouldn't be alone.'

They were so kind, and I knew they were sincere in their concern, for I had known them all my life. Lilian and my mother were particularly close, having been friends since the days when they were both young girls about town, and I knew too that Lilian's grief was probably as great as my own. Perhaps it was for that reason I felt I had to get away. I needed Corey Cove, needed the peace and the space and the pounding of the waves and the lack of pressure to do other than to mourn. So long as I saw those poor little hamster faces in front of me, I felt compelled to be cheerful and it was tearing me to bits.

I drove to the Cape in Mom's car, picked up groceries at the local store and continued to smile as I received condolences from all the kind people who had known us over the years. It was a relief to reach the house and to close the front door behind me. I leaned against it for a while, letting the atmosphere wash over me, conscious of my mother's presence not far away.

'I know you're there, Martha Crozier,' I called out; but there was no response, only the shush-shushing of the sea and the sound of the whirring of the old refrigerator in the kitchen.

I had expected to weep, and was not proved wrong. For two days I mooched about, not doing much but crying and sleeping and feeling sorry for myself and for her, because she had driven herself so hard and hadn't been able to enjoy the fruits of her labour. I kept thinking of different aspects of her life; the times when she'd forced herself to dress up and go out to some function when I knew she'd rather be at home with her feet up. The times when she was supposed to be on vacation but was always at the end of a phone, at everyone's beck and call. Then, suddenly, it was as if I heard her voice.

'That's enough! For Pete's sake, girl, pull yourself together,' she seemed to be saying, her voice as harsh and vigorous as ever. 'You've got as much backbone as a plate of Jell-O! You should be ashamed of yourself.'

I knew she was right. I made myself cook a proper meal, tidied the house, tidied myself, and felt a great deal better. The sadness was there, of course, and the sense of loss – it always would be – but somehow I knew that the paralysing helplessness had passed and that from now on I would be able to cope with the knowledge that I was on my own. Life went on – a platitude, but an inescapable fact.

I sat down and thought about my future. *Bower Street* was clearly on its last legs. I had wanted desperately to act, but over time I'd realised that I didn't really have what it takes to make the big time, and the thought of scraping around for second-rate bimbo parts like Mary Lou for the rest of a short acting career filled me with depression. A pretty face and good figure were useless without the talent to back them up. It was time, I felt, for my life to take a new turn – but in what direction?

I was, so Frank had assured me, a wealthy young woman. Maybe now was the time to do all the travelling I'd missed out on. That one trip to Europe had taken us to Paris and to Switzerland, which left hundreds of places to see, and the solitary school trip to Britain, though we had whizzed around some of the main tourist attractions, had merely whetted my appetite for more. Then there was Africa – the Far East – Australia—

Hey, hold on there, I told myself. First I had to decide what I would do about the apartment in New York, as well as this much-loved house. The first I would sell, I decided without any difficulty. It was far too big and too ostentatious for me. Not my sort of place at all. Frank had also advised me, as he had advised my mother, to sell the Corey Cove house. It was too big and rambling, needed too much attention, he'd said. It shouldn't be left empty. Something smaller and more modern would suit me better, be far less of a responsibility.

I'm sure he had common sense on his side, but selling was quite beyond me and I had no intention of doing so. I needed to know that this house was there in the background, waiting for me to come back to it, however far I travelled. Sorry, Frank, I said silently. Can't be done.

I went out the following day and walked along the beach, noting that things were changing. A few lots had been sold along the shore and houses were being built; still, the sea hadn't changed, nor the sky, nor the headland, nor the clean, fresh air. I breathed deep of it and felt a great deal steadier.

It was on my way back that I met Len Hancock, a neighbour we had known for years. He'd always been good to us – had kept an eye on the house when it was unoccupied and could be relied on to fix the odd tile or check the plumbing. We stopped and talked and he said how sorry he and Patsy had been to hear about Mom, and he reminisced a little about past incidents; the time he had taken us out in his Boston whaler and we'd seen a whole shoal of dolphins, and the night when we'd gone

21

over to his place for a barbecue and Mom had mixed lethal daiquiris.

'She was a heap of fun,' he said. 'Kind of gave the whole place a shot in the arm when she was around.'

I managed to smile and agree, and would have walked on, since I could feel the onset of tears once again. But he seemed reluctant to let me go. There was, it became clear to me, something else he wanted to say, though he seemed to find it difficult to begin.

'How's the family, Len? Is Patsy well?' I asked, making an effort to behave normally. It was all the spur he needed and he became animated.

Patsy was fine, he told me. And the children were fine, too. Doing real good, the lot of them. And his brother Hank – why, he'd left New York and was building a house just nearby. Only thing was, it was all taking longer than anyone had thought and so Hank and his wife were looking for somewhere to rent. It had crossed his mind – now, he didn't want to rush me or intrude on my grief – but had I thought what I wanted to do with our house? Maybe it was too soon to talk of such things, but if it was possible, Hank and Sally would love to rent it for six months or so, and even though he maybe shouldn't blow his own brother's trumpet, you'd go a long way to find finer tenants.

I said I would think about it; and the more I thought about it, the more it seemed like a good idea. I liked Len and Patsy, had met Hank and Sally and liked them, too. It would be a comfort, if I were truly to go on an extended holiday, to know that the house was occupied and looked after. When I returned to it after my walk I wandered up to my mother's room and stood looking out at the sea.

'Shall I?' I asked. But this time I heard no voices.

I turned and looked around the room. Any tenant would clearly want to use this as the main bedroom since it was the largest, had its own bathroom and commanded the best view. No point in being sentimental, I thought, looking at the dressing table where my mother had sat so often, and the desk where she had written her letters. I would have to bite the bullet and clear out all her belongings.

It was not a happy task. There were old, casual clothes hanging in the closet, and most evocative of her presence of all were a couple of bright silk kaftans she delighted to wear on summer evenings. I took them down and held them both at arm's length in front of me. They seemed to bear the shape of her slim, dynamic body and what I was to do with them, I couldn't imagine. I couldn't bear the thought of anyone else wearing them, yet they were far too good to throw away. Maybe I'd pass the buck and give them to Lilian.

On the dressing table were half-empty jars and bottles of make-up, a hairbrush with a few silvery-blonde hairs still enmeshed in it, and nail varnish in the clear red colour she liked best. In the drawers underneath underwear carried traces of her perfume.

All the drawers were neat, for Mom had hated mess and clutter. Scarves were neatly folded, pantyhose rolled and kept in little silk sachets designed for the purpose. I kept some things, threw away others. Dusted the empty drawers, and put them back. Then I turned my attention to the desk in the far corner of the room.

It was a bureau with a top that let down. As expected, its interior was incredibly neat, everything in little compartments. Curiously I took out the bundles of letters and photographs and old bills, feeling like an intruder. Not that there was anything particularly private or unexpected among them, though I was a little surprised to see an old, postcard-sized studio portrait of my father, who had died three months after I was born. The marriage had not been a happy one, and though I had seen the photograph before it had never been on display and was not something that I would have expected her to keep so carefully.

Tucked away as it was, she had probably even forgotten it was still in existence.

As a child, I was always curious about him, never having known him myself.

'I never knew him, either,' Jim said once, when I pressed him for information. 'I can't tell you what he was like. He wasn't around much. You'll have to ask Mom.'

I had already asked and had got nowhere. He was handsome, Mom had said, and a good actor. Beyond that I learned nothing.

'Why wasn't he around?' I asked Jim. He shrugged.

'Dunno. Just wasn't. I really don't remember him much.'

'He must have come home sometimes,' I reasoned.

'Guess so. He just wasn't the kind of dad who'd take a kid fishing or to a ball game. I don't think he liked kids much. To tell the truth, I was a bit frightened of him, he was such a stranger. He was kind of powerful,' he added, after a moment's thought.

'Powerful? How powerful?'

'Dunno. Just kind of—' He'd hesitated, trying to find the right word. 'Threatening, I guess. As if he could get real mad if a guy didn't behave.'

It wasn't until I'd been twelve, going on thirteen, that I'd learned the truth. All I knew until then was that my father had drowned in a boating accident. It took a mean-spirited older girl I'd beaten to a starring role in a school play to taunt me with the true facts. He'd been a drunk and a druggie, she said, and he'd fallen off a friend's yacht and drowned himself after an all-night orgy with a group of film actors and starlets.

'Well, that's what they said they were, but really they were nothing more than call-girls,' she'd told me in shocked tones, loving every minute.

'That's nonsense!' I'd said.

'No, it's not. My mom told me, and she knows all about it because it was in the papers. So *there!*'

When I confronted my mother, she confirmed that this account was largely true.

'You should have told me,' I flung at her bitterly. 'I felt such a fool, not knowing.'

'Maybe I should,' she admitted. 'I was going to, when you were older.'

'You might have known someone would tell me. After all, he was a famous actor.'

'Not so famous,' she said wearily, and sighed. 'Sure, it was a nine-day wonder, but I thought it had all been forgotten a long time ago. God knows, I've almost succeeded in forgetting it myself.'

'He was my *father!*'

She'd looked at me in silence for what seemed a long while, then she sighed again and put her arms round me.

'He wasn't a bad man, sweetheart. Just very weak and self-indulgent and quite unsuited to marriage. He couldn't take responsibility, you see. Not for himself or for anyone else. You won't grow up like that, not with me behind you. You mustn't let it worry you.'

It did worry me, though less and less as time went by, until in later years I'd hardly ever given him a thought. Until now. I studied the face of the man in the photograph with the utmost concentration. How terrible, I thought, if I turned out to be weak and irresponsible and self-indulgent, too. After all, here I was, twenty-three years old, a failed actress, with plenty of money but not an idea in the world of what I ought to do with my life. Did some gene lurk within me that would prevent me doing anything worthwhile?

The face, at least, was nothing like mine. I could see no likeness – never had done, neither to me nor Jim. He was good-looking, as my mother had said, but in a dark and smouldering kind of way. He would, I thought, have made a good Heathcliff.

As I studied the photograph, Jim's long-ago description came to mind. He did look both powerful and threatening, with an added touch of petulance, as if irritation were boiling just below the surface. It struck me that even if I had never heard anything

27

about him, I could have guessed that he was the kind of man to think only of himself, not of his wife and children at home. It was not the kind of face that appealed to me or would ever attract me, but even so I found I could not throw the photograph away. I put it in a shoebox I found in the wardrobe, together with various other pictures that were in the desk, mostly of myself and Jim when young.

I turned my attention to the desk again and found that in the centre was a small, locked drawer. It presented no problem for me, for I had seen the key in a little porcelain box on the dressing table. Inside there were more papers; private letters, for the most part years old and of no particular significance. I riffled through them, tore them across and threw them away. At one time my mother had opened an account with a local Corey Cove bank, and although she had closed it a few years later, beneath the letters was the half-used cheque book and a few bank statements. Under them was another letter consisting of several pages, and I unfolded them feeling nothing more than a mild curiosity.

How could I possibly have known that what I was to read would turn my world upside down?

Two

There was an English address at the top –
18 Cranleigh Road, the address that had
been Jim's, I recognised with a shock – yet
the letter was dated 9th July, 1990, nine
years previously and just over a month *after*
he had been killed. I remembered that
period so well. His body had been flown
back to New York and we had come to the
Cape immediately after the funeral service.
We had stayed for the rest of the summer.
    'Dear Mrs Crozier,' the letter ran.

I know that this will come as a shock to
you, and it is hard for me to know where
to begin. I am still in a state of shock
myself, and have not been able to bring
myself to write before. Now I feel I can
put it off no longer.
    I am aware that Jim never told you of
my existence. The truth is that we were
very close – in fact, we loved each other
and for the last four months of his life we
lived together.
    I am also aware that for some reason

you have an antipathy towards the British. This is why Jim never mentioned me to you – which was the only thing I can think of about which we differed. I felt that you should be told, particularly as we would undoubtedly have married had Jim lived.

The reason I am writing now is that only the week after he died, I had confirmation that I was pregnant. I am well into my third month of pregnancy, and our baby is due towards the end of January next year. I know that you and Jim did not see eye to eye about a good many things but, for all that, he felt a great affection and respect for you and I am certain he would want you to know about your prospective grandchild. What you do about it is up to you.

Neither of my own parents is alive. My father was in the army and was killed in Northern Ireland ten years ago, while my mother died last year. I have no brothers or sisters, so am very much on my own apart from my father's sister, who has always been very good to me. For this reason, I have no doubt that friends, when they hear of my situation, will urge me to have a termination, but this is something I have no intention of doing and I hope you will back me in this decision. This baby is a part of Jim, whom I loved with all my heart, and whatever the difficulties I will keep him and bring him up myself. For some reason I feel quite convinced I will have a boy!

I am a competent and experienced secretary, fluent in both French and German and up to date with all the latest information technology. I feel sure I could find work anywhere. If you would like me to come to America so that you could be part of your grandchild's life, I would be willing to do so as I have few ties here.

On the other hand, I am not asking for anything you feel unwilling to give. I am young and healthy and very independent. I am perfectly capable of fending for myself and my child, but thought it only fair to you and to Jim to let you know the state of affairs.

Hoping to hear from you, I am yours sincerely, Caroline Bethany.

Below the signature, in my mother's handwriting, was a further note:

One thousand dollars sent July 23, 1990.

And she never said a word to me! Not then, not since.

There was no other comment, no clue as

to what she might have replied to this un-known, bereaved girl. I read the letter through again, my disbelief growing. How brave was Caroline Bethany, how admirable her attitude. And how solitary she was! In my over-emotional state of mind I found the newly banished tears welling in my eyes again.

But then the importance of what she had written hit me in the solar plexus and excitement took the place of sadness. Somewhere in England I had a nephew – or a niece, I reminded myself, seeing that I had followed the unknown Caroline Bethany in assuming the child would be a boy.

It was clear that my mother had not invited her to America – unless, of course, she had sent the money so that Caroline could pay her air fare if she wanted to. Somehow I doubted it. The very fact that she had said nothing to me made me think that her reply had been cool, for why, other-wise, had there been no other communi-cation? No Christmas or birthday cards, no photographs? Surely these would have been in evidence if she had shown any kind of friendliness?

Of course, I had been very young at the time; I'd celebrated my fourteenth birthday only three days before that letter was written. Now I was much closer to the age that Jim had been at the time of his death, and the enormity of my mother's action took my breath away.

'My God, Martha Crozier,' I said to the spirit within that house. 'You could be a bitch when you put your mind to it.'

I had always known it, of course. She had laughed at misfortune and never gave in to despair during the bad times. She was smart and attractive, not demonstratively loving but casually affectionate and always reliable – but by heaven, she was hard-nosed. And she sure as hell didn't like the British.

Was it a boy, I wondered? I was on fire, suddenly, with the desire to find out, thrilled beyond expression to think that after all I was not entirely alone in the world. Somewhere out there was a nine-going-on-ten-year-old boy or girl who was Jim's child.

I dialled the number for international information and asked if they had a Caroline Bethany listed at the Chiswick, West London address I remembered so well from the days when I had written regularly to Jim.

I hardly dared hope that she would still be there, and of course, she wasn't. I put the phone back in its cradle and reread the letter. When I had done so, I sat chewing my lip, thinking hard.

Lovells, I thought. The firm of fine art auctioneers Jim had worked for. This was my only avenue of enquiry. There must surely be someone still working there who was there at the time of Jim's death, someone who would remember him and his girlfriend and would know where to find her. Maybe Caroline had worked there, too. Maybe she still did! I called International Enquiries once more to get Lovells' number and was about to dial it when I realised it was Easter Sunday and that there was hardly likely to be anyone at work. My call would have to wait for some future date.

Meantime, however, all my indecision had left me. I knew now what I had to do. The moment I was released from *Bower Street* I would fly to England, find Caroline Bethany wherever she was – surely it couldn't be difficult in such a small country? – rescue her from the life of drudgery I felt sure she must be living and bring her back to the States. My imagination leapt ahead. I certainly wouldn't sell this house now! It was a kid's paradise and Jim's boy would love it. There, I was doing it again! It could just as easily be a girl. It didn't matter. She'd love it, too.

I had one night in New York before flying back to LA and spent it going through Mom's papers there. There was certainly plenty to deal with. Letters of sympathy, a few bills, junk mail which still kept coming even though it was I and not she who had to throw it in the bin. There was also a list from

34

the Chapel of Rest of all the people who had sent flowers to the funeral. Some famous names were there, the cream of Broadway, but there were many whom I recognised as friends and acquaintances. Others were completely strange to me. Who, I wondered, was Olga Stanovsky? She sounded like a Russian spy. And as for Sir Timothy Crofthouse – well, he sounded just the kind of Englishman my mother couldn't abide. How she could ever have met him was a total mystery to me, but I assumed him to be an actor, even though I had never heard of him. I could almost see him in my mind's eye – grey and distinguished and probably very handsome in a military kind of way. That kind of man could often have a long, but totally unstarry career in Hollywood playing earls or lords or aristocratic roles. Sometimes they did very well as butlers, too. Whatever; I just hoped that receiving a wreath from him wasn't enough to make my Anglophobe mother turn in her grave.

I was more interested in the older papers I found in her office and spent a long time going through them just in case there was any more information about Caroline. I found no other references to her, but I did unearth a photograph of Jim and another guy which must have been taken a year or so after his defection to England. I remembered it arriving – remembered thinking how distinguished Jim looked in his grey suit with a smart shirt and a tie. Mom had been annoyed by it because in some strange and indefinable way her all-American son looked so English. It was the suit that did it, I guess, and the fact that they were standing beside an ancient stone wall covered in rambling roses.

'Steve and me in the garden of Summerton Manor,' he had written on the back.

We went there to work, but personally I just couldn't feel more at home in these stately surroundings. Sorry, Mom!

They were there because Lovells was holding an auction sale of someone's art collection. I also remembered how he had written a funny letter about it which Mom had read, straight-faced, before tossing it across to me. But of that letter or of others he had written, nothing remained.

I'd forgotten Steve, but remembered now that he had figured quite a lot in Jim's letters of the time. He'd worked at Lovells too, and now that I thought about it, I seemed to recall accounts of a holiday the two of them had spent in Europe. Hadn't they gone skiing together? And to Italy to look at art treasures? He had the kind of looks that I liked, I decided, as I studied the photograph – unlike those of the subject of that other picture I had found in my mother's desk. Thinnish face, dark hair, nice smile. Ten years older now, of course – thirty-threeish, perhaps. Yes, an attractive man was Steve; but Steve *who?* Had Jim ever mentioned his last name? If he had, I couldn't bring it to mind.

It was all such a long time ago, but at least it was one more tenuous link. And then and there I made another snap decision. Why bother to phone Lovells first, when maybe I wouldn't get beyond the telephone operator? To hell with wasting time with intermediaries. I would just go.

Back at the *Bower Street* studio, the pall of gloom that hung over the set told its own story. The soap's days were numbered. I felt sorry for the other members of the cast, who were worried about where the next job was coming from – but for myself, the parting of the ways couldn't have come at a better time.

I had to go back to New York to see to a few business matters, like signing various papers connected with my mother's will and putting the apartment on the market. I did a little shopping (something told me that spring in England might, for all that Robert Browning said about it, be somewhat chillier than Los Angeles), and I met Lilian for lunch, mainly to ask her advice regarding London hotels.

There was only one worth patronising, she told me. You could keep your Hiltons, ignore your Dorchesters and Savoys.

'You have to stay at Quentins! It's so cute and comfortable and you'll be looked after beautifully. Frank and I would never go anywhere else. Mind you, it's not cheap – but then you've no need to worry about that.'

'Is it somewhere central?'

'Oh, sure! Right off Piccadilly. You'll adore it. Wait – I have the phone number in my purse. You can call them right now.'

I took the card she produced but declined the use of her mobile phone. I'd do it from home, I said. I needed to contact the airline office first.

For some reason that I could not explain to myself, I had said not one word to Lilian about the cause of my sudden desire to go to London. It was as if I hardly dared mention the possibility of finding Jim's child in case I discovered that there was no child and no Caroline Bethany – that the whole thing was some pointless hoax, no more than a dream that would dissolve and dis-appear in the light of day. It meant too much to me. Still, it seemed that Lilian approved of my actions.

'I'm glad you're taking this trip,' she said, 'though I do wish you could find a friend to go with you. Isn't there anyone in the show who'd keep you company?'

'No. And anyway—'

'I'd come myself if it weren't for the fact that Frank's booked a cruise. I adore London, especially in the spring – though do take some warm clothes, dear. Maybe Frank could postpone our trip and then I could—'

'No, really, Lilian,' I said hastily. 'It's sweet of you even to think of it, but you mustn't dream of such a thing. I really don't mind going on my own. There's so much I want to see and do.'

'Well—' Lilian still looked dubious. 'I guess it'll do you good to get away.'

She insisted on driving me to Kennedy the next morning. We didn't talk much – or at least, I didn't talk, since Lilian herself had much to say about a production of *All My Sons* she and Frank had seen on Broadway the night before, particularly the actress who played the mother and was, in real life, having an affair with 'that simply divine English actor – the one who won all those awards'.

'My dear, she must be all of fifteen years older than he is! It seems almost obscene.'

I made suitable noises, put in the odd meaningless word. It was all Lilian wanted and I am sure she didn't notice my abstraction; the truth was that so wrapped up was I in thoughts of the search for Caroline and her child I could think of nothing else. In fact, my excited anticipation was growing with every second and once on the aeroplane I found myself unable to concentrate on reading or the movie that in any case turned out to be one that I'd already seen. A Wall Street trader in futures had the seat next to mine and did his best to engage me in conversation, but I could summon no interest in him either, and eventually he gave up the struggle and busied himself with his laptop while I stared out at the blue, blue sky above the clouds and tried to make plans, knowing even as I did so that it was a useless occupation. The entire enterprise was one huge question mark. I would have to take everything a step at a time.

Three

Quentins didn't look particularly impressive on the outside; it was just a big London house with steps up from the street, a shiny brass balustrade on each side. Once inside, however, I knew at once that Lilian had been right in recommending it so highly. There seemed an air of unobtrusive, efficient opulence about it, a warm, luxurious elegance, like the best of country houses in the heart of London.

A beautifully proportioned staircase swept upwards from the ground floor, but I was taken aloft in a cute little gilt elevator as far as the third, after which I had to ascend a few stairs that were dark and crooked and delightfully Dickensian. You would have found nothing like them in your Sheratons or Hiltons, nor was my odd-shaped room under the eaves like any other I had ever seen. I thought no worse of it for that, however. To me it all added to the delightfully olde English atmosphere which was clearly Quentins' speciality. I loved the trellised wallpaper, the flower paintings on the wall

41

and the antique bureau in my room, and thrilled to the panorama of rooftops and river that was revealed the morning after my arrival when I drew the drapes aside. The combination of excitement and jet lag meant that I'd hardly slept at all, but the adrenalin was pumping and I couldn't wait to get on with the day.

It had been dark when I arrived. Now London was laid before me – or at least, part of it was. On my way from the airport any ideas I might have cherished about it being easy to find Caroline in such a small country quickly flew out the window. I should have remembered from my previous school trip that the place was seething with people, crammed with houses and cars, and that London itself seemed to go on for ever. Still, I wasn't despondent.

The sun that was shining seemed a little diffident and the sidewalks glistened with the rain that had fallen during the night, so I thought it prudent to wear jeans, sweater and Burberry when I set out for Lovells. But before I ventured out I asked directions from the girl at the reception desk, who was, I discovered, the very same person who had spoken to me in New York when I'd booked the room. She was about my age, name of Sue, pretty as a picture and eager to help. My spirits were high as I swung along the shiny street where daffodils and tulips shouted at me from window boxes and the whole world looked newly washed. I felt quite certain, suddenly, that everything was going my way, a feeling helped along by the fact that Lovells and the hotel, quite by chance, proved to be in the same area, not very far from St James's Palace – a happy coincidence that seemed to augur well.

I found Lovells without too much trouble, though the entrance was so unimpressive that I walked right on past it and was forced to retrace my steps. Inside, I gained quite a different impression – something I ought to be getting used to, I told myself, remembering my reaction to Quentins. Apparently houses in England made a speciality of being bigger on the inside than on the outside.

There was, I could see from various notices, a sale that day, and the atmosphere was one of tightly controlled activity. Signs directed people to auction rooms somewhere to the right of the entrance hall, and already there was a considerable stream of people coming in from the street. Meanwhile, men in overalls were carrying pieces of furniture in another direction and young men strode purposefully around with files and clipboards.

There was a large reception area to the left, rather like a left-luggage office, except that it contained china and pictures and ancient pieces of furniture instead of suit-cases. I waited in line and eventually it was my turn to speak to the girl behind the counter. She was younger than I was and I wasn't at all surprised when she told me she had never heard of Jim. Was there anyone still working there, I asked her, who had been part of the Fine Art department ten years earlier when my brother was also there?

She chewed a thumb nail and twiddled a curl.

'Ten years ago?' she repeated incredulous-ly, as if I were asking for intimate knowledge of the early Palaeolithic age.

'Surely there's someone?' I urged.

'Well—' She glanced over her shoulder in a hunted kind of way. 'Maybe Mr Higgin-son. He's kind of—' She seemed to search her vocabulary for the right word. 'Old,' she finished, a little lamely.

'Could I see him?'

'Well—' She chewed her lip. 'He was around just now, but he's kind of important. I expect he's busy.'

'I don't mind waiting.' This statement did nothing to remove the worried look from her face. 'Meantime,' I went on, 'can you tell me if you have a Caroline Bethany working here?'

The girl shook her head.

'Not that I know of.'

'Well, maybe—' I dove into my purse for the photograph, suddenly remembering it. 'Maybe you know this man. His name is Steve.'

She took the picture from me, shook her head with the corners of her mouth pulled down, and was about to return it when she suddenly changed her mind and took another look.

'Hang on a mo,' she said. 'Maybe I do know him.' She looked up at me with a quick grin that made her look much prettier. 'Not bad, is he?'

Not bad at all, I thought – as indeed I had thought ever since I had discovered the photograph.

'That was taken roughly ten years ago,' I said.

'I'm sure I've seen him. Yes, I'm sure he's the one. He doesn't work here, but he comes to the sales quite often. He's a dealer. Hey, Viv.' She turned round to summon another girl who was crouched down in the far reaches of the reception area peering at the underside of a table. 'Have you got a moment? Come and look at this photo. Isn't it that chap from Richmond who bought the Queen Anne chairs last week?'

Viv, once she had straightened up, proved to be a more on-the-ball person altogether, several years older than the first girl and considerably more intelligent. I hastily outlined the situation, keeping to the bare essentials. My brother had worked for the company during the late eighties, I told her, but had died in an accident in 1990. Now I was in England I was anxious to trace his closest friend.

'I'm pretty sure that's the man who bought the chairs,' Viv said, having given the photograph her consideration. 'Ten years on? Thirty-something? Yes, I'll stick my neck out and say that's him.'

'You have his name and address?'

'They must be on file. Tracey, could you see to it? I must get into the auction room.'

Tracey retired from view into an inner office and, hopes rising, I waited – joined, at length, by a small man in a long overcoat staggering under the weight of a large card-board carton in which, he told me, he was carrying a collection of Goss china that was worth a small fortune.

'My old dad would have been amazed,' he confided to me once he had set the carton down. 'Common as dirt when he bought it, Goss china was, but worth a mint now, so they tell me.'

I made congratulatory noises, not knowing (or, I have to admit, caring) the remotest thing about Goss china. I was awaiting Tracey's reappearance far too urgently to pay much attention to him. Tracey, however, seemed unaccountably delayed.

A tall, thin man with rimless eyeglasses and an air of authority strode past, checked at the sight of me and the Goss china gentleman, and came over to us.

'Is there no one to attend to you?' he asked. 'There should be a girl—'

'She's finding some information for me,' I explained. 'An address.'

'Oh?' He looked disapproving, as if this was no part of her duties, and I smiled at him placatingly without any visible thawing on his part. He had a little, pursed mouth under a sharp nose and a way of lifting his head to peer through the bottom half of his eyeglasses which gave him an unpleasantly disdainful expression. It occurred to me suddenly that since he was past the first flush of youth, he could conceivably have been with the firm in Jim's time – might even be the elderly Mr Higginson that Tracey had referred to. I ignored the disdain and flashed him my very best Mary Lou McAllister smile.

'I wonder,' I said, 'if there's any chance that you could help me? My name is Crozier – Holly Crozier. Jim, my brother, used to work here. Maybe you remember him?'

'Ah!' I had all his attention now. His eyes, seen through the bottom half of his eyeglasses, were very large and very pale and were staring at me with a sudden sharpening of interest.

47

'You *do* remember him!' I said excitedly.

'Of course.' He gave a thin smile. 'How could I ever forget him, Miss Crozier? He was in my department – and, I may say, he was the first and last American we have ever employed at Lovells.'

'Oh? Why do you say that?'

He shrugged his shoulders, still with that same superior smile on his face. 'He was a forthright young man, as I recall. You Americans rather pride yourself on that, of course. No, your brother had no time at all for what one might call the niceties. He knew his job, I have to admit, though perhaps not so well as he thought. His problem was a lack of diplomacy. He rubbed people up the wrong way. Still—' Suddenly he seemed to collect himself, to remember that Jim had met an early death. 'It was a very sad accident, Miss Crozier. A tragic business.'

'It sure was.' I managed to control my anger at the way he spoke of Jim, though it hardly endeared the man to me and I certainly didn't recognise his description of my brother. Apart from his arguments with Mom, he had been the most equable, easygoing of characters, with not an enemy in the world.

I turned to Tracey, who had returned from the inner office and was giving Mr Higginson a small, scared smile as she approached me.

'Just finding an address, Mr Higginson,' she whispered breathlessly, clearly scared to death of the man. She handed me the paper before turning to deal with the Goss china man. On it she had written: 'Steve Maitland, 2 Mermaid Passage, Richmond, Surrey.'

'This man,' I said, holding the paper towards Mr Higginson. 'I believe he was a friend of my brother's. Did you know him, too?'

'Ah,' he said again. He took the paper and looked at it with a a kind of amused sneer, his eyeglasses glinting in the light.

'Young Mr Maitland!' He handed it back to me. 'Yes, I seem to remember that he and your brother were friends. He left us some years ago to open his own business, the foolish fellow! Like all the young, he wouldn't be advised by those who knew better. On his beam ends now, of course.'

'Did you also know Caroline Bethany? She was a friend, too.'

I could have sworn that the name rang a bell with him. There was a sudden flicker in those pale eyes, but even so he shook his head.

'My dear young woman, I had no knowledge of your brother's private life, nor did I want it. I'm sure he had many friends. From what I remember, he and Mr. Maitland

49

enjoyed – er – what one might call an active social life. Rather too active, I would venture to say.'

I decided to ignore that, too, but the way he spoke made my hackles rise.

'Caroline Bethany didn't work here, then?'

'Not to the best of my knowledge. Of course, I can't be expected to remember everyone. People come and go.'

'If you do happen to remember her, you could always contact me at my hotel. Look, I'll write the name down.' I delved into my purse and found a card engraved with my name. Hastily I scribbled 'Quentins Hotel' on it and handed it to him. He took it absently, his attention now attracted by Tracey who appeared to be having some trouble with the Goss china gentleman.

'Just leave it, sir,' Mr Higginson said, his tone somehow managing to express exasperation with both parties involved. 'The girl is no more than a receptionist.'

I couldn't remember when I had taken such a dislike to anyone. Tracey might not be the brightest girl in the world, but nothing could excuse the dismissive scorn in his voice.

'Goodbye, Tracey,' I said. 'Thanks so much for your help. You were great.'

I turned abruptly towards the door, pointedly avoiding any such farewell to Mr Higginson, but had gone no more than a few steps when I heard his voice calling my name.

'Yes?' I turned to face him.

'Miss Crozier—' He was smiling at me now, but it was a salesman's smile, a politician's smile. His eyes glinted as coldly as ever. 'May I ask your purpose in coming here and asking all these questions? If I'm to help you at all, I think I ought to know.'

'Do you?' I had given up any attempt to be other than icily cold towards him. 'I can't honestly see why. Anyway, I thought you said you weren't able to help me.'

'I don't think I can, but clearly you consider there might be a chance I could remember something. Otherwise, why give me the name of your hotel?'

I thought this over. He had a point, but somehow I felt a great reluctance to confide in him about Caroline's pregnancy. Or about anything, come to that. I felt quite sure that anything I said would somehow be turned against Jim.

'I – just want to meet the people who were Jim's friends,' I said. 'That's not unreasonable, is it?'

'Well, I'm not at all sure I agree. No good ever comes of dwelling on the past.' He was still smiling that false smile, and his tone had softened considerably. 'A word to the wise. Take it from one who's been on this earth considerably longer than you, my

51

dear. I'm not unsympathetic, but it's been a long time. For your own happiness, put your grief behind you and concentrate on the future.'

Patronising bastard, I thought, and gave an equally false smile of my own.

'You're right, of course,' I said.

'As for finding his friends – well, my dear young lady, I don't want to discourage you, but really it's an exercise that's doomed to failure. London has a very shifting population, you know. People move away, can't be found. You're here on holiday, and I hate to think of you wasting your precious time following all kinds of blind alleys. Why don't you simply enjoy all the country has to offer?'

If there was one thing I was not, I thought, it was this gentleman's dear young lady. My hackles rose even higher.

'Perhaps I will,' I said. 'After I've looked up Steve Maitland, that is.'

He shook his head at me, apparently more in sorrow than in anger. I turned and walked away towards the door, but when I got there I was forced to stand back and wait a moment as a woman staggered in with a large oil painting. And as I waited I turned and glanced back the way I had come.

Higginson still stood there, staring after me, his expression blank, the light catching his spectacles again. Then, as if seeing he was observed, he swung on his heel and strode away.

I had no idea how far Richmond was from London. Wherever it was, it seemed a good idea to telephone ahead, so I went back to the hotel. The friendly receptionist, who told me she had lived in London all her life, said that it was on the river, not far at all, and that I could get there on the tube. Meantime, she would find out the telephone number and put me through right away.

I listened to the phone ringing at 2, Mermaid Passage, Richmond, with my heart pounding so hard I could hardly hear myself think. A male voice answered.

'Maitland Antiques.'

'Is that Steve Maitland?'

'Speaking.'

'It's Holly Crozier here. Jim Crozier's sister.'

'*Holly Crozier!*' He sounded astonished. 'My God, what a surprise! Are you over on holiday? We must get together.'

Suddenly I found it hard to breathe, still more to find words.

'Yes,' I said. 'Yes, I'd like that. In fact, I – I really want to talk with you. It's awfully important.'

'Yes?' He sounded mildly bewildered. 'This isn't just a social call, then? How

53

can I help?'

'I'm desperate to find Caroline.'

'Caroline?' The bewilderment had intensified. 'Caroline Bethany? I'm afraid I haven't seen her for years. I've no idea where she is now.'

The disappointment was shattering and it took a second or two to pull myself together.

'What happened to her? Did she leave London?'

'Well, I assumed so. It was just about the time that I was going into business on my own.' He paused, and when he resumed speaking his voice seemed hesitant, regretful. Even guilty. 'I'm sorry to say we lost touch. I had an awful lot on my plate around then.'

Just when she needed all the friends she'd ever had?

I managed not to say it, but there must have been some outraged quality in my silence that reached him over the wire, for he hastened to explain further.

'I phoned a couple of times and left messages on her answerphone, but she never rang back. Then one day when I was in her area I called round at the flat. The woman in the flat above said she'd gone away without leaving an address. I was sorry. She was a great girl and I know she was shattered when Jim died, but I thought maybe she just wanted to get right away from everything that reminded her of him. You know – start a new life somewhere else.'

'What about the baby?' The words burst out of me in a rush, far too loud, far too hectoring. There was another momentary silence.

'*What?*' he said faintly.

'She was having a baby when Jim died. Didn't she tell you?'

'Not a word. My God.' He sounded shocked and concerned and it was a second or two before he got his breath back. 'Poor Caroline! What must she have felt? Look, Holly, I can understand now why you feel you want to trace her, but I honestly can't help you. I only wish I could. How the hell did you find out about it, anyway?'

'It's a long story.' I sighed, my optimism knocked out of me. I'd banked so much on Steve Maitland providing all the answers and the disappointment was devastating. 'Steve, can't you think of anyone who'd know where she went? She must have had other friends.'

'I suppose she must.' He seemed to be thinking this over, then I heard him sigh. 'It's no good. I met one or two people round at her place, but they were just names. There was a Liz, I remember, and someone called Sarah. Who they were and where they are now I haven't a clue. Mostly, though, it was just her and Jim. They were everything to each other.'

It was my turn to sigh.

'I was banking everything on you.'

'I'm sorry. But listen.' His voice changed a little, grew more positive and upbeat. 'We must meet. Something might occur to me. Besides, I feel I almost know you already. Jim spoke about you a lot. He thought the world of you.'

'It was mutual.'

'By the way—' he was sounding mildly amused now '—just out of interest, what does your mother think of this quest of yours? I seem to remember Jim saying she would have a fit at the thought of him marrying an English girl.'

'She died last month.'

'I'm sorry. That means you're alone, doesn't it? Or are you married? I've lost track of how old you must be.'

'Old enough,' I said. 'But no, I'm not married. You?'

'No.'

'I kind of figured it would be great to discover a niece or a nephew somewhere in England.'

'Have dinner with me tonight,' he said. 'There's a little Italian place in Notting Hill where Jim and I used to go. It's gone up-market since that bloody film, but it's still pretty reasonable and they do a damned good fettucini. Where are you staying?'

I told him, and there was yet another silence.

'Very nice,' he said after a moment, a touch dryly, I thought. 'I hope you brought the contents of Fort Knox with you. Well, Luigi's will make an interesting contrast. I'll pick you up at eight, if that's OK with you.'

It was OK with me and I told him so, but I still felt weak with disappointment about his lack of knowledge regarding Caroline. Or maybe it was just plain tiredness.

I napped after lunch – just couldn't keep awake. My body clock must have been all over the place, but I felt much better when I finally opened my eyes at four thirty. I phoned room service and ordered coffee (I knew it ought to be afternoon tea in these surroundings, but couldn't bring myself to rise to the occasion; coffee was what I needed).

Having drunk it I became positively optimistic again. Steve would think of someone who would know the whereabouts of Caroline. And if he didn't – well, there were surely other means. You were supposed to be able to find anyone on the Internet, so I'd been led to believe. Maybe Steve would know how to do it. And wasn't England the kind of place where everyone was charted from cradle to grave? People couldn't just disappear, could they?

Steve would know, I told myself again. I

couldn't wait to meet him. He had sounded nice. Kind. Even Mom couldn't have complained about his voice, which had none of the arrogance she detested. Higginson, now – oh, my gosh! What would she have made of him? He sounded like he had a whole treeful of plums in his mouth.

I studied Steve's photograph again, trying to tie in the voice I had heard with the face that was before me. The cumulative impression was one of warmth and humour, added to which was the fact that Jim, whom I had always looked up to, had thought a great deal of him. Also, it had to be admitted that Tracey had erred on the side of caution when she had described him as 'not bad'. From where I was sitting, Steve Maitland looked very good indeed – even if he was, as the horrible Mr Higginson had suggested, on his beam ends. And ten years older, I reminded myself. He could look quite different now.

I spent a long time on my hair, a little amused by the fact that the finished effect looked definitely tousled. But artistically so, I assured myself.

I changed my clothes a couple of times before deciding on a pair of skinny black trousers I'd picked up in Saks before leaving New York, my Gucci boots, and a white silk blouse that was a particular favourite and had a collar that looked good over an adorable jacket that had been one of my mother's last presents to me.

I looked long at the final result in the full-length mirror, changed my earrings several times, added a few gold chains, took them off again and finally settled on a spectacular pendant that had been yet another present from Mom. It was then that I admitted to myself that I was very nervous indeed.

Why on earth? I could only assume that I was transferring to Steve some of the hero worship I had felt for my brother – which made no sense at all! I had no need to be nervous, I assured myself. I, who had been wined and dined by stars of stage and screen.

I lifted my chin and gave myself a supermodel's arrogant stare – then sagged with a rueful smile. Who was I trying to kid? The outward appearance might fit, but I'd never felt easy in the glitzy showbiz world in which I had moved with such apparent assurance – the LA world where grass was bought by the yard and unrolled like a carpet, and smiles were so often as false as plastic flowers. I might have looked much like every other blonde starlet, but hidden beneath wide-eyed, unsophisticated Mary Lou McAllister was wide-eyed, unsophisticated Holly Crozier, and I was far from confident that Steve would like me. So what? I asked myself, lifting my chin once more. What did the approval of one hard-up antique dealer matter to me?

Inexplicably, quite a lot. I took a deep breath, picked up my purse, and made for the door.

Four

I was too impatient to wait for the elevator so took the stairs that led me down to the reception area.

Steve was already waiting there, and I saw him a second or two before he saw me. He was a little taller than I had imagined, and broader than in his photograph, his hair not quite so dark as it had appeared. Essentially, though, he was unchanged and I would have known him anywhere. As I came down the last few stairs he turned and saw me. He took a step towards me, and as he smiled at me I was conscious of a great thump in my chest and a wonderful, heady feeling of excitement, as if sparks were flying – as if a laser beam had suddenly zipped between us.

Is this *it*? I thought, half delighted and half afraid. Could it be? It just might. It really might! I felt like letting out a whoop and a holler, but it helped, being an actress. Even a not-very-good one. I smiled and calmly approached him, giving no clue as to the turmoil inside of me. I went towards him with my hand outstretched and he took it in both of his.

'Hallo, Steve Maitland,' I said. 'I feel, somehow, that you are a very familiar presence.'

'I'm – dazzled!' He shook his head, laughing. 'I would have said the same until now, but the girl Jim told me about had pigtails and braces on her teeth.'

'I've changed. Just a little.'

'You certainly have!'

There was a pause while we assessed each other, a moment of slight awkwardness which we filled by grinning at each other like zanies, neither of us appearing to know quite what to do or say next. I liked the shape of his smile, his clear grey eyes and their shapely winged brows. Even the marginally oversized nose seemed just right. His clothes were OK, too. I don't know quite what I expected, not being experienced in dating Englishmen, but the chinos, dark blue shirt and casual jacket would have passed muster anywhere.

'Well!' we both said together, and laughed.

'Would you mind if we made a fairly rapid exit?' he said. 'I've left my car on a double yellow line.'

'Sure.' I turned at once for the door. Outside Quentins' flight of steps there was a vehicle the like of which I doubted they had seen many times in their long history. It was a large, rather battered station wagon long past its first youth, and it clearly had many utilitarian uses.

'It's not exactly first-class travel,' he said apologetically.

'It's just fine,' I told him; but, as we pulled away from the kerb, I remembered what the odious Mr Higginson had said with such glee. It looked as if he had been right about Steve and his business. I hadn't been in such a ramshackle vehicle since I was in high school. And I didn't give a damn! I was just so glad to be there, sitting next to Steve. Once the initial shyness wore off we talked nineteen to the dozen, as if we truly had known each other for years. His laugh, his hands on the wheel, the way his lips quirked when he was amused – it all seemed familiar to me in a quite astonishing way. I know this man, I thought. I *know* him! I wanted to throw back my head and laugh at the miraculous, incredible turn of events, but I continued to play it cool – or, at least, no more than lukewarm.

'What was Caroline like?' I asked him.

'In appearance? Dark-haired, brown-eyed. Rather Gallic, I suppose.' He smiled when he spoke of her, as if he had only happy memories. 'Actually, she was of French extraction, way back. I remember her saying so. There was a sort of—' He hesitated, his eyes screwed up in thought. 'I dunno – it's hard to describe. There was a sort of quickness about her. A vivacity that was very attractive; but she was a good listener. Maybe that's what I remember most of all. She really listened. She wasn't one of those ghastly girls whose eyes roam all over the place while they're talking to you, checking that someone more interesting hasn't just entered the room. That wasn't Caroline. There was a feeling of – oh, I don't know how to put it! I suppose "calmness" describes it best, though that sounds dull and she definitely wasn't that. I suppose it was a kind of assurance, as if she had life all sussed out.'

'You must have liked her an awful lot,' I said, feeling, ridiculously, rather jealous of this unknown girl.

He nodded. 'I did.' He turned his head and gave me a swift grin. 'But not in the same way that Jim did ... Hold tight – we turn just here.'

He pulled off the main road and brought the car to a clanking halt. It heaved and puffed for a moment after he had turned off the engine.

'Now, don't say anything rude to hurt the old girl's feelings,' he said warningly. 'She and I have been together a long time.'

'I wouldn't dream of it,' I assured him.

'I don't suppose it's the sort of thing you're used to.'

'It got us here, didn't it?'

We walked back towards the street of shops we had left and in only a few moments arrived at Luigi's, a small restaurant that I could see through the windows was already half full.

Inside, it was warm and colourful and throbbed with a hubbub of voices. A small, dynamic man with a shock of white hair surged forward to greet us, arms stretched wide as if to embrace us both. He stopped short of this, however, but reached to give Steve a friendly clap on the shoulder and an enthusiastic shake of the hand.

'Signor Steve!' he cried expansively, his voice heavily accented. 'How pleased I am to see you. Long time no see – and now you bring this lovely lady!' He bowed towards me, brown eyes sparkling with life. 'You are most welcome, signorina.' Again he turned to Steve. 'It's been too long, signor. I tell Mama you book table for tonight and she say she come out to see you and say hallo. Come. I give you my best table in the corner.'

We had barely seated ourselves before a plump, smiling woman emerged at a run from somewhere backstage, coming straight over to give Steve smacking kisses on both cheeks.

'You naughty boy, so long you don't come,' she said, standing back and shaking a finger at him. 'Why you forget your friends, eh?'

'Anna, as if I'd ever do that! I've been busy, that's all.'

'Busy making lotsa money, yes?'

'Er – no! I wouldn't go that far. Still, we get by. Hey, let me introduce you to Holly. Do you remember, years ago, I used to come in here with a friend called Jim? Jim Crozier?'

Anna's good-humoured face fell into sorrowful lines.

'The nice American boy who had the accident? I will never forget him.'

'This is Holly Crozier, his sister.'

'Hi,' I said, stretching out across the table to offer her my hand.

'Ah!' Anna seized it and pumped it up and down with great energy. 'Such a tragedy, and such a nice young man. But it is good you come here, Mees Holly. Your brother loved my cooking – isn't that right, signor?'

'Absolutely.'

'Then it's a sure thing I will too,' I said.

'You're bound to, Holly,' Steve said. 'It's the best.'

'Huh!' Anna pretended disbelief. 'The best, eh? So that's why you not here for so many weeks?'

'Not from choice, I promise you. But now I am here, tell me the news. How are you, Anna? You're looking marvellous.'

She laughed dismissively.

'No, no – not marvellous!' She patted her stomach. 'Oh, healthy, yes, but my trouble, I eat too well. What is a woman to do when all her life she is in the kitchen with good food all around?' She lifted her hands, palm upwards in entreaty, her mouth pulled down.

'You look great to me,' Steve said. 'And tell me, how's the family? Are they all well?'

'All *very* well, thanks be to God. Gianna has another another bambino. Luigi, she call him. Gianni will get his degree this year. Francesca and Lisa are doing well at school.'

'That's great.' He was involved, I could see – genuinely interested, not just putting on an act, and I could also see the pleasure he was giving Anna. 'What does Francesca want to do with herself?'

'She wants to cook! I tell her, computers are the thing, not cooking stoves, but she not listen! She wants to go to Italy for a year, then maybe to college here.'

'Well, good for her. Doing something you enjoy is what matters most.'

'Like you enjoy the furniture, yes?'

Steve laughed.

'Like I enjoy the furniture. Some of it, anyway. And what about Lisa?'

'This week, a model. Next week, maybe a film star. Later – who knows? She a clever girl. We hope she go to university, like Gianni.'

'They're all a great credit to you and Luigi.'

Anna tapped her forehead with her finger-tip.

'The brains they get from Luigi,' she said. 'Now I must go. Maybe we talk later, yes?' She still lingered a moment, however, to pat him on the shoulder. 'Is good to see you, signor,' she said, adding in my direction, 'This a good man, my dear, with a warm heart. He do Luigi and me very, very good turn. We don't forget, even if he makes out it was nothing.'

'Some welcome,' I said when she had hurried back to the kitchen. Steve was laughing, a little embarrassed.

'I bribed her,' he said.

'It sounded pretty spontaneous to me.'

'Well, we go back a long way.'

'What was the good turn?'

'It was nothing, really.'

'Anna said you'd say that.'

'Well, it's true. They were pretty hard up when the business first started and I managed to get them a good price on some nice old pieces they wanted to get rid of. Apparently they'd been offered peanuts by other dealers. Their English was very poor in those days and I gathered that there were those who saw them as an easy mark. I just happened to recognise the quality and find the right buyer, that's all. I was only doing my job. Now—' He was clearly trying to dismiss the subject. 'Don't you think it's time we got down to the serious business of the evening? Have a look at the menu. It's on the blackboard on that far wall.'

It was that kind of place. Chequered cloths on the tables, candles in Chianti bottles. Nothing fancy, but there was undoubtedly a wonderfully warm atmosphere, which clearly made Luigi's restaurant popular in the neighbourhood, for by this time it was full and would-be diners who had neglected to book were being turned away. We made our choice, both of food and wine, and Luigi himself took our order.

'I guess he or Anna wouldn't know what had become of Caroline?' I said thoughtfully when he had gone.

'Well, we can ask him, but I doubt it very much.'

His doubts were confirmed when, a moment later, Luigi brought over our wine and two glasses. No, he said. He had no idea what had happened to Jim's girlfriend. He couldn't even remember the young lady clearly, though he did recall that one had come several times with Jim.

'It was a long time ago,' Steve reminded me when he had left us.

'I guess so. Tell me more about her.'

He took a thoughtful sip of his wine.

'I've told you what she looked like, the

kind of girl she was. I don't quite know what else to say. There's no doubt that she was something special. I used to tell Jim he was lucky that I hadn't met her first – not that I kidded myself it would have made any difference if I had! She didn't have eyes for anyone but Jim, and as for him – well, he was just crazy about her. They were great together.'

'Where did they meet?'

'At someone's house.'

'*Whose* house, Steve?'

He chewed at his lip for a moment, then shook his head, defeated.

'If I ever knew I've forgotten. But I think—'

He paused and I waited, hanging on his words.

'What do you think, Steve?'

'Now I think of it, I believe it was somewhere on the river. Henley, or Marlow – somewhere like that. I remember hearing about a boat that Jim nearly capsized. It was a joke between them, that Jim came close to drowning her before they'd been properly introduced. They're pretty grand houses in that neck of the woods so I guess it must have been someone with plenty of loot, someone out of our usual class. Jim knew people that I didn't, of course. Various Americans, people connected with the art world, and so on.'

'You must have known where Caroline worked.'

'Yes, of course. She was PA to the managing director of a property development company in the City. Greenway Development, it was called. I don't know that I ever heard the boss's name.'

'Might he have lived in any of these places you mentioned?'

'I suppose he might have done. Now I come to think of it, I believe Caroline did socialise with him a bit – his wife, anyway. Jim got a bit agitated about it towards the end.'

'Why?'

'She was demanding. Wanting Caroline go to here and there with her. Oh, I don't suppose it was a big issue between them – just that Jim mentioned it once when we were having a beer together. He said that this woman – can't remember her name – was becoming a pain.'

I took out a notebook.

'What was the name again? Greenway Development?' I wrote it down, but as I glanced up at him I saw that he was looking at me with a dubious expression on his face.

'It's an awful long time ago, Holly. Don't get your hopes up. People forget, move, retire – die, even.'

'So that horrible guy in Lovells said. He remembered Jim, though, even if he wasn't any help.'

'Higginson?' I'd already mentioned my encounter with him to Steve, and to my far from flattering description of the man he had instantly added some acid, highly amusing comments on his own account.

'Higginson,' I confirmed. 'I could have killed him! Whatever low opinion he had of Jim, he could surely have kept his feelings to himself in my presence. He was barely polite.'

'To say the two of them didn't get on is the understatement of the year. Jim couldn't stand the man. Of course, being in his department, he had a lot more to do with him than I did.'

'He seemed to imply that Jim's social life interfered with his work. Yours, too.'

'That simply wasn't true, not for either of us. Jim loved his job.' He stopped as if something had just occurred to him. 'Actually, the boot was on the other foot. Jim complained sometimes that Higginson was less than meticulous.'

'In what way?'

Steve took another sip of his wine as if thinking his answer over carefully.

'I don't want to make unwarranted accusations,' he said. 'There have always been forgeries in the art business, and mistakes happen in the best-regulated companies. A place like Lovells has to be on the lookout

72

all the time; its reputation is on the line at every sale, but even experts can be fooled and it's still possible for the odd fake to get through the net. I remember there was one occasion when someone brought in an alleged—' He hesitated. 'Monet, I think it was. No – I remember now, it was a Corot. Higginson authenticated it, but Jim didn't agree – and, being Jim, he told him so.'

I laughed at that.

'Yeah – Higginson said he was forthright.'

'I think some pretty forthright opinions were exchanged on both sides that day.'

Conversation was interrupted as our food was served, but was resumed after a suitable pause for appreciation of the delicious aroma and taste. Maybe the salad wasn't the most imaginative in the world, but Anna sure could cook pasta.

'Jim loved this place,' Steve said. 'It hasn't changed since the days when we saved up our pennies for an occasional splurge.'

Saved up? *Jim?* To come *here*?

I must have looked as surprised as I felt.

'Lovells are notoriously mean,' he explained, seeing my expression. 'The prestige of working there is supposed to compensate for low salaries, and we were pretty hard up in those days.' He gave a short laugh. 'So what else is new?'

'Is business bad?'

'*Comme ci, comme ça.*' He tipped his hand

this way and that. 'It's not so bad as it was – in fact, things seem to have been picking up quite nicely lately. It's a damned shame I didn't have more capital to stock up a few years ago, before everyone began to feel a bit more affluent. People were keen to sell off the family treasures in those days. Now everyone's more inclined to buy than to sell.'

'But that's good, surely?'

'Yes, of course, up to a point – just so long as you have the stuff to sell. And of course, to acquire stock one needs capital...' His voice trailed away and he was silent for a moment.

I was still thinking about Jim, realising with astonishment that while we were living in luxury in the States, he'd had a tough time making ends meet. As far as I knew, he'd never mentioned it or asked for anything. Well, good for him – but it made me madder than ever about the paltry thousand dollars that Mom had seen fit to send to Caroline.

'A penny for them,' Steve said.

I hesitated, then told him about my mother's niggardly response to Caroline's letter. The easy relationship that had sprung up between us encouraged me to speak frankly. My mother, much as I loved her, had always possessed the ability to make me more angry than any other living soul, and I

74

was conscious, suddenly, of saying more than I should. Conscious, you could say, of revealing myself as the worst kind of daughter.

'I find it awfully hard to make excuses for such a total lack of generosity,' I said hastily, by way of explanation of what seemed like terrible disloyalty to my recently dead single parent.

Steve shrugged tolerantly.

'Well, a thousand dollars is a thousand dollars,' he said. 'Not a sum to be sneezed at. Maybe it wasn't such a good time for her.'

'She could spend twice that in a month on clothes and visits to the beauty parlour. If she'd sent Caroline ten times that amount she wouldn't have noticed the difference. Even better, she could have told her to come to the States. Welcomed her into the family.'

I'd been looking down as I spoke, feeling – in spite of my undoubted justification – somewhat ashamed of my disloyalty to my own mother. His silence seemed to go on for quite a while, and when I glanced up I saw he was looking at me with an expression on his face that I couldn't interpret. There was a blankness about it, a sort of stillness. He looked away, not meeting my eyes.

'Well,' he said almost absently. 'What's done is done.'

I sensed a change of mood, a kind of

withdrawal of warmth. There was a distinct feeling of disappointment. Had he expected better of me? Had I failed some test? Maybe I had sounded disloyal and shrill and quick to condemn. I've blown it, I thought drearily. Just when I thought that maybe, just maybe, Steve Maitland might supply the answer to all the questions I've ever asked myself.

It was an atmosphere hard to define, for we continued to talk through pasta and dessert and coffee, finding no shortage of topics to discuss, from American politics to the current bestseller list. Among other things, Steve told me about places I ought to visit in London, plays to see, others to miss.

'Not that I go to the West End a lot,' he said, having given me a rundown on what was playing at the National Theatre. 'It's too damned expensive these days – but there are often try-outs in Richmond and I try to catch those. You really ought to see the new Tom Stoppard while you're here, though. It had wonderful reviews.'

I said something non-committal, more aware of the impersonal tone of his voice than what he was saying. All the spontaneity seemed to have been dissipated, all that warm feeling of familiarity that had wrapped us round from the moment of our meeting. It wasn't that Steve had suddenly become less charming or less polite – far from it. He was too polite, too considerate, as if I were a maiden aunt he was entertaining out of duty, or a busload of tourists he was paid to entertain. Without doubt, a mysterious blight had fallen on the evening, and I felt certain I was to blame for it.

Luigi offered us brandy on the house, but Steve declined it because he was driving. I felt bound, therefore, to do the same, though I wouldn't have minded another drink, simply because my spirits had dipped, if not to zero, then not far above it.

He paid the bill, looked at his watch, smiled his charming smile.

'Well, I don't suppose you'll want a late night,' he said. 'And I have an early start tomorrow.'

Oh, *pul-lease*, I thought. Don't let me keep you out of your beddy-byes one more minute than necessary.

'Let's get going, then,' I said, as if going or staying was all one to me. The heart that had leapt with joy at the sight of him not three hours ago lay heavy in my breast. I didn't need to be an expert in extrasensory perception to get the message that he'd gone off me in a big way. Well, his loss, I told myself as I stalked out of the restaurant ahead of him.

As if in tune with my mood, if was raining when we left the restaurant. The street was wet and shiny and a car accelerating away from the sidewalk contrived to spray my new black trousers with the contents of a puddle. Steve expressed annoyance on my behalf, but coolly. To me the incident seemed quite appropriate, for there were no sparks flying between us now.

As we drove away he talked of some Georgian silver he was going to see the following day, out of London in some town I'd never heard of. I listened to him in a state of panic, suddenly desperate that I should be given another chance. The journey was passing rapidly. Wasn't he going to say *anything* about helping me to find Caroline, or seeing me again? I recognised a street quite near to the hotel and panic turned to desperation.

'About Caroline – what do you suggest I do now?' I burst out, interrupting a prolonged silence.

'Well—' He looked a little surprised. 'You could check the birth certificates at St Catherine's House for – when? January 1991? At least you'd know if Caroline had a boy or a girl.'

'That's true.' It would be good to know, even if it took me no nearer finding her. 'I guess the girl at the hotel can tell me how to get to wherever it is.'

'Then I think in your place I'd put ads in the personal columns of all the quality newspapers. The girl will give you the name of them, too. Then there's Greenway Development, where she used to work. You can find their number in the phone book.'

'Sure.' I lifted my chin and stared out at lighted shop fronts shimmering through the rain. I was damned if I would give any indication of needing his help. I wasn't *that* desperate! Why, I'd turned down better, richer, more fascinating men than Steve Maitland a million times. Who the hell did he think he was? Then a thought struck me and my attempt at self-sufficiency fell by the wayside. 'The aunt!' I cried eagerly, turning towards him. 'I completely forgot the aunt! Caroline mentioned her in the letter. She was her only relation, she said, and had always been good to her. You must surely have met her.'

'Yes – yes, I did, just once.' It was clear that he had forgotten her, too. 'She came over at Christmas to Jim and Caroline's flat in Chiswick.'

'From where, Steve? Think!' But he shook his head, unable to tell me.

'Near enough to come for the day. That's all I can tell you.'

'Maybe she was the one who had the house by the river?'

'I suppose it's possible – but no, on second thoughts, I don't think so. I got the distinct impression that this was the first time she'd met Jim.'

79

'You've got a lousy memory,' I said bitterly.

'Haven't I just?' He spoke lightly, as if this whole issue had somehow ceased to concern him. 'But then I didn't know it would be put to such a test, did I? As far as I recall, she was a scholarly kind of woman – a teacher, that was it! I remember her talking about it. She was – oh, in her late fifties, I suppose. She wore an interesting old ring,' he added, inconsequentially. 'Sorry, but that's the sort of thing that sticks in my memory. I remember her saying that it was left to her by her French grandmother. I told her that if she ever fell on hard times, it would probably be worth a tidy sum. She said she'd never sell it – that it would be Caroline's one day.'

We had drawn up at the hotel by this time and still he had said nothing about seeing me again. I thanked him for a pleasant evening – outwardly polite, still controlled – but to my annoyance the panic was back and I didn't want to part like this.

'About the theatre,' I began. 'The play you mentioned. Have you seen it? I mean, I'd love to, and I'd welcome a chance to return the hospitality.'

'A nice thought, but I think you'll find they're booked up.'

'I could try.'

'By all means.'

The street lights cast a strange-looking light on us, but I could see quite clearly that he had that polite, impersonal smile on his face again; and in that moment I felt, suddenly, totally in sympathy with my mother and her feelings regarding the British. He was cold and heartless and unfeeling and I could cheerfully have beaten him over the head had some suitable weapon been handy.

I turned and fumbled at the door handle, but before I had worked out the way to operate its archaic mechanism, he had gotten out of the car and come round to open it for me. To my jaundiced eyes it seemed more like a desire to get rid of me rather than common politeness. Still, he paused at the foot of the hotel steps and in the light of the lamps that stood on the gateposts I saw him looking at me. He wasn't smiling any more. Maybe it was just a trick of the light, but it seemed to me now that he had an expression of real sadness on his face. What was going on? I just couldn't figure out this guy at all.

'It really has been good to meet you,' he said softly. 'Jim would have been so proud of you. You are a very lovely lady, Holly Crozier.'

'Well, thanks. And thanks again for a great evening.' I knew my manners, after all. It was another thing Mom had taught me.

Neither of us moved. It was as if we were both suspended in a moment of time, not breathing, not conscious of the thin rain that still drizzled down, and for one crazy moment I thought he was going to kiss me. He didn't, though. He just gave a tight kind of smile and raised his hand to touch me on the cheek.

'Take care,' he said. Casual once more, he stepped back, lifted his hand in a kind of half-salute, and was gone.

I stood for a moment watching the back of his disreputable wagon as it disappeared down the street, then pulled myself together, afraid that that he would see me through the rear-view mirror positively radiating wistfulness. Where the hell had it all gone so wrong?

I turned and walked briskly up the steps of the hotel, head up, smile on face, doing my best to look like any girl returning from an enjoyable night out.

So that was it, I thought, far from smiling on the inside. All those fireworks when we met; all that elation. Had I over-exaggerated the excitement? Made a drama out of a simple encounter that meant nothing?

Up in my room I stared at myself in the mirror. I still looked OK. No spot or blemish that I could discern. No lipstick stains on my teeth. No bolognese sauce down my shirt. What had I done to make Mr Stephen

Maitland of Richmond, Surrey, drop me like a hot coal? Even the compliment he had paid me as we stood outside the hotel had a kind of dying fall, as if he had no intention of seeing me again.

I could think of no reason for this other than the way I had spoken of my mother. Well, maybe I had been too harsh in my criticism. Disrespectful. Maybe it was the British way to put mothers on a pedestal, admitting to no fault in any of them. Indeed, I did feel a bit ashamed. On the other hand, my outrage at the cavalier way she had treated Caroline was something I had felt sure that Stephen would share, and I still boiled with rage whenever I thought about it.

Well, the hell with him, I thought. Who needed Mr Stiff-Upper-Lip Stephen Maitland? He'd proved himself the worst kind of unemotional, uninvolved, passionless Brit, and I could do without any help he was likely to be able to give me. I'd go in search of that birth certificate first thing in the morning, and I'd ring the newspapers and put ads in all of them. And if that failed, then I'd hire a detective. Some friend he turned out to be, I thought, as I wiped off my make-up in swift, angry swipes.

But once in bed, the light switched off, I couldn't help remembering the way it had been at the start of the evening; the rapport and the ease and the feeling that I had known him for years. And yes, the excitement, the sheer sexual chemistry. He'd felt it too, I was certain. You can't mistake that kind of thing. The thought that, no matter whose fault it was, we had somehow managed to make a hash of it made me more sad than angry.

But then a thought struck me and, no matter what I told myself, there was no doubt that I found it offered a crumb of comfort. For all the feeling of finality, he hadn't actually said goodbye, had he? Maybe, after all, we'd both get a second chance.

Five

I located St Catherine's House without too much trouble and, though all was confusion inside, by asking various officials I finally found what I was looking for; an enormous tome listing all the births that had taken place in Britain in the first quarter of 1991.

And there it was. The twentieth of January, a male child, to Caroline Bethany in Oxford. So it was a boy! We had both been right. But why Oxford, I wondered? And was it possible that she could still be there?

I found a telephone and patiently tracked down the number I had to ring to contact Directory Enquiries. I felt very grateful to Caroline that she wasn't called Smith or Brown, and it only took a few seconds to learn that there was a C. Bethany listed at an Oxford number, which I wrote down in my notebook with a considerable feeling of triumph. Suddenly, miraculously, it seemed that I was on the right track, and I congratulated myself on proving to be such a good detective. Maybe I could take it up full time now that it appeared my acting career had taken a nosedive! Almost trembling in my eagerness, I put coins in the slot and dialled the number I had been given.

And it rang and rang. Unwilling to give up hope, I let it ring until long after it was reasonable to do so; finally I had to concede defeat and leave the telephone to the poor woman who had been waiting, more or less patiently, to use it after me. It shouldn't have been a surprise to me to find no one home, I told myself. No doubt Caroline had to work to maintain herself and her son. I would try again later.

Meantime, I was left not knowing quite what to do. It was pointless to put ads in the papers or phone Greenway Development if I had truly found Caroline without doing so. I began to walk back along the Strand in the direction of Piccadilly. On the advice of Sue, the receptionist, I'd acquired an A to Z street guide and, as I studied it, I happened to see that I was very close to Covent Garden. I instantly decided I would go in search of it.

I found it without difficulty and was at once captivated. The rain of the night before had stopped long since and now the sun was shining, making it pleasant to wander about, stopping every now and again to browse in shops or enjoy the street entertainers.

I was drawn towards the far end of the

piazza by the strains of classical music and sat down at one of the tables close by, both to enjoy it and to order a coffee. There were two musicians currently performing, I found: a girl playing the flute, a boy the violin. Students, I guessed, and was entranced by the sound they produced together. The music was beautiful, though unfamiliar to me, and their playing was of a very high standard. But what attracted me almost as much as the music was the beauty of the musicians themselves. They were so young, so – I struggled to find the word – so gloriously, innocently unblemished. And so much in love, I saw, as the music finished and they turned to smile into each other's eyes.

Call me a sentimental fool, but it was so piercingly sweet that a knife seemed to twist inside me and I sat there, watching and listening and sipping my coffee, envying the happiness that seemed to enfold them like some holy aura. Would it ever be like that for me? It never had been, not yet. Oh, I'd had lovers, of course. I'd been attracted to men, and men had been attracted to me. Some had sworn they were in love. But me? Never! Excitement, yes: love, no. I'd always felt just slightly detached.

The night before, when I'd seen Steve, it had seemed for a little while as if for once things might be different; and it still hurt like hell to think how everything had changed, between one breath and the next, before I had lived long enough to know if anything could develop between us. It was hard to understand. Surely if he had felt even one-tenth of the attraction I'd felt for him, a few ill-chosen words regarding my mother wouldn't have affected the issue? After all, he must have known from Jim that she wasn't always the easiest person to get along with.

Now, more than twelve hours later, I wondered if I had imagined that sudden cooling of the atmosphere. Maybe he was preoccupied – busy – tired. Oh, there were endless excuses and explanations for his behaviour for one who longed to find them.

Maybe I'd phone him later on when he was back from his trip. After all, by evening I might have spoken to Caroline, and there would be a lot to tell him. I could even pursue the matter of the theatre ticket, or ask him to the hotel to dinner. Thank God, in this day and age a girl didn't have to sit around sewing a fine seam while she waited for the male to take the initiative.

For the moment, however, he was out of reach. Over a sandwich and yet another cup of coffee, I took Caroline's letter out of my purse and read it again, and as I did so I had a sudden desire to go and look at the street where she had lived with Jim, and to see for myself the spot where Jim had been so cruelly mown down and left for dead. Laver Street, it was called. The name of it was carved deeply in my memory. Was it morbid, to want to visit the scene of this long-ago tragedy? Yes, possibly. Still it was something I felt I had to do before I left England, and now seemed as good a time as any.

Outside the cafe I hailed a cab and told the driver I wanted to drive around Chiswick, just to look at one or two places. He professed himself willing to take me there and back, but looked loftily amused at my pronunciation of the name of the place. Not Chis-wick, he told me. Chizzick. Well, I said, how's a poor ignorant American supposed to know these things? To which he shrugged his shoulders and continued to look amused.

He assumed from the outset that I was interested in buying a property in the area, though I had said nothing to imply this. It so happened, he told me, that he lived in Chiswick himself, and he proceeded to deliver a non-stop rundown of the area's many amenities as we drove towards the western suburbs.

Instead of allowing him to continue, I was unwise enough to tell him I had no interest in buying a house there or anywhere else, but simply wanted to see the place. There was something in the ensuing pause that seemed to say this confirmed all his suspicions – I was definitely a few nickels short of a dime – but it only took a few minutes for him to launch into conversation again. He supposed, he said over his shoulder, projecting his voice through the gap in the glass that divided us, that this was a sentimental journey of some kind. Americans were like that. Sentimental. They let it all hang out, like. Well, we couldn't all be the same, could we?

I allowed that we could not.

'Take that Jerry Springer,' he said. 'And Oprah, and all that lot. You'd never get an English audience carrying on like that, all them tears and shouting and that. And confessing everything about their sex lives. I saw a telly programme the other day – cor luvaduck, you'd never credit what they were saying, all out in public. You'd never get a Brit carrying on like that, oh dear me no. It's the reserve, you see. We're more, like, strong and silent.'

'Really?' I couldn't help the note of amused surprise in my voice. Strong he might have been. Silent he certainly was not.

He continued not to be it all the way to Chiswick, where he parked in a convenient place, allowing me thankfully to escape the sound of his voice while I wandered a little way along Cranleigh Road. Number 18 was attached to number 20 and was its mirror image. Indeed, all the houses in the street seemed absolutely identical, give or take the odd tree. All were built of yellowish brick, which seemed very popular in that part of London, and all had square bay windows, top and bottom. It made little sense for me to stand and stare at number 18, but still I did so, thinking of Jim alive and happy and loving Caroline. There was a bright yellow flowering shrub in a tiny strip of garden at the front behind a low brick wall. I wondered if it had been there ten years ago – if, in fact, Caroline had planted it.

The door of number 16 opened and a woman with a child in a buggy bumped down the step, giving me a suspicious look, so I turned away and went back to the taxi.

'Seen enough?' the driver asked, eyebrows raised, his expression that of someone humouring a child.

'Yes, thank you. I'd like to go to Laver Street now.'

'Where?'

Even though he was a resident of the area he had never heard of it and had to resort to looking it up in the A to Z he had in the front of the cab – A to *Zed*, as I must remember to call it. I could tell that these kind of verbal differences seemed to increase his irritating assumption of superiority.

I assured him it couldn't be too far away. I knew it was somewhere near the Thames, for it was in the fields bordering the river that Jim used to take an early morning run. Laver Street led down to these fields, or so it had been stated at the inquest.

'You want to go *there?*' he said incredulously, having found it on the map. 'There's nothing there, you know. I didn't even know it had a name.'

'I'd just like to see it, if you don't mind,' I said. Now more exasperated than amused, he swung the cab round and drove off through a few residential streets, clearly more doubtful than ever of my sanity. We crossed a kind of freeway (motorway, I guess it's called over here) and went down to what looked like an industrial area, though one that definitely appeared to have seen better days. There was a derelict, abandoned air about it and as if to make it more unappealing than ever, a light rain had begun to fall once more. The buildings were smoke-grimed and forbidding, the windows broken, tall weeds growing around the gates where lorries had presumably once come and gone. In front of them were walls studded with broken glass to deter intruders.

The taxi came to a halt.

'There you are,' the driver said. 'Laver Street. The river's down the far end.'

I could see the name set high up in a brick wall. The street was narrow, barely more than an alley, potholed and stony, running between two of the derelict warehouses. No wonder the driver thought me mad! Why would anyone in their right mind want to come to a place like this?

With my hands deep in my pockets and my collar up around my ears I got out of the taxi and stood looking bleakly at the ugly little street. It was no longer than fifty or sixty yards. On one side was the continuation of the wall with its pieces of glass along the top; on the other, a similar wall ran halfway down the length of the street, giving way after a while to a high wire-link fence. I walked down towards it, as if expecting it to be able to give some clue about what had happened to my brother.

Of course, it did no such thing. It was just a fence, quite impenetrable, with a 'Dangerous Chemicals' sign fixed on it. Everywhere there was evidence of decay and desertion. If dangerous chemicals had once been stored there, then they were long gone.

Exactly where had it happened, that long-ago tragedy? And *why* had it happened? There had been a river mist that morning, it had been stated at the inquest. Visibility had been poor. It had seemed some sort of explanation at the time, but now, seeing the location for the first time, I felt bewildered. What kind of vehicle would be coming down this narrow street in the early morning, so fast that it would hit and kill a solitary runner, on his way to the fields that lay beyond it beside the river?

I carried on right down to the end. There were flimsy buildings here – sheds or garages, now as derelict as everything else. Beyond them, to the left, the road disintegrated completely into a muddy track and bent round behind the buildings to follow the course of the river. To the right, however, there were playing fields of some kind. I could see goalposts, a smart clubhouse in the distance, signs of regeneration. The river was glassy, with willow trees on its banks.

As I looked, a police launch chugged from left to right, and as the noise of its engines died away I heard the sound of pounding feet behind me. I turned to see two men in running strip panting their way down Laver Street and I watched as they passed me on their way to the open fields. Runners still used Laver Street as a short cut to the river, then, just as Jim had used it that fateful morning. I felt chilled to the bone, as cold as I had ever been.

'Seen all you want to?' the driver asked as I returned to the cab. I nodded, unable to speak for a moment. Then, desperate to tell somebody – *anybody* – I blurted it out.

'My brother died down there.'

'Blimey!' he said. 'What happened?'

I couldn't, at first, find the words to answer him, and when he saw my dilemma, he softened towards me.

'You look like you could use a nice cuppa,' he said. 'There's a place I know not far away from here.'

I allowed myself to be taken there, and together we sat at a plastic table and drank tea out of plastic cups, the driver less voluble now. I felt rather sorry for him. How could he have known when he picked me up that he was being thrust into the company of someone as emotional as I was proving to be?

The tea restored me a little and I managed to smile at him.

'Thanks,' I said. 'Sorry about that. I didn't realise how it would affect me.'

'Recent, was it?'

'No. It happened about ten years ago.' Briefly I recounted the facts – how Jim was in the habit of taking a short cut down Laver Street every morning to go running by the Thames, and how one morning he had been knocked down by a hit-and-run driver and left for dead.

'And they never found the geezer what done it?' he asked. I shook my head. 'What a bastard,' he said.

He took a few gulps of his tea, then looked at me, a look of mystification on his face.

'Hard to understand, eh?' he said. 'I just don't get it. I mean, a little road like that, why would anyone be in that kind of hurry, going down there?'

'I was wondering that myself,' I told him. 'I suppose if those factory places were open then, there would be more traffic than there is today—'

'But it's a sharp corner no matter which way you approach it. Anyone turning in there would have to slow down, stands to reason. How far down the road did it happen?'

'I don't know. I don't think I ever heard. Anyway, places change, don't they? Maybe it was all different, ten years ago.'

'Yeah, well – I s'pose that could be it. Must have been a lot busier then. Even so—' He broke off, still looking unconvinced.

'At the inquest, they said visibility was bad.'

'Yeah? What else did they say?'

'I don't know. I was only young at the time. My mother came over from the States for it, but she never talked about it afterwards.'

He took a few more thoughtful sips of his tea.

'There are some villains about, and no mistake,' he said. 'Fancy not stopping! You wouldn't credit it, would you? Maybe the driver was drunk,' he added after a moment. 'Or evil.'

'Evil?' I stared at him. 'Of course he was

evil! Anyone half decent would have stopped. If Jim had been rushed to a hospital he might have survived.'

'What I mean is, *really* evil, like he meant to do it. You gotta admit, if you want to wipe someone out, it's as good a way as any other. Didn't have no enemies, your brother, did he?'

I thought this question in lousy taste and was quick to deny it.

'Of course not! It couldn't have been anything like that. You watch too many cops and robbers programmes on TV. There was never any question of that, as far as I know.' I waited until he had drained his cup, then got to my feet. 'Thanks for bringing me here, but I really must get back to town.'

The visit to the scene of Jim's death might have depressed me even more than I had expected, but I cheered myself with the thought that I had actually found Caroline and would be calling her shortly. Suddenly I was more impatient than ever to get back to the hotel, but our progress towards Central London was incredibly slow. The thickening traffic all around us was evidence of the fact that the rush hour was in full swing, and I chafed at every delay. Still, it was reassuring to think that, like all the people around me, Caroline was probably on her way home at that very moment.

The cab driver had switched off his meter

a long time before we arrived back at the hotel, and I had a shrewd suspicion that if I'd understood British money a little better, the amount he demanded in payment would have seemed astronomical. He had, however, put up with my incomprehensible demands manfully and had plied me with tea when I most needed it, so I was grateful to him and paid up without quibbling. I felt, in fact, as if he and I had spent several lifetimes together, and we parted like old friends.

I was in a fever of impatience to call Caroline now and I hurried up to my room, shrugged off my coat, found her number in the notebook in my purse and dialled it once again.

This time it was answered on the third ring.

'Is that Caroline Bethany?' I asked, so excited that I stuttered over the name.

'Yes. Who is that?'

'Caroline—' My voice still sounded shaky. 'Caroline, this is Holly Crozier, Jim's sister. I've only recently discovered that you exist, so I've come over to England to find you.'

I paused, hoping for some reaction, but there was only a pause in response. Then, at last, she spoke.

'*Jim's* sister?' She sounded bewildered, as if this was beyond belief; in fact I had the distinct impression that she was more suspicious than delighted, as I had expected.

'Well, you see—' Hastily I rushed into an explanation of the situation. 'I was very young when Jim died, as you know, and my mother never told me about the baby or anything. It must have been simply appalling for you, being left on your own like that. I just wish she'd told you to come—'

'I think,' said the rather dry voice at the other end of the phone, 'that you are labouring under a misapprehension, Miss Crozier. Your brother was living with my niece, who was also called Caroline. We share the same name.'

'Oh!' The anti-climax was disappointing, but I rallied quickly. 'Still, you must have her address. Do tell me where to find her! Is she living with you?'

The other Caroline Bethany laughed shortly.

'Good gracious, no! I haven't seen or heard of her for over eight years.'

'Oh,' I said again, thoroughly deflated. This piece of information surprised and dismayed me so much that for a moment I could think of nothing to say in reply to it.

'She came here to have the baby,' Miss Bethany said. 'But I'm afraid we – we fell out. You must understand I was a busy woman with a career and interests of my own. Having a baby here was – well, inconvenient, to say the least. Broken nights, the washing machine in constant use, all the disruption – I found I simply couldn't take it. So she made arrangements to leave.'

'To go where?' I asked. 'She must have told you.'

'Well, somewhere in the West Country, I believe. Initially, that is. But she didn't stay there long and now I have no idea where she is.'

'She didn't keep in touch?' I must have sounded incredulous. I know I felt it, for Steve had implied that Caroline and her aunt were very close.

I heard Miss Bethany sigh.

'I'm afraid people can be very ungrateful, Miss Crozier,' she said at last. 'I won't say I wasn't hurt when she failed to contact me, but that's the way it is. I don't know where she is.'

'But didn't you make any attempt to find her?'

'As I said before, Miss Crozier, I was a very busy woman in those days – the head of English in a large girls' school. And I would point out that *I* haven't moved! She knows exactly where to find me if she wants me.'

'Aren't you worried about her?'

'Why should I be? She's not a child, you know. Caroline is a most capable and independent woman who has chosen her own path. If her pride prevents her from getting in touch with her only relative, then so be it.

So there it is, Miss Crozier – I'm afraid I'm quite unable to help you. I'm sorry to have to say this. I liked your brother.'

'I'm sorry, too,' I said. 'By the way, what name did Caroline give the baby?'

There was a short silence, and when Miss Bethany spoke again, I could swear there was a softer, more kindly note in her voice.

'What else but James?' she said. 'Jamie, she called him. He was a lovely baby, I have to say that.'

She sounded almost sorry that Caroline had left her and that she had thus been deprived of seeing Jamie grow from a baby into a little boy, but in view of what had gone before I remained unimpressed. I had not warmed to this Caroline Bethany, for it seemed to me that she had been both unsympathetic and unhelpful. Of course babies were disruptive! I didn't know much about them, but I knew that. What else had she expected? Broken nights didn't go on for ever, and the baby's mother must have suffered considerably more than she did.

Still, there seemed little else to say. We exchanged a few meaningless pleasantries, I told her where to find me in case any information came her way, and I put the receiver down, my spirits once more at an all-time low. I had no expectations of ever hearing from her again; indeed, I gained the strong impression that she was hardly listening to me when I told her the name of my hotel. She had, it appeared, closed the book on her niece.

How odd it seemed that the aunt Caroline had written about in her letter, the aunt who had always been so good to her – the same aunt who owned a valuable ring she was determined to leave to her – should prove, in the end, so hard and unfeeling. Why, she had sounded as if she didn't care a bit whether Caroline lived or died!

There was, I felt sure, much that she hadn't told me. The more I thought about it, the more I felt that no matter what temporary strains had been caused by one small baby, they surely could not have been sufficient to nullify all the goodwill and affection of previous years. It didn't make sense.

It was not only inexplicable, but devastatingly disappointing. All day, through all the dismal activities at Chiswick and the nagging anxiety regarding Steve's altered attitude towards me, I had been buoyed up by the thought that I had found Caroline. Now I knew I had achieved nothing.

Back to square one, I thought drearily. A whole day wasted. I could have gone to Greenway Development and put the ads in the papers, but now it would all have to wait until tomorrow. And none of this, I told myself, would seem half so bad if I had someone to talk it over with. Someone who would commiserate with me. Someone, perhaps, like Steve.

No, dammit, I wouldn't phone him! I might have thought of it earlier in the day, but Caroline wasn't the only one with a fair quantity of pride.

I found a miniature bottle of brandy in the minibar and poured it into a glass, sipping it slowly, feeling lower than a snake's belly. What is it with these people, I asked myself? There was Steve, seeming one minute to be delighted with me, the next colder than the Russian steppes, and Caroline Bethany the elder turning against her niece, who had been grieving for Jim at the same time as struggling with a tiny baby. If ever there was a reason for post-natal depression, this surely was it! How un-understanding could you get?

Was this why my mother was so anti-Brit all her life? Had she found, the hard way, that you couldn't rely on any one of them to stay the same for two minutes together? I sipped my brandy and found, as I did so, that I didn't really buy this theory. After all, Jim had thought a lot of Steve – and what about Luigi and Anna? Their fondness for him was obvious in the warmth of their welcome at the restaurant. A good man, Anna had called him, and whatever Miss Bethany was like, I couldn't really believe that he was as rigid and unbending as she appeared to be.

By the time the brandy was finished, I found I had come to a decision. I *would* call Steve after all and tell him what Caroline's aunt had said. To hell with pride and to hell with wondering if it would make me seem forward or pushy to do so; I simply needed to hear his voice.

Without hesitating further I put down my empty glass and reached for the phone.

Six

All I heard in response was his answering machine. He was, it seemed, still away from home.

I left a message asking him to call me but had a horrible suspicion that he wouldn't do so – or, at least, wouldn't do so immediately, which was what I had in mind. I should have made my message sound more intriguing, I thought. Said I had something important to tell him. My hand hovered over the telephone while I wondered whether to call again with a kind of postscript to my previous message, but decided against it. If he phoned, then he phoned; if not, I'd manage without him. It was in the lap of the gods.

What a day, I thought a little later as I consumed my solitary dinner in the hotel dining room. What a lousy, rotten, disappointing day. The sooner it ended, the more thankful I would be. I would have an early night and try to forget it; get some rest so that tomorrow I could be all bright-eyed and bushy-tailed as I set out once more on my quest. And then I remembered that tomorrow was Saturday and offices would be closed and that a dreary weekend yawned before me with nothing to do and no one to do it with. Well, I'd have to act like a tourist, I thought. There were trips I could go on, sights to see. Unless, of course, Steve phoned and suggested something different...

By nine, still without a call from him, I was in my room – clothes discarded, face creamed, teeth cleaned – when the phone rang.

'Hi,' Steve said. 'It's me.'

'You got my message?'

'Message? No. I've not been home yet. I called because I wanted to. How are you and what are you doing?'

Sheer surprise at hearing his voice made me breathless. I sat down on the edge of the bed and did my best to gather my wits.

'It's been a terrible day,' I told him. 'I'm about to draw a veil over the whole thing and go to bed.'

'At nine o'clock on a Friday night? That's positively immoral. Possibly even illegal. Friday night is party night, didn't your mother ever tell you? Come on – come out and have a drink.'

He sounded in high spirits, and his voice was persuasive. Even so—

'I don't know,' I temporised. And it was true, I didn't. Ninety-five per cent of me longed to rush out to meet him, but the remaining five per cent was still wary and unforgiving. How did I know this wouldn't end in another let-down?

'Why was today so terrible?' he asked.

'Well—' It was hard to know what portion of this disastrous day to pick. My mission in Chiswick? The disappointing phone call to Aunt Caroline? I decided on the latter.

'I managed to track down Caroline's aunt, and she knows nothing. They fell out, she said, and she hasn't seen Caroline in years. Can you beat that?'

There was a short silence from Steve as he digested this.

'No,' he said at last, sounding mystified. 'That's the oddest thing I ever heard.'

'That's what I thought. I got the impression they were devoted to each other, but the aunt sure didn't sound it.'

'It doesn't add up at all. Listen, come out and tell me all about it. Please! I'm not so far away – I just managed to find a meter close to the Athenaeum with ten minutes on the clock, which is the kind of thing that doesn't happen twice in a lifetime. I was sure it had to be a lucky omen.'

'Give me ten minutes,' I said, making up my mind. I couldn't help laughing at myself, a touch derisively. Last night I had been consigning Steve to hell, yet on the other hand I had never managed to rid myself entirely of the hope that we would meet again and all would be as it had seemed at the beginning of the evening. Was I being a fool? Well, possibly – but there was no time to debate the issue. I sprang into action, flung on jeans and a sweater, washed my face, fastened my hair with a barrette, pulled on my boots and was ready for action. I might even have made it in five minutes.

I waited for him at the entrance and ran down the steps when I saw his car drive up. The awkwardness of the previous night seemed to have evaporated totally. We were both so pleased to see each other than spontaneously we kissed, just lightly, like old friends. Then he looked at me a little warily.

'I had an awful feeling we weren't going to see each other again,' he said. 'I – sort of blew it last night, didn't I?'

'Sort of,' I agreed.

'I'm sorry. I suffer from this chronic case of idiocy, you see.' He started the engine and pulled away from the sidewalk. 'I've had it from childhood. Just as I think I'm over it, back it comes.'

'So long as it's not contagious. Or terminal.'

He said no more, and I still had no idea what had caused his change of mood, but I resolved to leave it right there. Maybe he'd explain, maybe he wouldn't. I found myself so pleased to be with him again that it didn't matter any more. I felt, suddenly, less despondent about my terrible day. It was going to be all right. I didn't know how, or why, but somehow I felt quite sure of it.

He took me to a wine bar somewhere near the river. We managed to find a secluded corner where we could talk and there I gave him a blow-by-blow account of all that had happened.

'At least you know that the baby was born safely and that she called him after Jim,' he said. 'But I still can't get over her aunt's attitude. It doesn't add up in any way to the impression I had of her. I can't believe they didn't keep in touch – they seemed so close! *Someone* must know where she is. We must get those ads in the paper and try to scare up some of her old friends. I just can't believe she would have dropped everyone.'

'You're sure you want to be in on this?' I asked him. 'I know you're busy, and I don't want to be a nuisance.'

For a moment he looked at me without speaking, eyebrows raised, lips pursed. Then he gave a grunt of rueful laughter.

'I deserve that,' he said. 'Holly, I want to be involved. I'm sorry I seemed so detached last night. I can't tell you what an effort it took for me to walk away from you like that.'

'It was – disconcerting,' I said, sticking to my resolve to ask him nothing.

My hand was resting on the table and

when he covered it with his I could feel the electric shock right through to my backbone.

'I told you, I was an idiot,' he said. 'Please don't hold it against me.'

'Do you get these unfortunate attacks often?'

He didn't answer, but looked at me with his bottom lip caught between his teeth as if the question required thought. He had relinquished my hand, but I still felt shaken. What was it about this guy?

He chose not to answer my question.

'Another drink?' he said, and picking up both our empty glasses he went to the bar while I observed him, still puzzled but liking what I saw, even from the back. He was tall and rangy and his butt was kind of – well, sexy, I guess. No other word for it. He was wearing jeans and a navy-blue sweater yet somehow managed to stand out in the crowd. There were two miniskirted girls up at the bar eyeing him appreciatively and, knowing I was being both childish and foolishly unsophisticated, I felt pleased that they would see he was with me. See, I said to myself, didn't I say that Mary Lou McAllister was a clever bit of typecasting? Was it not true that she and I were sisters under the skin?

'Tell me about your day,' I said when he came back to the table. 'Have you had a good one?'

His expression lightened immediately, but whether with relief that the previous subject was dismissed or with enthusiasm at the treasures he had found, I couldn't tell.

'Yes, I did. I had a great day,' he said. 'That's what's so incredibly fascinating about my job – I just never know what's round the next corner. I was after silver and managed to buy a bit, but there was some absolutely wonderful porcelain I didn't expect at all. Worcester, but quite rare and very beautiful. I could have bought more if I hadn't set myself a limit. There was a marvellous Queen Anne desk I positively lusted after!'

'Was it the contents of a mansion, or something?'

'Not just one house. The sale was at auction rooms, down in Sussex. A town called Lewes.'

'I'm not too sure where that is. My geography is hopeless.'

'Maybe you need to get out more.'

'Nothing I'd like better. Perhaps I should go to auctions, too, and buy something really fabulous to take back to the States with me.'

'Yeah. Why not?' He smiled at me but I seemed to detect a distinct look of caution in his eyes that I couldn't attempt to explain. I felt as if, all unwittingly, I had said

111

something wrong. Hastily I rushed on.

'What made you so crazy about antiques?' I asked him.

'Oh, I learned about good craftmanship at my grandmother's knee. Her house was stuffed with lovely furniture and every piece seemed to have a story attached to it. I was hooked from a tender age. When she died she left various bits and pieces to different members of the family and I came in for a Sheraton worktable and a couple of Chippendale chairs. I wouldn't let anyone else touch them and insisted on having them in my room and dusting them myself. What a poisonous little bastard! Though, mind you, I did have my reasons.'

'Like what?'

'Well, dusting and polishing was never much of a priority at home. My parents were too busy and too unworldly to care if they ate off orange boxes. They were left quite a number of lovely things but most were sold right away. Possessions meant very little to them, you see. A table was a table, and money meant that more could be spent on good works. There was a mission station in Uganda that profited mightily, I seem to remember, much to my annoyance at the time. I was of the Charity Begins at Home tendency.'

His father, he told me, was vicar of a large parish and their home was chaotic, never

112

without a full complement of hard-luck cases, battered wives and assorted down-and-outs.

'Did you really mind?'

He considered the question.

'Sometimes. Yes – there were definitely occasions when I felt they had more time for other people than they did for their own kids. As my brother Andy once said in a burst of totally uncharacteristic non-PC-ness, you get tired of having the place littered with quadriplegic, blind, one-parent lepers.'

'*Lepers?*'

'He exaggerated. But a houseful of unfortunates of one kind or another was something we grew up with. That's the way it was.'

'Is it still like that?'

'Not any more. Well, not so much. My dad's retired now, and although he still gets hauled out to take services here and there, they left the vicarage years ago. They're still in the same village, but they live in a two-bedroom, highly efficient modern box.'

'Do they hate it, after the vicarage?'

'Are you kidding? They keep warm in winter for the first time ever. And the roof doesn't leak whenever it rains.'

'What about brothers and sisters? Any more besides the politically incorrect Andy?'

'I have a sister. Karen. Andrew's the clever

one – a research scientist, three years older than me, highly successful. He's working up in Scotland at the moment, doing something incredibly technical to do with the oil industry. More, better, faster – you know the kind of thing. He's married to a journalist called Mary and they have two kids – a girl and a boy, Charlotte and Hugh. My sister, Karen, is younger than me by two years. She's nursing in the Middle East, engaged to a doctor. They're supposed to be coming home to be married in the autumn.'

'You're all close?'

'Very.'

'That's wonderful. I envy you.'

'We've been lucky. Not that I thought that when we were young! Andy and I hated being the children of the manse. We always felt we were expected to be cleaner than clean in word, thought and deed and we were *never*, under any circumstances, allowed to miss Sunday school! The vicar's family is always on show, you see. Andy and I thought it most unfair.'

'How about Karen?'

'Well, she was better at toeing the party line. A good actress, was Karen. Very prim and proper on the outside, but in fact artful as a wagonload of monkeys. She could get away with murder. We teased her like mad, but really we rather respected her for it.' He laughed, reminiscently. 'Many's the time

Andy or I, or both, ended up carrying the can for something she'd done. Dad was always so bloody *sorrowful* when we'd transgressed. I used to wish he'd swear a bit and belt me one, like my mate Joe's dad. Get the whole thing over, you know?'

'I think it all sounds rather idyllic.'

He laughed at that.

'I suppose it was, in a way. We knew just where we were with them, what was expected of us, that nothing we did shook the way they felt about us and that they'd always be there, like twin Rocks of Gibraltar. I think that's the biggest gift any parents can give their kids, don't you?'

'Yes, I do. And I suppose, for all I say about my own mother, that's what she tried to do. It wasn't easy, on her own.'

'It can't have been. And then losing Jim—'

'I don't think she ever got over it. I don't suppose you would, losing a child. It was bad enough for me.'

I found myself telling him about that terrible time, and the way the house on Cape Cod had somehow come to represent safety and security to me. I told him about the New York apartment and how I was determined to sell it.

'And your work?' he asked. 'I suppose you're between jobs at the moment.'

'I kind of feel I'm between everything at

the moment,' I said. 'Where to live, what to do. I've given up all idea of going on with acting.'

'Why on earth?'

'It's a world I don't like very much. I don't fit into it.'

'No?' He raised a sceptical eyebrow. 'My bet is that you'll go back to it.' He was looking at me with the crooked smile I found so attractive. 'You have the looks and the personality, and you have the right contacts. That must help.'

'Talent helps more,' I said. 'And that, unfortunately, is in short supply.'

'I don't believe it.'

'With all due respect, Steve, you may know your Chippendale from your Sheraton, but you don't know the first thing about my acting ability. From all you tell me, your sister Karen might be more of a success than I'll ever be.'

'What do you want to do?'

Even after considering the question for the hundredth time, I still shook my head, defeated.

'I don't know,' I said. 'I have this strange feeling that maybe if I just wait – if I'm receptive to new ideas – something irresistible will offer itself.'

'I think you're wise.' He grinned at me. 'Look, this offer may not come into the irresistible class, but why don't we have a

116

day out somewhere in the country this weekend? I have to stick around the shop tomorrow, but I'm free as air on Sunday. I feel it my solemn duty to show you a little of Britain's heritage. How about Bleinheim? Have you been there?'

'No, I haven't, but I've heard of it. It's a stately home, isn't it?'

'It's a palace, the seat of the Duke of Marlborough, and it's in Oxfordshire. No self-respecting tourist should miss it.'

'I'd love to see it.' I would, I admitted to myself, probably have said the same no matter what destination he'd suggested, but Blenheim would do very well. 'So you'll be working all day tomorrow? Why don't you come and have dinner with me at the hotel tomorrow night?'

'Wow!' He opened his eyes wide. 'Dinner at Quentins? That's an offer I'm incapable of refusing! Thanks – I accept with pleasure.'

So, I thought as a little later we drove back to the hotel, I'd be seeing him tomorrow and the next day, too. And I smiled to myself, thinking it had turned out to be not such a bad day after all.

The dinner was superb. It did occur to me during the course of it that maybe Steve might want to make a night of it, but though he stayed late we didn't move beyond the hotel lounge which, rather to my relief, we had to ourselves. What would I have said or done if he'd made any move that indicated he wanted to stay? Gone along with it, I think; but in a way, much as I was attracted to him, I was glad he didn't. I had a sense that the time wasn't right.

The next day, Sunday, dawned bright and sunny, and as we drove out towards Oxford I felt happy and optimistic, looking forward to a day in Steve's company and quite content to put all thoughts of finding Caroline on hold.

We found no lack of things to talk about, though there were periods when we were silent, happy to enjoy the countryside, with its woods and fields and little woolly lambs.

We drove through the lovely village of Woodstock and, at the end of it, turned into the grounds of Blenheim, the first sight of which took my breath away.

'My God, what a place,' I breathed. 'Surely it's even grander than Buckingham Palace?'

'Gift of a grateful parliament to the duke,' Steve said as we parked the car and walked round the building to take a proper look at it.

'They sure must have been grateful.'

'He won a great battle for them. But nothing changes, you know. Apparently his wife, Sarah, had constant battles with the

118

architect and the builders because they didn't finish on time. *And* she was fighting with them on her own because the duke was off heaven knows where, having the military equivalent of a heavy day at the office.'

'Nothing changes!'

'She was a feisty lady, our duchess – and a great favourite of Queen Anne. Let's go for a walk in the park first, shall we, while the sun shines? We can see the house later.'

We set out round the lake and Steve sketched in some of the background to the original duke and duchess, their lives and loves. Maybe it was the thought of all these lords and ladies that reminded me, for I suddenly thought of Sir Timothy Crofthouse, the man who had sent flowers to Mom's funeral. I asked Steve if he had ever heard of him.

'Crofthouse? Certainly I have. He's quite a power in the land.'

'In what way?'

'Anything Artful and Crafty. His family is immensely wealthy. They owned Crofts.'

'What's Crofts?'

'The supermarket chain. Not that he has anything to do with that now – I believe they sold out to some German company years ago – but he's on numerous quangos. Quasi non-governmental organisations,' he added, seeing my uncomprehending expression. 'He's also some kind of adviser to the government on things to do with the arts. There's a Crofthouse Gallery at the Tate and an annual Crofthouse Prize for young musicians.'

I frowned, as much in the dark as ever.

'I wonder how he ever got to know my mother,' I mused. 'Through his interest in the arts, maybe – though she was never really interested in "the arts" in an abstract kind of way. All she knew was who and what was saleable. At that she excelled.'

'The Crofthouses live at Fincote, not far from where my grandmother used to live. It's a very grand house.'

'As grand as this?' I gestured towards Blenheim Palace, which we could now see across the lake, looking even more impressive from a distance than at close quarters. Steve laughed.

'Not quite – but pretty damned grand, I'm telling you. My grandmother told me that time was when the aristocracy looked down on the Crofthouses as 'trade', but that was three or four generations ago. I think your Sir Timothy is the third baronet. Very establishment!'

'I simply don't understand,' I said. 'He can't have been a close friend. You know how Mom felt about Englishmen!'

'Maybe she made an exception for baronets.'

'I would have expected that to put her off

more than anything else.'

'I've seen him on TV and he comes over as a nice guy – not that I know him personally.'

'Well, it's a complete mystery to me. I just can't imagine how their paths could have crossed.'

'You could always drop into Fincote and ask him,' Steve said. 'As it happens, I'm going that way tomorrow – there's a viewing at a country house in the Surrey Hills. Look, why don't you come, too? Lovells are auctioning the contents on Wednesday and I have a shrewd idea I might find a few things to interest me.'

'That'd be great.' I responded with enthusiasm, my main emotion being one of joy that having had dinner with me the previous night and then spent this entire day in my company, he was still coming up for more. 'And, hey,' I went on, 'maybe I'll see something I'd like to buy for myself.'

'Why not?' he said lightly. Innocent words, yet somehow I sensed the faintest of chills. I came to a halt so that he was forced to turn and look at me.

'Something wrong?' he asked, frowning.

'Not with me,' I said. 'But I feel some strange vibes from you. What is it, Steve?'

For a moment he didn't reply, but just sighed and looked away past me, away into the distance.

'Look,' he said after a minute. 'There's

something I've got to tell you.' There was a bench a few yards ahead of us and he took my arm and led me to it. I was so apprehensive about what was coming next that I kept my mouth shut and waited for him to get to the point.

We sat down side by side and for a moment there was silence between us, as if he were having difficulty knowing where to begin.

'Thursday night,' he said at last. 'I owe you an explanation.' I began to protest, but he imprisoned my hand in his and gave it a shake as if to signal me to stop. 'I've just got to get things clear,' he went on. 'It's important to be straight with you, right from the beginning.'

The beginning of what? I almost asked him, straight out, but managed not to.

'Go on,' I said, in a neutral kind of voice.

'Well – I told you I wasn't married. That was true,' he added hastily, seeing my puzzled look. 'But only just. I was divorced six months ago.'

'But you still love her?' I was struggling to understand what this confession was all about.

'No – no, not at all. Well, I did once, of course, but not lately. I was just thankful when the whole thing was over.'

'Well, I'm sorry if you were unhappy, but Steve—' I paused and looked at him, still puzzled. 'What has this got to do with Thursday night?'

Distractedly he ran a hand through his hair.

'I'm telling this all wrong,' he said. 'Let me start again.' He gave a kind of glancing smile in my direction. 'The whole point is that my wife – Tanya – married beneath her.'

'What?' I was laughing now.

'She always thought so, anyway. She was – is – very beautiful and her parents are filthy rich. They live in the stockbroker belt in a vast, ten-year-old Tudor Gem in Sunningdale, right by the golf course. None of that seemed to matter at first. Not to her, anyway, though I have to say her parents never approved of me. They believed, quite rightly, that I would never be able to keep her in the manner to which she was accustomed. She didn't mind, she said. She had a soul above sordid details such as paying the grocery bill – and anyway, Daddy would always help out if the worst came to the worst. Without going into all the sordid details, I'll just say that it didn't work out.' He gave a mirthless grunt of laughter. 'And believe me, that's the understatement of the year.'

'Were there children?'

Steve shook his head.

'No, thank God. I – we – both wanted them, to start with, but when Tanya got

123

tired of living the simple life she said she wouldn't dream of having a kid before I'd come to my senses and taken the mind-numbing job her father was currently offering me. I wouldn't. *Couldn't.* Honestly, I considered it, and I tried in the interest of harmony to agree to it, but there was no way I could have lived like that, no matter what I was paid. So then she found someone else—' He broke off. 'Look,' he said, facing me, one elbow on the back of the seat. 'I was as much to blame as she was. I know I'm pig-headed and single-minded about my work. It's a passion with me, not just a job. She was pampered all her life, brought up in the kind of home where it's impossible to hold up your head if you don't own an Olympic-sized swimming pool. I told you what my childhood home was like, and nothing could be more different. The only pool we had was on the landing where the roof leaked and the rain came in. We were chalk and cheese, with different outlooks, different priorities.'

I let this hang in the air a bit before I spoke again.

'So now you're a free man again,' I said after a moment. 'That's good, surely?'

'Except that she took me for every penny she could get. God knows why the court was so generous towards her. It just about wiped me out financially.'

124

'That was tough, with your own business to run. Couldn't you appeal?'

'I considered it; then I thought, to hell with her – with all of them. I just wanted to walk away, forget it all, start again.'

'And you will,' I said, reaching to touch his arm. 'I'm sure you will. But I still don't quite understand what was with you on Thursday night.'

He gave a breath of laughter.

'You can't make the connection? Can't see why I should have had a sudden fit of déjà vu when confronted with a beautiful girl who I suddenly realised was also loaded?'

'Not unless you were planning to ask me to marry you over the tagliatelle.'

He laughed again.

'No,' he admitted. 'I hadn't got that far. But I did feel a certain – shall we say *frisson*?' He gave the word an exaggerated French pronunciation and quirked his eyebrows in a kind of stage-Gallic manner, mocking himself. 'Then, over dinner, all my defence mechanisms went into action when I realised that once more I'd frissoned over a girl who was way out of my league.'

'Is this friendship, or a game of baseball?' I asked him, happy and relieved now that I recognised the problem. It had been the money, all along! Of all the crazy things!

He leant and kissed me on the cheek.

'Friendship, I hope,' he said.

'Me, too. Don't let's complicate things with money. It couldn't be less important.'

'Only people with plenty think like that. I'm skint, Holly. It's not a comfortable thing to be.'

'But you turned down the chance of a well-paid job to do the thing you love, so you're not beyond hope.'

He laughed, then sighed, but somehow his confession seemed to have cleared the air, made him happier.

Getting to his feet, he reached for my hand and pulled me to mine.

'Come on,' he said. 'Let's go and see the house.'

'No, wait! You must swear not to let filthy lucre spoil a promising friendship?'

'I'll try,' he said, then he paused a moment, his hands on my shoulders. 'How promising?' he asked.

'That rather depends.'

'You can buy Lovell's entire stock and I won't turn a hair,' he promised. 'I swear it! Tomorrow is still on, isn't it?' He pulled me a little closer, adding softly, 'Or have you had enough of me?' His face as suddenly still, his eyes questioning. Deliberately provocative, I smiled up at him, feeling for the first time in control of the situation.

'I'll tell you after tomorrow,' I said. 'What time do you plan to leave?'

He grinned at me, those clear grey eyes suddenly alive and a network of lines fanning out from their corners. He pulled me even closer and wrapped me in a bear hug, laughing delightedly.

'If you're at the shop by about one, we can grab a pub lunch and shoot off as soon as maybe.' He took my hand and we set off once more down the grassy path. 'Ideally, I'd like to get away before, but it can't be managed. I haven't any help at the moment, so I have to close up the shop when I'm not there.'

'That must be inconvenient.'

'I'll say it's inconvenient – but it can't be helped. Assistants are an expensive luxury.'

I looked at him and marvelled, thinking that to run a business in this way was surely like doing so with one hand tied behind his back – but I made no comment, the subject of money being taboo.

'Let's go and inspect the palace,' I said.

My main preoccupation the following morning was to place the ads asking for information about Caroline. I contacted all the papers that Steve had suggested, and after a lot of thought I dictated:

BETHANY. Would Caroline Bethany, last heard of in Oxford in 1991, or anyone with any knowledge of her

whereabouts, please contact James
Fenton (Jim) Crozier's sister urgently,
view friendship and support.

I'd omitted Jim's full name in my first draft,
but then thought that maybe it would be as
well to print the whole lot. The notice
would, I was told, appear in the personal
column of the newspapers the following
day, under a box number. So that was taken
care of.

I then looked up Greenway Development
in the directory and copied down the
address. I had made up my mind that I
would pay them a visit rather than contact
them by telephone, feeling that I was more
likely to find someone to help me if I were
standing before them in person. And
indeed, the way I was passed from hand to
hand when I got there made me feel that I
had made the right decision.

The company seemed to have a policy of
employing only the young and trendy, none
of whom had heard of Caroline Bethany. I
was directed, eventually, to the office of the
human resources manager who, despite the
impressive title, looked about fifteen. After
proclaiming himself baffled, he suggested a
visit to the accounts department, where I
would find a certain Doreen Mortimore
who had been with the company 'for ever'.

I did not find this difficult to believe.

Miss Mortimore was angular, with a thin nose, even thinner lips, and little round eye-glasses. She could have been any age between forty and sixty. I put my question to her and for a moment she did not answer but merely looked at me suspiciously, that forbidding mouth folded into a tight little circle. After a moment, still in silence, she turned to her computer terminal and punched a few more keys, staring at the screen as if she did not at all like what she saw. I hovered beside her, trying to be patient.

'Caroline Bethany,' she said musingly at last, turning her head to look at me with ice-cold eyes. 'Of course I knew her. I remember her well. Why do you want to know?'

'I'm trying to find her,' I explained, and launched into my spiel. Over from America, anxious to contact my late brother's friends, et cetera, et cetera.

'She did have an American boyfriend, that's true.'

'That was my brother. Please – have you any idea where she is now?'

'None,' she said briefly, and turned back to her computer, apparently once more absorbed in the columns of figures on the screen. Was that it? I continued to hover in the hope that something helpful might yet be forthcoming.

'To tell you the truth,' I said, when she

continued to disregard my existence, 'I'm beginning to get a little anxious about her. She seems to have dropped out of existence.'

Miss Mortimore permitted herself a thin smile, her eyes still on the monitor.

'One thing I can tell you for certain,' she said. 'She'll be all right, wherever she is. Caroline Bethany is a survivor. She knows exactly how to take care of herself.'

'What makes you say that?' I asked.

She arched her neck and massaged it a little, not answering for a moment. Then she shrugged.

'We joined Greenways at about the same time, Caroline and I. She was younger than me, less experienced all round. She was taken on as a junior secretary. I came into the accounts department. Now I'm in charge of it – responsible for all this.' Vaguely she lifted an arm to indicate the rest of the room, where half a dozen other girls were busy with their own computers.

'Congratulations,' I murmured, and she laughed derisively.

'Congratulations? Fifteen years it's taken me. Fifteen years!' She paused again and bashed a key or two. 'In six months Caroline Bethany had become secretary and personal assistant to the managing director.' She turned and looked at me, her mouth set in a bitter little smile, her eyes hard and cold.

'You can draw your own conclusions from that.'

'Perhaps she was simply very good at her job,' I said.

Doreen Mortimore gave a snort of laughter.

'Let's say she was a pretty girl who was very good at making up to the right people! Mr Quigley was MD at the time, and in no time at all she was arranging social events for him, going to parties at his house, taking shopping trips with Mrs Quigley, going to the ballet and opera and art exhibitions – we all knew about it. It was the talk of the place.'

'Is he still here, this Mr Quigley?'

'No. He left years ago. Eleven or twelve at the very least.' She turned to her screen once more, with an air of finality. 'I'm afraid that's all I can tell you. I really am very busy, so if you'll excuse me—'

'Can't you tell me where to find him?'

'No, I can't.' She had reached for a file now and was studying it carefully, making it abundantly clear that she had no more time for me. I sighed.

'Well, thanks,' I said, and left her.

I was walking a little disconsolately down the corridor towards the elevator when a thought struck me which made me turn right around and find my way to the human resources guy again.

'I'm awfully sorry to bother you,' I said to him. 'I wonder if, perhaps, you have Mr Quigley's home address in your files? Miss Mortimore tells me he was the managing director here in Caroline Bethany's time. Before—'

'Before Mr Miller-Formby? Yes, that's right. I never knew him, but I've heard the name and seen his signature on various old documents.' He looked at me doubtfully. 'I suppose we must have it somewhere, but I can't possibly divulge it. It wouldn't be ethical.'

I gave my best smile and batted my eye-lashes at him, feeling a little guilty as I saw the tide of red that flooded his face.

'I wouldn't want you to do anything that wasn't strictly above board,' I said sweetly. 'How about his phone number? It's his wife I really want to speak to. It seems she was friendly with Caroline, and I'm so anxious to find her. This is the best lead I've had yet.'

He cleared his throat, eased his collar, and looked away from me, biting his lip. Then he glanced in my direction again, still blushing, and gave a small, uncertain smile.

'Well—' he said doubtfully.

Lightly, I touched his arm.

'You know what?' I said. 'British men are just the sweetest in the world, and the most intelligent. Now, if you were American you'd simply stick by the rules without using your brain at all.'

I seemed to hear Grandma McAllister's voice in my ear, saying, 'Mary Lou, may you be forgiven!'

'I suppose if it's Mrs Quigley you want to see...' His voice trailed away as he considered the matter further. 'Well, I can't see the harm,' he finished, suddenly making up his mind. 'Hang on a moment.'

He disappeared and was away for five minutes or so before coming back with a scrap of paper in his hand which he gave to me with a nervous smile.

'Just don't let on it was me who gave it to you,' he said.

'I won't,' I said. 'I promise.'

Full of glee, I left the offices of Greenway Development and managed to find a telephone in the street outside where I wasted no time in dialling the number I'd been given – first ensuring that I had a pocketful of change, as I had no idea of the location of the Quigley residence. It could, as far as I knew, be in the north of Scotland.

I soon found it was not that far away. It was a woman who picked up the phone, and the words she used were enough to cause me a flutter of excitement.

'Henley 00963,' she said.

Seven

'*Henley*!' I said to Steve when we met for lunch. 'Wasn't that the place you said was on the River Thames? So it could have been at the Quigleys' house that Caroline and Jim met.'

'Could be,' Steve said. 'Didn't you ask?'

'I thought it could wait until we met – but surely it has to be, Steve. Caroline and Mrs Quigley – Rose – were friends and, according to Doreen Mortimore, spent a lot of time in each other's company. Which, I may say, our Miss Mortimore didn't approve of one bit! She was practically spitting nails about it, even after all this time.'

'What did you and Rose arrange?'

'She said she didn't think she could help but that she'd like to meet me and to talk about Caroline, so I said I'd go out there tomorrow morning. I might learn something useful, who knows? I'll hire a car and drive myself.'

Steve looked dubious.

'Are you happy about that? I wish you'd let me drive you. Only thing is, the morning's absolutely out for me – I've got two appointments I really mustn't miss. I'd be glad to take you later in the day, though.'

I can't say that driving out of London on the wrong side of the road to a place I didn't know was particularly appealing, and for a moment I was tempted by Steve's offer. In the end, though, I shook my head.

'No, Steve. Thanks all the same, but Rose seemed to imply it would be better for her if I went in the morning, and that's what I agreed to do so I'd better abide by it. Besides, it'll stop me just sitting around feeling frustrated. I guess it's time I got to grips with driving in England. All I need is someone to point me in the direction of Henley.'

'For God's sake be careful.'

'I will,' I promised him. 'Believe me, I'm a good driver. Honestly! And I have this kind of hunch that says if you can drive in New York you can drive anywhere.'

'Rose,' he said musingly, apparently accepting my assurances. 'Now you mention it, I think I remember Caroline talking about her. I never met her, though. My impression was that seeing her was more in the line of duty. I wouldn't have said they seemed really close.'

'Then who *was* she close to, Steve? Think!'

We were in the pub by this time, drinking beer and eating ham sandwiches, and for a moment he chewed reflectively. Then he shook his head, defeated.

'It's no good. I've racked my brains ever since you asked me before, but I don't think I ever heard the last name of any of her friends. You must remember I didn't know Caroline until after she was heavily involved with Jim and to say they didn't have much time for anyone but each other was the understatement of the century. You know how it is.'

I know, I thought, how I'd like it to be, but I confined myself to nodding without speaking.

'Maybe the ads will winkle someone out,' he went on. 'Like I said before, London's a bit of a transit camp. People move on, everyone's rushing around with no time for anyone but themselves. For which,' he added unhappily, 'I have to take my share of guilt. It's frightening to think now how I took it as quite normal that Caroline should want to drop out. I was so busy trying to get the resources together to go into business on my own that I didn't pause to wonder why on earth she'd do such a thing.'

'You think it was out of character?'

'Yes, I do, now I think of it. Way out of character. The whole scene, I mean, from not saying anything about the baby to having this split with her aunt and never getting in touch with her again. I can't get my head around that. It simply doesn't tie in with anything I know about her. She had a warm, spontaneous kind of nature and though I can imagine her flying off the handle under pressure I can't believe she wouldn't attempt some kind of reconciliation.'

'It does seem strange, doesn't it?' I thought it over. 'Unless—' I began. Then interrupted myself. 'No, that's too silly.'

'What were you going to say?'

'Only that – well, maybe something happened to her. Something to prevent a reunion, I mean.'

'Like what?'

'I don't know. I can't help wondering...'

For some reason the taxi driver had come into my mind, with his talk of Jim's accident not being an accident at all, that he could have been run down deliberately. I'd dismissed it out of hand at the time, but now I couldn't help thinking – suppose the same thing had happened to Caroline? Who would know? Her aunt was her only living relative and under the circumstances she might not have got to hear of it. I guess my face expressed my emotions.

'What is it?' Steve asked. 'You look as if you've just thought of something.'

For a moment I said nothing. It all seemed so crazily melodramatic, so utterly impossible. This was, after all, peaceful England, not downtown Los Angeles. Steve would

137

surely laugh at me, tell me I was foolish to harbour such a thought for one second. But in the end I told him, and he didn't laugh. He merely sat staring at me, brows drawn together.

'I never heard any such suggestion at the time,' he said after a moment. 'What happened to Jim was an awful, shocking, horrific tragedy and no one had words bad enough for the driver of the car, but I never heard it suggested that it could have been anything more than an accident.'

'But Jim ran down that road to the fields every day, didn't he?'

'Almost every day, I think. He liked to keep fit.'

'So his movements were predictable?'

'Yes, I suppose so. But Holly, this really is in the realms of fantasy. What possible reason could anyone have had for killing him deliberately? He was just a nice guy, lived with a nice girl, loved good paintings and Italian food and playing squash and having fun. He never did any harm to anyone, so any kind of conspiracy theory doesn't make any sense. Yet, on the other hand—'

He paused and I looked at him uncertainly.

'On the other hand, what?'

'There's no doubt that Caroline's disappearance is a bit of a mystery. Why would

138

she cut off all communication with the people she knew before? Is it remotely possible that she and Jim knew something – saw something—?'

Suddenly I found I had lost all appetite for my sandwich.

'No – no, I don't suppose so. I expect there's some perfectly normal explanation.' He continued to look uneasy, though, as he looked at his watch. 'We ought to be off if you've had all you want.'

By mutual consent we didn't talk much about Jim and Caroline on the way down to Fallowlands, the large house just beyond Dorking where the sale was to take place. We talked instead about holidays: where we'd been, where we'd like to go. It seemed a delightful coincidence to discover that we both cherished the dream of sailing up the Amazon.

'And I really, really want to see the Great Wall of China,' I said.

'Been there, done that.'

'When?'

'Before I went to university. I backpacked around Australia and the Far East. Doesn't everyone?'

'That must have been fun!'

He laughed at that.

'Yes, it was. Maybe more fun in retrospect than it was at the time. We often slept rough, and sometimes didn't have enough to eat, but I wouldn't have missed it for the world.'

'So then you came home. Where did you go to university?'

'Bristol. It's a seaport in the south west—'

'I know where Bristol is! I'm not that ignorant.'

'Oh, beg your pardon, I'm sure! I suppose it was there I really got hooked on antiques. There are some fantastic old shops in the back streets – were, anyway. It was all a long time ago. I expect they've all gone upmarket by now.'

'Is there something particular you're looking for today?' I asked him.

'Mm.' His expression was a touch rueful, as if all depended on whether he could raise the funds. 'I've been lusting over the catalogue ever since I got hold of it. There's a Victorian scrollback sofa that I'd love to get my hands on. I have just the buyer for it, ready and waiting if only it goes for the right price.'

'What about pictures? Will there be any?'

'Yes, quite a lot – but not for me. That's not my field.'

My mind zoomed back to Jim, whose field it was. And, of course, Caroline.

'I do hope we get a lead from those ads,' I said, and in response Steve took one hand off the wheel and rested it momentarily on my trousered thigh. It was a casual, asexual touch that was meant to bring comfort, but to me it seemed to burn like fire. Maybe to him, too, for his touch didn't linger and his voice sounded a little strained when he spoke.

'Patience,' he said. 'We can only wait and see.'

Fallowlands turned out to be an impressive, solid kind of house. Victorian, Steve said, and a bit of a monstrosity, but I rather liked its Gothic turrets and irrelevant balconies. It seemed to me to demonstrate the enormous self-confidence, the total lack of self-doubt that must have informed those old Empire-builders.

We approached it by a sweeping drive lined with trees and were directed around the back to park the car and to enter by what I imagined was the tradesmen's entrance. Steve manoeuvred his battered Ford alongside a gleaming red Porsche.

'Maybe one day,' he said, looking at it longingly.

'Thou shalt not covet thy neighbour's automobile,' I said, and he laughed.

'That belongs to someone who's more a neighbour of yours than mine. Rupert Craven. He has a gallery in St James's Street, specialising in Victorian watercolours. Guess he's interested in the Marleys.'

I'd never heard the name of that particular artist but wasn't about to confess my ignorance, so said nothing. In any case, he had spoken absently, as if his mind were elsewhere, and I guessed that it was his own affairs that were uppermost in his mind.

Once inside, amongst all the other dealers and various members of the public, it interested me to see how he became, suddenly, very serious and professional. From various things he had said to me I understood that his feeling for fine craftsmanship was almost like a love affair; it thrilled him much as a Beethoven symphony thrilled a music lover, the grain of a piece of wood giving him as much pleasure as Jim would have found in a Rembrandt or a Vermeer. It was clear, too, that he enjoyed the thrill of the chase – the feeling that *this* might be the day that he would discover some magnificent piece at a bargain price.

Here, on his own ground, I hung back, letting him go ahead to do his own particular thing. I saw how he was greeted by other dealers – could see that they liked and respected him – and it gave me vicarious pleasure to witness it.

I tried not to watch him too obviously and began to inspect the lots for myself, but after a few moments I looked round and saw that he was squatting down to peer at the underside of a small table. As I watched, a small, elderly lady tapped him on the shoulder with her catalogue and he looked up at her with a smile, standing up at once to answer the questions she was clearly asking him concerning that particular piece of furniture. He pointed out different features, stooping again to show her the curve of the legs.

He was unhurried, good-humoured, and I could see that she was charmed by him, smiling to herself long after he had raised his hand in farewell and gone on to look at something else.

I'm right about him, I thought, seeing this byplay. He's a nice man. A *really* nice man, of the kind that I had signally failed to meet at any stage in my life before. But the attraction I felt for him wasn't just because of his niceness. Chemistry was at work as well – so powerfully that I had an over-whelming urge to go over to his side and put my arms around him. Instead I made a great effort and turned my back on him, wandering over to a piece of furniture that caught my eye. I looked it up in my catalogue – Lot 239, a Sheraton worktable in satinwood. It felt silky to the touch, and the shape of it was as satisfying, I thought, as a good meal. This, if nothing else, illus-trated Steve's point; nothing was more beautiful than good wood and excellent craftsmanship. It would be interesting to know about such things; to learn how to distinguish the fake from the genuine article. Maybe he would teach me, I thought hopefully. Well, a girl can dream, can't she?

The pictures were in an adjoining room and, resolutely leaving Steve to himself, I went through to see what was on offer. A group of watercolours caught my eye. I looked them up in the catalogue, too, and saw that they were described as being 'attributed to Augustus Marley'. It took me a moment to realise that the man who was studying them earnestly only a yard or two away was none other than Mr Higginson, the man I had taken such a dislike to at Lovells. He glanced at me indifferently and turned away again before apparently realising my identity and looking once more in my direction to nod stiffly in greeting.

I nodded back but said nothing, moving a few feet away from him to study a large oil painting which had pride of place on an adjoining wall. It depicted a family dressed in eighteenth-century costume. There was Papa in his wig and velvet jacket looking ahead proudly, head erect. Beside him was Mama who, in an elaborate, diaphanous blue dress, gazed fondly upwards at her husband, several angelic-looking children draped artistically around her knee and a small lapdog leaping up on his two hind legs.

'Happy families!' said a voice in my ear. 'Such sentimental twaddle! The mother was

144

no better than she should be, the father was a sadist and the child on the right grew up to be transported to Australia for fraud.' It was Higginson who had come up to me unawares and was standing at my shoulder. 'Zoffany,' he added.

'Zoffany?' In my ignorance I had never heard of this artist, any more than I had heard of Augustus Marley.

'Currently one of the most valuable eighteenth-century painters of the English conversation piece. Second rate, in my opinion, but there you are – that's the art world for you. Fashions come and fashions go. Collectors in this materialistic age suddenly appear to see virtue in this kind of faithful reproduction of clothes and furniture and smug, happy families.' He sniffed disparagingly. 'Sentimental nonsense,' he said again.

'Well, it sure beats dead cows in formaldehyde in my opinion,' I said. 'Actually, I think it's great. You can feel the texture of that curtain and the mother's dress.'

His lips twitched in disdainful amusement.

'If that's what you want, of course ... Well, I have no doubt it will attract a good price from a like-minded buyer.' What he meant, judging from his expression and the tone of his voice, was 'like-minded moron'. He moved away, back towards the watercolours, which were far more impression-istic. 'These, now, are more to my taste.'

It occurred to me that Higginson might know if Jim had made any enemies in the art world, preposterous though this might sound to me, and after a moment I followed with the intention of asking him. However, before I could open my mouth we were joined by a tall, smiling man who looked as if he had been typecast as a member of the aristocracy in a Hollywood movie. He had handsome features, fair hair brushed back over his ears, and was wearing clothes that looked both studiedly casual and fabulously expensive.

'Ah, there you are, Higginson.' The voice went with the face. It was well-modulated, relentlessly upper class. 'I wondered where you'd got to.' He gave me a charming smile. 'But now I've seen your delightful compan-ion, I don't blame you for dallying a little.'

I smiled back, but restrainedly. Crazy about himself, I thought – and was inwardly amused at the thought of what my mother would find to say about him.

Higginson directed his tight-lipped and utterly unconvincing smile in my direction.

'Miss Crozier,' he said. 'May I introduce Rupert Craven?'

The owner of the red Porsche, I remem-bered. I acknowledged the introduction and noted, with interest, that Craven's blue eyes

146

appeared to sharpen as he registered my name.

'Ah – so *you're* Jim Crozier's sister,' he said, smiling down at me.

So he'd heard of my presence here; Higginson must have mentioned it. But why would he have done that? When I'd spoken to him at Lovells there had been nothing in his manner to indicate he'd rated my presence sufficiently interesting to report to anyone.

'Yes, I'm Jim's sister.'

'I was so sorry when he died. A tragic business.'

'Miss Crozier,' Higginson said, 'has come to England with some misguided idea of trying to trace her brother's associates, though what she hopes to gain from this is somewhat obscure.'

I ignored this and turned towards Craven.

'How well did you know Jim?' I asked him.

'Quite well. In fact, I'd say we were good friends. I frequently bought at auction – still do, of course – so I often came across him in the way of business, but apart from that we often met socially. I first met him at the home of a mutual friend – someone I happened to meet at the American embassy – and after that we played squash and socialised.'

'Did you know Caroline?'

'Did I not?' He smiled reminiscently. 'A

delightful girl. Believe it or not, it was I who introduced them. I'd taken Jim with me to my sister's house one Sunday for lunch.' He turned to Higginson politely, as if wishing to include him in the conversation. 'You've met Rose, haven't you? She and George were having a bit of a party—'

'Rose is your sister? Rose Quigley?' I stared at him in astonishment. 'That's an incredible coincidence! I'm going to visit her tomorrow.'

'Well, isn't that strange?' He twinkled at me engagingly. 'Though perhaps not so strange as all that. George Quigley is something of a collector and the art world is quite a small one. We all move in the same circles, round and round and round. I had no knowledge of Mr Higginson's movements today, but I'd have bet any money on running into him. I knew he'd be enticed by the Marleys. Aren't we all?'

'I suppose it's no use asking you if you know where I can find Caroline?' I said. 'Your sister said she had no news.'

'Your visit will surely be rather a waste of time, then,' Higginson said, a touch waspishly. I wondered why he should care either way, but refused to rise to the scornful note in his voice. I smiled at him sweetly.

'Mrs Quigley said she would welcome it.'

'And I'm sure she would,' Craven said lightly. 'Poor Rose doesn't see many people these days. Well, Miss Crozier, it's been a great pleasure to meet you, but I regret that duty calls. By the way—' He indicated the watercolours with an inclination of his beautifully coiffed head. 'What do you think of these?'

I looked once more at the pictures, six in number, and though I was conscious of an unworthy desire to pronounce them hideous simply because Higginson liked them so much, I couldn't find it in my heart to do so. No way! They were simply lovely – delicate and understated yet somehow radiant with light.

'I think they're wonderful,' I said. 'But why do they say "attributed" to Augustus Marley? Is there some doubt that he actually painted them?'

'Oh, I don't think so,' Craven said, genially dismissive. 'What's your opinion, Higginson?'

'There's no doubt whatsoever.' Higginson had moved nearer still and was peering at the pictures. 'They have all the trademarks – that distinctive lightness of touch and way with colours. Absolutely no doubt at all.'

'How much will they go for?' I asked.

'Who can tell?' Higginson shrugged his shoulders. 'It rather depends what dealers are present on the day. I gather, though, that there's considerable overseas interest and my guess is they'll fetch anything from twenty to thirty thousand each. Pounds, of course. Not dollars. Could be even more.'

'Are you going to bid for them, Mr Craven?' I asked.

He smiled inscrutably, and refrained from making any reply.

I became aware, suddenly, that Higginson very much wanted this conversation to be over. There was something in the way he jerked his head to look first at me and then at Rupert Craven, the impatient way he was jingling the change in his pocket. Well, like him or loathe him, I thought, he probably wanted some shop-talk with the gallery owner.

'I mustn't keep you from your deliberations,' I said. 'Nice to have met you, Mr Craven.'

'My pleasure,' he assured me, inclining his head politely. 'Do give Rose my love when you see her.'

Poor Rose, he had called her. Why 'poor'? Perhaps my visit tomorrow would give the answer to that question – as well, hopefully, as those to many others.

I said my goodbyes and left them, making my way back into the main room where I could see Steve standing a little apart from the crowd, talking to a tall, lean, bespectacled woman wearing a dashing red cape and a vast pair of beaten metal earrings. He saw me come through the door and waved to me, clearly inviting me to joint them.

He introduced his companion as Serena Newbold, art correspondent of the *Sunday Chronicle*. She looked, I thought, a touch intimidating at first sight, but I soon forgot first impressions when Steve told me she had known Caroline.

'You *did?*' I turned to her eagerly.

'Well, I knew your brother better. I was so sorry when I heard about the accident. He was a great guy, a laugh a minute. We often met at auctions and exhibitions and so on, and I thought a lot of him. And of Caroline, too. I was working at the Sylvester Galleries then – but as I've been telling Steve, I haven't seen or heard of Caroline for years, so I can't be of much help to you, I'm afraid.'

I tried to hide my disappointment in the interest of good manners.

'I guess that's something I'm getting used to,' I said ruefully. 'But it's good to meet you, anyway. I really love talking to people who knew Jim.'

'Holly was just a kid when he died,' Steve said.

'Yes, she must have been.' Serena smiled at me. 'He was definitely a brother to be proud of, Holly. A bit difficult to live up to, maybe—'

'Difficult? In what way?'

151

She pursed her lips, shrugged her shoulders.

'He was a very—' She hesitated. 'Upright young man. I suppose that makes him sound a bit dull – just the tiniest bit holier than thou – but he wasn't like that at all. Far from it. He made me laugh all the time, but he'd never compromise his standards. Not like some.'

'How do you mean?'

'There's skullduggery in the art world as much as any other. I've known experts such as Jim be offered bribes by gallery owners to authenticate certain dubious so-called treasures. And be leaned on by other experts to do the same. It's dog eat dog out there, I'm telling you, with enormous fortunes to be made.'

I had only to remember the sums mentioned by Higginson regarding those few Marley watercolours to know she wasn't kidding.

'But Jim was incorruptible?'

'One of the good guys,' Serena said.

'Didn't I tell you?' Steve put an arm round my shoulders and gave me a squeeze, as if wanting to lighten the moment. 'Tell me, what did you think of the Marleys?'

'I loved them,' I said. 'In fact, there are lots of things I'm just crazy about. This place is crammed with beautiful things.'

'Yeah!' Steve was grinning down at me. 'I

saw you talking to one of them when I took a look into the next room. For one moment I thought I was to be abandoned in favour of a ride home in a Porsche.'

'No sister of Jim Crozier would be taken in by that great phoney,' Serena said.

'Phoney? Rupert Craven?'

'Oh, nothing proven, of course. Maybe I'm biased – I just can't stand that particular brand of spurious charm. Not that he bothers to exert it in my direction! We crossed swords long ago and now he'll hardly give me the time of day. Personally I wouldn't trust him even as far as I could throw him. Well—' She hitched her cape more comfortably on her shoulders. 'This won't get the column written. I must go and formulate a few coherent ideas about the Marleys. The alleged Marleys, I should say.'

'Higginson says they are beyond doubt.'

Serena smiled and shrugged her shoulders again.

'He's the man who knows,' she said. She wished me good luck in my search for Caroline and left us, Steve bearing me off immediately to show me the Victorian scrollback sofa and one or two other items that he thought I would appreciate.

He was so involved and enthusiastic that I didn't want to break his train of thought by introducing the subject of Rupert Craven and his sister, and it wasn't until we were sitting in the car, about to leave, that I told Steve about what I had discovered.

'Isn't that the oddest coincidence?' I asked him.

He was suddenly still as if struck by an unwelcome thought, his brows drawn together in a frown.

'I'll say it is!'

'And it *was* at Rose's house that Jim met Caroline. Craven said he knew Jim quite well and that he took him one Sunday—'

I fell silent, for it was clear that Steve was busy with his own thoughts and hadn't heard a word of this. He was sitting in the driving seat, not turning the key, just staring in front of him and chewing his lip.

'What is it? What's bugging you?' I asked him.

For a moment he seemed undecided whether to tell me or not. Then, starting the car, he said, 'Tell you over tea. And I know just the place.' He appeared to shake off his preoccupation and turned to smile at down at me. 'Just the cutesiest tea room in the cutesiest little village you ever saw. Guaranteed to delight the heart of any visiting American.'

'Don't you patronise me, you arrogant Limey.'

'As if,' he said gravely.

We followed the main road for a mile or so, then turned down a narrow lane that

154

swooped up and down hill through country-side that was as pastoral as any of Mr Marley's watercolours. There was the sheen of fresh green on the trees, and sheep with their lambs in the fields.

'I like this part of the country,' Steve said. 'My grandmother lived around here when I was young and I always loved coming to stay.'

'I can imagine.'

And I could, too. I had this sudden picture of Steve as a small boy, exploring these woods and fields and wading over that stream, and I stared out of the car window, afraid that some instinct would tell him how much it affected me.

After a few miles we came across an old farmhouse and a cluster of buildings, and beyond them crossroads where Steve made a left turn that quickly brought us into the main street of a small village, complete with village green and duckpond and half-timbered buildings of the kind that to most Americans typify the image of Merrie England. I was no different. I got out of the car and looked around me with delight.

'It's wonderful,' I said. 'You sure hit the nail on the head, Steve – I adore it! Is it for real? It's straight out of a picture book. What did you say it was called?'

'Simmings Cross,' Steve said. 'Look, there's the cross, just by the church. It dates from the middle ages. So does the inn.'

'I love it, I love it! Can we have a look round the church after tea?'

'Why not? If you still want to,' he added, as if for some obscure reason I might have changed my mind by that time.

'Oh, will you just look at that row of cottages?' I begged him. 'They couldn't be more perfect!'

'The big one at the end is where we're having tea.'

We lifted the latch on the heavy oak door and went inside. Apart from one elderly couple, who were already gathering up their things to leave, we were the only people in the cafe – which, I have to admit, had rather gone overboard with the cuteness. There were dark wood wheelback chairs at the round tables, and a wealth of old china, dried flowers, polished brass and chintzy curtains.

A pleasant, fluffy, middle-aged woman in a flowery apron turned from the departing couple to greet us. I guessed she was the owner; she looked, somehow, like a lady who would own a cute tea shop.

'How nice to see you,' she said warmly to me, as if I were an old friend. I thanked her. Such courtesies – probably insincere – are not uncommon in the States and I accepted it as quite normal. But then she added, as we took our seats at a corner table, her voice

156

one of friendly enquiry: 'Are you going to be staying long this time?'

This did faze me a little and briefly I hesitated.

'Just long enough to have some tea, I guess.'

'Oh—' For a second she looked disconcerted, then she gave an embarrassed laugh. 'You're American! Do forgive me. For one moment I thought you were someone I knew, but I can see now I was mistaken. Silly of me! Now, what can I get you?'

I left it to Steve to order tea and scones. He'd tried them before, he said, and they were the best he'd tasted anywhere.

'Now,' I said once she had left us. 'Give! What was it you were going to tell me over tea?'

He drew a long breath.

'Rose Quigley,' he said. 'If she's Rupert Craven's sister, then she must be Piers Craven's sister, too. He's an artist. Of a kind.'

'Famous?'

'More infamous, I'd say.'

'For what?'

He hesitated for a moment or two, his expression troubled.

'Go *on*,' I begged him. 'Don't keep me in suspense.'

'Well, then—' But still he hesitated.

'*Steve!*'

157

'I suppose you ought to be forewarned before you see Rose. Just remember, nothing was proved.'

'*Steve*,' I said again, on the brink of fury.

'All right. I'll tell you. There are those who think that Piers Craven could be guilty of murder.'

I stared at him.

'And he knew Jim,' I said softly. 'He must have done.'

'And Caroline,' Steve said. 'But Holly, we'd be daft to jump to conclusions. He was tried and acquitted for a crime that took place long after Jim died. There was never the slightest suspicion—'

'But they moved in the same circles,' I said. 'They inhabited the same small world.' When Steve said nothing, I looked at him searchingly. 'Tell me what you're thinking, Steve. Do *you* think he was guilty?'

Still he hesitated for a moment.

'I don't know,' he said at last. 'I wouldn't put it past him.'

Eight

I said nothing, for the tea-shop lady had emerged from the kitchen with the tea and scones. In a fever of impatience I waited for her to set out the cups and plates, the butter and jam and cream, the milk and sugar, and the moment she had gone I leant forward anxiously.

'You mean you think he's guilty of the murder he was charged with?' I asked him. 'Or do you mean Jim's?'

'No, no—'

'But you think he would be capable of it?'

'To be honest, I'd believe him capable of almost anything, up to and including necrophilia, but whether he was actually guilty as charged in this instance is another matter.'

'Tell me about it.'

'It's a pretty sordid story,' he warned me. 'Well, let's face it – anything connected with Piers Craven is almost bound to be. He's the complete opposite of Rupert. Rupert bends over backwards to appear suave and worldly-wise, the crème de la crème of the establishment, but Piers is a kind of *enfant terrible* of the art world. Well, let's say he *was*. He's a bit beyond the *enfant* stage now.' He was silent for a moment as he poured the tea, as if taking time to pick his words. 'He's a gifted artist, no doubt about it. A complete original. He won the Turner Prize when he was quite young and was hailed as a kind of prophet of modern art. People put up with his foul language and loutish ways because he was glib and anarchic and funny, and there was a time, about seven or eight years ago, when he was the darling of television chat shows. Any controversial topic connected with art of any kind, and you could be sure of Piers Craven being wheeled out to give his opinion on it. Not any more, though.'

He handed me a cup of tea and proffered the sugar, which I declined with a shake of the head.

'Go on,' I said. 'What happened?'

'Booze happened. And drugs. In the beginning he was outrageous but, as I've said, amusing. Then he became more outrageous and less amusing, then finally the outrageousness became offensive and abusive and he wasn't amusing at all, just extremely embarrassing. There was the odd talk show when he was completely out of his head, and now, I gather, there isn't a TV company who wants to know. He made a few much-publicised attempts to dry out,

160

but he wasn't news any more – until suddenly there was a scandal that involved under-age kids of both sexes. The tabloids had a field day, as you can imagine. Even if one discounts a proportion of the dirt they uncovered, there's no doubt that Piers Craven is bad news in any language. He must have been a terrible headache to poor, respectable Rupert. Very bad for that well-bred, upper-class image!'

'I can imagine.'

'He went to prison for a while for drug dealing – not for very long, in the end. Six months, I think it was. And when he came out he maintained he was a changed character. He was certainly a lot quieter, less in your face all the time. In fact, he disappeared from the London scene altogether and the next thing I heard, he'd founded a kind of commune somewhere on a Welsh hillside – a community of like-minded artists, apparently, whatever that means. Like-minded perverts, I suspect. They live in a decrepit old farmhouse, miles from anywhere, and God knows what goes on there. Certainly he hasn't produced any more paintings worth having. It's as if he's burnt out somehow – as if he peaked too early. You can't help wondering about their background, can you? Piers and Rupert – both so different but both screwed up in their own way. And now Rose.'

'We don't know that she's screwed up.'

'No. Something tells me it would be safe to bet on it, though.'

'I'm determined to go with an open mind. But Steve, what about this murder? The one you mentioned in connection with Piers?'

'Alleged murder,' Steve corrected me. 'I can't really remember all the ins and outs, but there was some sort of rave-up at the commune and a young girl died. A respectable girl, apparently. Yes, that was it – she wasn't really part of the commune, but someone had met her in the local pub and invited her to a party. The cause of death was said to be a drug overdose plus too much alcohol, and though there wasn't any suspicion of foul play, exactly, Piers was the owner of the house and it was his party. He was very severely reprimanded by the judge.'

'But you think there was more to it than that?'

Steve shrugged.

'I don't know,' he said. 'The father of the girl tried to say so and was paid a fantastic amount for the story by one of the Sunday papers, but I was inclined at the time to give Piers the benefit of the doubt. It goes against the grain to make excuses for the bastard – in fact, I'd go so far as to say I never in my life took such a dislike to anyone. Even so, it's hard enough keeping track of teenagers at any kind of party, never mind the sort of free-for-all that this one must have been. It seemed that an accidental overdose was the most likely explanation. But then another man died.'

'What? How? Another overdose?'

'No. He was—' He pulled himself up suddenly as if something had just occurred to him.

'What is it, Steve?'

'He – he was one of the artists who lived in the commune with Piers.' He spoke slowly, almost unwillingly. 'He was quite a young chap, I believe. Piers and all the others swore it was an accident, but this guy had a girlfriend and she wasn't convinced. She went to the police and, as you can imagine, there was more scandal, more newspaper reports, but again, in the end, no conviction. Once more Piers Craven had emerged whiter than white.'

He still hadn't told me how this young man had died, but a chilling suspicion had already entered my mind. I could hardly manage to voice my question.

'Steve, was he – was he run down?'

Steve didn't answer in words, but he reached out and took my hand as if knowing I would need his support. 'Oh, my God,' I whispered.

'D'you know, I'd forgotten. I never connected it. Never thought...' Steve shook his head as if at his own obtuseness. Then he increased the pressure on my hand. 'But Holly, it could so easily have been an accident.'

'I know.' And I did, of course. People were killed in road accidents all the time, every day, every minute of the day, hadn't I read somewhere? Even so, it was impossible not to brood on the coincidence.

Other people came into the cafe, a family with three young children, talking, laughing. The owner appeared once more and Steve took the opportunity of paying our bill.

'You haven't eaten much,' she said, a note of reproof in her voice. 'Was everything all right?'

'Just fine, thanks,' Steve assured her. 'The scones are as wonderful as ever, but when it came to the point we weren't very hungry.'

I managed to smile at her and say goodbye, but my thoughts were still in turmoil.

'Jim knew Caroline who knew Rose who is Piers Craven's sister,' I said, breaking the silence as Steve drove away from the village green, both of us forgetting that we'd had every intention of looking at the church. 'It's like a jigsaw puzzle with half the pieces missing.'

Steve's glance was sympathetic but seemed to contain a warning, too.

'Don't let your imagination run away with you, Holly. There was never any question at the time of Piers being remotely connected to Jim's death, if that's what you're thinking. I don't even know if Jim knew him personally, though I admit it's probable that he did since from what you tell me he was friendly with Rupert. I suppose Caroline might have known him through Rose, but as far as I can remember, Jim died before Piers's meteoric rise to fame. I'd never heard his name until long afterwards.'

'"Poor Rose",' I said, after a moment or two's silence. 'That's what Rupert called her. Why would he have done that?'

Steve shook his head.

'Heaven knows. I don't imagine she's poor in the material sense.'

I was silent again, my thoughts twisting and turning, getting nowhere, finding nothing but blind alleys. And then it struck me that everywhere I turned, there also was Higginson.

'You know, Steve, Higginson told Rupert about me,' I said, remembering. 'Isn't that the strangest thing? Why would he have done that? When I saw him at Lovells he treated me like I was nothing but a waste of space, so why did he consider my search for Caroline important enough to mention it to Rupert?'

'Perhaps he knew she was Rose's friend and mentioned it casually.'

'But when I first went to Lovells he told

me he'd never heard of Caroline!'

'Maybe you'll learn more when you see Rose Quigley – *hey*!' He jammed on the brakes suddenly and backed a few yards. 'I nearly forgot to point Fincote Manor out to you. I told you it was around here, didn't I? Well, there it is, behind all those trees. That's where your friend lives. It's a lovely old place.'

'My friend?' I looked at him in some bewilderment.

'Sir Timothy Crofthouse, Bt.'

'Oh!' Our present problem had put all thought of that gentleman's existence out of my mind, but at Steve's words I looked through the open wrought-iron gates. Although much of the house was hidden by the trees he had mentioned, I could see that it did indeed look very fine. And very old.

'Elizabethan,' Steve told me. 'It's been in the family for a long time. My grandmother took me to a garden party there once, years ago, when I was just a kid.'

'Did you meet Sir Timothy?'

'No. Well, to be honest, I don't remember. I suppose I could have done. I do remember being expected to smile and say "How do you do?" to what seemed hundreds and hundreds of people, all as old as Methuselah, but the only thing that sticks in my mind is the coconut shy.'

'Why in the world would he have sent

flowers to my mother's funeral?' I mused, momentarily distracted. It seemed of little importance compared with our other worries, however, and the subject of Sir Timothy was dismissed as Steve continued our journey towards London. For a while neither of us spoke. What Steve was thinking I don't know, but my thoughts were still circling around Higginson, trying to fit him into the equation in a way that made sense.

'Steve,' I said, after a while. 'Aren't there tests available these days to prove the age of a painting? I was thinking about those watercolours,' I explained in response to his questioning glance. '"Attributed to Augustus Marley", the catalogue said, but Higginson said he had no doubts.'

'Well, he's the authority. You heard what Serena said. He may be an unpleasant bastard, but he's held in high esteem. Sure, there are tests, but they're very costly and in most cases an auction house relies on the expertise of the man in charge.'

'And if the man in charge is mistaken, or corrupt?'

'Well, that's why buyers patronise reputable auction houses, like Lovells or Sothebys or Christies. Their integrity is assumed to be beyond doubt.'

'Yet,' I said after thinking this over, 'you told me that Jim thought Higginson wasn't always careful enough. That seems strange,

167

if his reputation stands so high.'

'Well – look, Holly, you know I thought Jim was a hell of a bloke? We were good mates, no doubt about it, but I have to admit that I – everyone, really – thought he was a bit over-cautious. And he and Higginson didn't hit it off, to put it mildly. At the time it didn't really seem a big issue. I kind of assumed it was all part of the ongoing battle between them. Still—' He was silent a moment, chewing his lip. 'I do see what you're getting at,' he said at last. 'If Jim was seriously concerned about a series of authentications that he thought were badly off beam...' His voice trailed away and I knew he was taking the possibility seriously.

'Serena said there was big money in it.'

'She wasn't wrong.'

'But if Higginson ignored his concerns, wouldn't Jim simply have gone to someone higher up in the firm to voice his suspicions? Surely there was some ultimate authority he could appeal to?'

'Higginson *is* the ultimate authority when it comes to watercolours, and he's been with the firm for years. The chairman, Friedman, is no art expert. He's more an administrator with an excellent knowledge of furniture and as far as he was concerned, Higginson can do no wrong. Couldn't when I was there, anyway. There are other experts in the firm, of course, but unless they were all of one mind and made some concerted representation to Friedman, I doubt that he'd take any notice. You must appreciate that Higginson is a sort of god in the art world. No one likes him much, but no one questions him.'

'So only Higginson is likely to have known that Jim thought he was wrong about certain things. Wouldn't Jim have told you if he was seriously worried?'

Steve thought this over.

'I don't know,' he said at last. 'As I've said before, I'm no art expert. And anyway—' He sighed, sounding unhappy. 'It's possible he might have thought I'd been unsympathetic in the past. I did tell him once he should lighten up a bit – not feel that every mistake was his responsibility. I did a conscientious day's work, often over and above the call of duty, but in my view we weren't paid enough to carry the can for the bosses. Maybe I underestimated the problem. You have to remember, he was with Caroline then and we weren't spending so much time together.' He glanced at me. 'I'm sorry,' he said. 'Really sorry.'

'You weren't to know. If he told Higginson he was wrong about things, it would certainly explain why Higginson disliked him so, wouldn't it?' I said.

Enough to kill him? Have him killed? I

didn't say the words, but I thought them just the same – and I thought of Caroline. If Steve was right, and Jim had told her what he suspected—

Steve took one hand off the steering wheel and reached for mine.

'Look, we don't *know* anything,' he said. 'All this is pure speculation.'

'You're right,' I told him. We looked at each other briefly, our smiles strained. 'But you've got to admit,' I said after a moment, 'it sure as hell hangs together, doesn't it?'

We drove straight back to Richmond where, for the first time, I saw Steve's apartment above the shop. It was small and cramped and I pretended not to notice when he whisked a shirt and sweater off a chair and threw them into a cupboard. In spite of this I thought it pretty tidy for a bachelor pad and, as I might have expected, it contained a few choice pieces of furniture.

He checked the answerphone and his e-mail before doing anything else.

'Hope springs eternal,' he said. 'I must be the supreme optimist. I always arrive home thinking I'll find some stupendous cash offer awaiting me.'

This time, as, I suspect, on most others, he was out of luck. The only message was one from his bank asking him to contact the manager as a matter of urgency, which caused him to swear under his breath and run his fingers distractedly through his hair.

'Problems?' I asked.

'I strongly suspect there are.' He attempted a laugh, as if making light of them. 'At intervals I get summoned to the bank so that the manager can tell me that he's worried about the size of my overdraft. Not nearly so worried as I am, I tell him, but strangely he seems to find this of little comfort. Oh, to hell with him! Let's have a drink.'

He fetched a bottle of red wine from the tiny kitchen and poured a generous measure into two exquisite, cut-glass wine glasses.

'Those are lovely,' I said. 'Antiques?'

He nodded, but said no more as he handed me one of them. In spite of his dismissal of the message from the bank, I could see that it had seriously worried him.

We sat down side by side on a leather sofa and I glanced at him, wondering if it would be tactless to press him to talk about it. He'd devoted himself to my concerns for days. It seemed only fair that I should concentrate on his for a while.

'I suppose you can understand the poor man's disquiet,' he said, while I hesitated. 'The bloody overdraft isn't exactly getting any bigger, but it's not getting any smaller either. And now the lease on this property has run out and the landlord is putting up the rent by thirty per cent. I don't know how I'm going to cope with that.'

'The bank must have had faith in you, to give you an overdraft in the first place.'

'Yeah, well – I somehow get the impression that their faith is running out. Here's to bank managers,' he said, raising his glass, making a good attempt to put his financial problems aside. 'May they all be filled with the milk of human kindness.'

I could offer him a loan, I thought. Easily. The only thing stopping me was that I knew he wouldn't take it. On the other hand—

'I'm looking for a good investment,' I said cautiously after a moment. 'Maybe—'

'No, Holly.'

'You haven't heard what I was going to say! How much do you need to wipe out the overdraft? And how much interest does the bank charge?'

'Too much,' Steve said. 'But don't even think of it, Holly. There's no way I would take a loan from you – but thanks, anyway, for harbouring the thought. It was a very kind one.'

I looked at him with exasperation.

'It wasn't kind at all,' I said. 'Seeing the way you feel about antiques, about that lovely furniture – well, it's kind of made me interested, too. I'd love a stake in something like this. No strings. Strictly business.'

He looked at me, laughing a little as if I

had said something to amuse him.

'You're sweet,' he said. 'But I couldn't do it.'

'Stiff-necked Limey bastard,' I said, without heat. 'That's what my mother thought about Englishmen, and if you ask me, she wasn't far wrong. At any rate,' I went on, 'dinner is on me tonight, so don't even think of arguing about it.'

'OK,' he agreed. 'I don't mind you buying me an Indian takeaway. There's one a couple of doors down the street.'

'I was thinking of something a little more salubrious.'

'Round here? We might have trouble getting a table this time of the evening – and really, the Indian's awfully good. Trust me.'

I trusted him. And eventually he was proved right, but we were in no hurry to eat. He telephoned to order the food, and until it was ready we sat drinking our wine, straying from the Caroline problem by talking with a sudden passionate intensity – heaven alone knows how the subject arose – about the implications of Clinton's misdemeanours. Suffice it to say that he seemed to know a lot more about what was involved than I did, which made me a little ashamed.

But at last he opened up a little gatelegged table. Being totally ignorant about such things, I couldn't identify its style or maker, but I could see with half an eye that it was

173

something rather special.

He ran downstairs for the food, leaving me to set the table and uncork another bottle of wine.

The meal, when at last we sat down to it, was lip-smackingly good.

'Best in the west,' he said. 'Didn't I tell you?'

'And didn't I believe you? And what's more, it's served with such style!' I was looking, as I spoke, at the candle in a Georgian silver candlestick that he'd placed in the middle of the table. 'I have to say that for someone on the breadline you sure live elegantly. You know, you never told me whether you were going to bid for anything you saw today.'

'The sofa,' he said at once. Then he sighed. 'Though I suppose that depends on the bloody bank.'

I said nothing – didn't even refer to my willingness to help. It was when we had eaten and he was standing up to clear away the dishes that he brought the subject up again, pausing with the plates in his hand.

'I wonder if I could touch Andy for the odd couple of thousand?' he said thoughtfully. 'He might come across – but then again, could I bring myself to ask him? On the whole, I think not. I might ask his advice, though.'

He wouldn't let me help him clear away or

get coffee, pleading lack of room in the kitchen, so I went to sit on the sofa again and thought hard about his problem.

'Look,' I said when he returned. 'I've been thinking—' He cocked an eyebrow at me. 'Steve, please, *please*, just for one moment, will you stop being the archetypal stiff-necked Englishman? No – just *shut up* and listen to me! I've got money to spare and I want to invest in your business. You've got enthusiasm and flair and know-how, but anyone can see that you're hamstrung without capital.'

He wasn't smiling as he came to sit beside me once more.

'Holly, no. I mean it.'

'But I've got faith in you! You say yourself that the climate is right for this business. People have money now and prices are going up. Look – I've got investments in all kinds of weird and wonderful concerns back home, things that I couldn't care less about. I don't even know what some of them are *for*, for God's sake! Think how much more fun it would be for me to have an interest in your business.'

I think he was tempted. He turned to look at me, taking hold of my arm. But then he shook his head hopelessly.

'No, Holly. It wouldn't do. It's sweet and generous of you—'

'Will you stop it? It's not sweet and

generous at all. I'm on to a good thing.' Still he shook his head. '*Why?*' I demanded.

He turned and poured out coffee without saying anything, handed me my cup, offered the sugar. Then he sighed.

'Look,' he said softly, turning towards me again, one elbow on the back of the sofa. 'Holly, ever since we met, I've been conscious of—' He hesitated. I looked at him questioningly. 'I have known,' he went on, his expression serious, 'that there's something between us – or could be – and it's ridiculous to think that anything could be strictly business, with no strings.'

I just watched and waited and said nothing. He took a breath and continued.

'I don't know what's to become of us. Of you and me. Frankly, the whole deal terrifies me. As I said before, you're way out of my league. However, one thing I do know; money will only complicate matters. It always does, and God knows things are complicated enough already. You must see that for yourself.'

'I see nothing of the sort,' I said stubbornly.

'Oh, Holly!' He laughed, reaching out to touch my cheek lingeringly with the back of his fingers. I put my cup of coffee down on the table beside me. If he was going to start that sort of thing, I thought, then the further I was from scalding hot,

176

spillable liquid the better.

'You'll go back to the glamorous life you left behind and you'll forget all about scruffy antique dealers who live over their shop without a penny to bless themselves with.' All the time he was speaking he was gently rubbing his fingers against my cheek. For a moment we looked at each other, not speaking, and I could feel the arm that had been on the back of the sofa tighten a little around my shoulders. Irresistibly we drew closer together so that his lips were only an inch away from mine.

'On the other hand...' he said.

'On the other hand?'

He was so close I could see the gold flecks in his eyes and the tangle of lashes that surrounded them, and every nerve ending I possessed seemed to be screaming at him to come closer, to kiss me. He put both his hands flat on each side of my face. Now, I thought – *now!* I wanted him, I realised, as I'd never wanted anyone or anything before.

'Maybe I'm just making difficulties. Maybe we should just follow our instincts. Take things lightly, just a step at a time. Settle for the fun option.'

I swallowed with difficulty.

'I think,' I said tightly, 'that I might find that quite tolerable.'

Now where did I get a word like that from, I asked myself? To me it sounded as if it had leapt straight from the pages of a Jane Austen novel. Maybe I was getting the hang of this British understatement thing.

'But the trouble is,' he continued, his voice husky, 'I don't think I'm very good at taking things lightly any more. That's what terrifies me. And given your position and my position, lightly is the only way I can take it. I have this picture of the future, you see: you, coolly beautiful as ever, waving good-bye at Heathrow. Me, emotionally screwed up yet again, left in the departure hall.'

I pulled away from him and looked at him without speaking for a moment. The spell was broken and I felt righteously angry, and not in the least Jane Austenish.

'What a strange, distorted picture you have of me,' I said at last. 'And what's all this crap about position? *Position*, for God's sake! Anyone would think I was the lady of the manor and you the serf at my gate. Maybe my mother was right about the British. They're stuck in the Middle Ages.'

'I'm talking money, Holly, and, as you know damned well, Americans take it as seriously as we do. Maybe more seriously. You're rich and you're beautiful—'

I looked at him, feeling as if I were on some kind of emotional switchback. How *dare* he assume that money was all-important to me! But oh, I did want him so.

'And I'm lonely,' I said, coming a little

closer again and putting my hands on his shoulders. 'And a little bit lost. And Steve—' I hesitated a little, but went on after a moment. 'If I'm not in love, then I'm most definitely on the brink.'

Time seemed to hold its breath while neither of us moved. Then he gave a sigh that was almost a groan and took me in his arms. His kiss was long and searching and just the most wonderful thing that had ever happened to me. It was everything I could have imagined. It was a kiss that seemed to make every inch of my flesh sing aloud with happiness, and as we drew away a little and looked at each other, I knew – and so did he – that nothing would ever be quite the same again.

'Oh, Holly,' he whispered. 'You're lovely – so lovely. What's going to happen to us?'

'Do you have to have everything so cut and dried?' I asked him. 'What happened to the step-at-a-time bit?'

He laughed and pulled me to my feet and kissed me again.

'I think I just fell from top to bottom,' he said.

Later, held close in his arms, I nuzzled against his bare shoulder, loving the smell and the taste of him.

'Mmm,' I murmured contentedly. 'This is nice.'

'Nice, but terrifying,' he said.

'Hey, I thought we were settling for the fun option! Terror is definitely out. Regard this as a fling.'

He propped himself up on one elbow and looked down on me.

'Just shows the fallacy of the old adage,' he said.

'What?'

'Flings ain't what they used to be.'

'Oh, gee, I get jokes as well?'

The fun option, I reminded myself. Hold on to that. No one could predict the future, but this, momentarily, was our world, our piece of heaven, and nothing outside it seemed wholly real.

Not even the bank manager. Not even Caroline.

Nine

The receptionist at the place I hired the car was full of good advice. Just keep going west, she told me; straight up Piccadilly, round Hyde Park Corner—

Hyde Park Corner! Sounds simple, huh? I still have no idea how I ever circumnavigated it without being mown down by far larger vehicles on either side of me, still less how I found the right exit. I plunged into the maelstrom of traffic that, in fits and starts, took me past Harrods and out into unknown country beyond until suddenly, by the grace of God, I found myself on the freeway, heading in the general direction of Heathrow, as instructed, and realised that I was truly on my way at last. Words cannot express how overjoyed I was when the name 'Henley' actually appeared on a sign.

Rose Quigley had given me instructions how to find Willow Cottage, her house by the river, and I located it without too much difficulty. It was some cottage! Despite the cute eaves and the thatch and the heavy wooden door with its iron hinges, it was only marginally smaller than Blenheim Palace. It had a sweeping semicircular drive and a garden bright with spring flowers, laid out and maintained by someone who was clearly an expert.

The door was opened by a tall, slablike woman in a pink nylon overall who barely had time to open her mouth to greet me before a man emerged from a room opening into an entrance hall of much the same dimensions as Grand Central Station. He strode forward in a masterful way to take over the situation, his hand outstretched.

'Miss Crozier? Glad to meet you. I'm George Quigley.' He smiled at me, the smile very white in a pudgy kind of face. 'Come in, come in! How very good of you to call. Thank you, Dora.' He turned and smiled equally dazzlingly to the hired help. He was a dazzling man altogether, with his snowy shirt and dark suit, highly polished shoes, gold cufflinks and ring. A big man, affable and full of energy and charm and confidence. 'Perhaps you'll be good enough to bring us coffee?'

Where was Rose? There was no sign of her in the lavishly furnished sitting room into which he ushered me. Like the garden, it was immaculate – like a show room in an expensive store, I thought. It was decorated in pale pastel colours with an off-white carpet, thick as snowfall, and shimmering oyster satin drapes opulently swagged and tailed. The paintings on the walls were gold-framed, lit from above; every ornament, every lamp looked as if it had been placed there by an interior designer. There were no books, no photographs, no apparent sign of everyday occupation.

George Quigley waved me towards a deep sofa and sat down himself in an armchair close by.

'Good of you to come,' he said again. 'I must apologise for my wife's absence. I'm afraid she's not at all well.'

I was a little taken aback by this.

'Oh – oh, gee, I'm so sorry. I wouldn't have come if I'd known.'

He brushed my apologies aside.

'No, no, I'm glad you did. I'm very pleased to have the chance to talk to you. After all, I knew Caroline too, you know.'

'Yes, of course you did. She worked for you, didn't she?'

'That's right. I saw something of her socially, too, as she became very friendly with my wife, even after I moved on from Greenway Development. I have to say Caroline was quite a remarkable secretary. The best I've ever had, or am likely to have. Really, a most competent and charming girl. Rose was extremely fond of her. She took it very hard when she simply disappeared without a word. It seemed out of

183

character, somehow.'

'Strange you should say that. It seems—'

'It wasn't like her to be so thoughtless. Not when she knew how Rose felt about their friendship. I should explain about my wife, Miss Crozier.' He leaned forward confidentially and lowered his voice a little, his face falling into more sombre lines. 'Not to put too fine a point upon it, she is neurotic. Hopelessly neurotic. I don't like admitting it, but it will help you to understand the – the *obsession* she had for Caroline. Because that's what it was. No doubt about it. Ah, thank you, Dora.' He flashed his smile again and a pause ensued while the coffee was placed on a table, two cups poured, milk and sugar offered.

'My wife,' George Quigley continued when at last we were alone again, 'is easily upset, and the subject of Caroline Bethany is one that upsets her more than most. Quite frankly, I persuaded her that it wouldn't be wise for her to see you this morning.'

'I'm sorry,' I said again. 'When I spoke to her, she seemed—'

'She's up and down,' Quigley said, not letting me finish. 'Yesterday was a good day. Today – well, I was heartily relieved when she agreed to stay in her room, I can tell you. Talking about Caroline does her no good at all. You see, Caroline came into our life at a time when Rose was at a particularly low ebb. She was desperate for children but had suffered a series of miscarriages and then was told that she'd never carry a child full term. Her – mental trouble started at about that time. Caroline was sensitive and understanding beyond her years. She seemed, somehow, like the daughter Rose always longed for, yet she was mature enough to see that Rose needed help. She was pretty and bright and amusing and Rose came to dote on her. Then, of course, Caroline met your brother right here in this house, and everything changed. Oh, she was kind – she still visited, still went to the theatre with Rose occasionally, met her for lunch, that sort of thing. She didn't drop her in any heartless way, but what could we expect? The girl was in love.'

'I suppose she was bound to—'

'Rose felt left out.' He was like a steamroller, I thought, ploughing on no matter what the obstacles. 'It simply wasn't the same relationship any more, and she just couldn't take it. Most people would accept that philosophically, but not Rose. She was hurt, tearful, and when your brother died, she wanted to help despite the fact that she hadn't seen so much of Caroline. They met once or twice, but then, suddenly, there was nothing. No calls, no letters. It was hard for my wife – so hard, in fact, that although I was annoyed with Caroline for dropping her like that, I tried to do what I could to find her, for Rose's sake. That's why I'm so glad to have the chance to speak to you myself, because if your aim is to find Caroline, which is what I understand it to be, I can save you a great deal of pointless effort.'

'Well, naturally I'd be grateful for any information—'

'I have no information, Miss Crozier.'

'What?' I could hardly believe it, after such a build-up.

'I have no information and nothing to tell you. That's the whole point. I simply want to warn you not to waste your time and money looking for Caroline Bethany. To all intents and purposes she seems to have vanished off the face of the earth.'

For a moment I just stared at him.

'Are you sure you covered—' I began.

'Oh, yes. I spent a great deal of effort and money looking for her. More money, I have to say, than most would have thought reasonable. I employed a private detective, the best in the business, who would have found her if she'd still been anywhere in Britain. Or anywhere else, come to that. I told Rose she must have gone abroad.'

'I suppose she could have done.'

'Without a word of farewell? It doesn't seem likely. Even her aunt—'

'She'd fallen out with her aunt.'

'Even so, I can't believe she would have

186

left the country without informing her next of kin – can you? Of course,' he went on, 'the alternative is almost too dreadful to contemplate.'

I looked at him again, digesting this.

'What – what do you mean?' I asked, knowing all the time.

'She could be dead,' he said.

'Why would you think that? Surely you're being overly dramatic?'

Quigley spread his hands, shrugged his shoulders.

'One doesn't like to think it, of course, but bearing in mind the minuteness of my man's search, it is something we have to face. It seems the only alternative.'

I frowned at him, thinking this over.

'But there would be a record, wouldn't there?' I said, thinking of all those great books in St Catherine's House, where I had found out about the birth of Jamie. 'Maybe – maybe she married. Changed her name. As you say, she might have left the country.'

'My man would have found her. He has contacts in almost any country you care to name.'

'But what about a death certificate?'

'My man discovered no less than three unknown girls who died at the right time and who could have answered her description. Two accidents, one suicide. Believe me, he explored every avenue.'

'You know she had a son?'

'Oh, yes. We traced them both as far as Oxford. Then, nothing. No, my dear, I greatly fear that this is the only alternative that's left to us. Caroline Bethany doesn't exist any more. It's as if the waters closed over both their heads, hers and her son's.'

I felt chilled by the metaphor.

'But that still doesn't mean—' I broke off, thinking suddenly of the girl in Wales, the man who had been run over and, inevitably, of Jim; and I remembered then that this concerned, plausible man of consequence was the brother-in-law of Piers Craven. Perhaps he had good reason to think I should never find Caroline or her son. Perhaps he'd made sure she was dead. Perhaps he knew for certain that she was one of the unknown girls. His story of the detective could be a total lie for all I knew.

'Are you interested in art, Mr Quigley?' I asked him after a moment. He looked rather astonished at the change of subject and cocked his head on one side to look at me, a small frown drawing his brows together.

'Indeed I am,' he said cautiously. 'My wife, too. Why do you ask? Her brother, Rupert Craven, is the owner of a gallery – as, of course, you know. You've met him, I believe.'

So Rupert, too, had seen fit to pass on the news that he and I had met. I tucked this

188

snippet of information away for consideration later, merely noting that, for some reason, my arrival seemed to have set this small corner of the art world buzzing.

'And Piers Craven?' I went on. 'Rose's other brother? I understand he is a most gifted artist.'

'He was, Miss Crozier.' Quigley sighed as if with regret. 'He paints very little now.'

'Such a pity,' I murmured. 'Why is that?'

There was something in his expression that made me think I had trespassed on ground he would rather not have to think about, but before he could say anything in response we were both distracted by the sound of raised voices in the hall. He half rose and just as he did so the door burst open to admit a small woman, waiflike to the point of emaciation, wearing a crumpled white boiler suit. She hurtled over to Quigley, her face contorted with emotion, and seized his arm.

'George, *please!* I must—'

'Rose! What on earth—? Darling, I *told* you—'

'I wanted to see her. Why shouldn't I? I wanted to see Jim Crozier's sister. I've got something I want to show her. Look—'

Quigley had put a restraining arm around his wife, but she elbowed him aside with surprising vigour and came straight over to me, flinging herself down beside me on the sofa. 'I found this. It's a picture of Caroline and me, taken in the garden that very summer she met your brother. Isn't she lovely? You can't blame him for falling for her, can you?'

I gave her what I hoped was a calming smile and took the photograph from her trembling hand, eager to see the girl who was the reason for my presence. She was sitting on a garden seat, laughing at the camera, and looked very lovely indeed; a happy girl in a summer dress, dark hair touching her shoulders.

And Rose, too, looked happy. Happy and almost unrecognisable. In the photograph her hair was ash blonde and attractively cut. There was flesh on her bones. Now she looked gaunt and pale and hollow-eyed, and her streaky, stringy hair, dark at the roots, was pushed behind her ears.

'Oh yes,' I said as I looked at Caroline. 'Yes, she's lovely.'

'I'll never understand it!' Rose's voice was high and querulous. 'Never understand why she didn't write. Not so much as a Christmas card!'

'Darling, I told you she'd left England,' her husband said, his exasperation all too obvious despite the endearment.

'She could still write, couldn't she? I mean, they do have post offices overseas, don't they?' She turned to me, so tense, so brittle that I had the impression she could be snapped in half with a twist of the fingers. 'We were so close, Caroline and I. So very, very close! She was twelve years younger than I was, almost to the day, but still we were the closest friends. She saved my reason, do you know that? Did George tell you? I wanted to die. I almost did! I tried—'

Tears welled in her eyes. Poor Rose, I thought. She sure was one flaky lady and I couldn't believe that Caroline would have been heartless enough to abandon her completely. Not willingly, anyway. Nothing I had heard about her pointed that way. With a distinct chill of apprehension, I felt the stirrings of belief in the theory that she was dead. And the boy? Young Jamie? Was he dead, too? I couldn't even bear to think about that.

'I explained everything to Miss Crozier, darling,' George Quigley said, adding: 'I rather think she was about to leave.' His eyes caught mine across the room. They carried a irrefutable order and I was aware, suddenly, of the strength of the man, of his implacable will. He was someone who would stop at little to get his own way; I could sense it without any doubt. I wouldn't want to be Rose, I thought with a tremor of fear.

Obeying the message, I rose to my feet.

'I'm very glad to have met you after all, Mrs Quigley,' I said. 'But your husband is right. I really ought to get back to town.'

'But I wanted to talk about Caroline!' Rose stood up too, as pouting and petulant as a child. 'George, why can't she stay? You never let me do what I want! She can keep me company while you go to your meeting. Let her stay – *please!*'

'That'll do, darling.' George was smiling but quite inflexible. 'You're embarrassing Miss Crozier. Dora?' he called, raising his voice a little.

Dora, the maid or nurse or whatever she was, had been hovering outside. She now came into the room and took Rose's arm.

'Come along, dear,' she said, her voice steely. 'Let's not have any tantrums.'

I held out my hand towards Rose.

'I really do have to go,' I said. 'It was so good to see you. Goodbye, Rose.'

She didn't speak or smile, but she took my hand briefly. Her touch was cold and dry as if there was no life in her. Clearly unwilling, but without further protest beyond a jerk of her shoulders, she allowed herself to be led from the room, as if she recognised that further protest was useless. Quigley watched her, saying nothing, waiting for the door to be closed before turning to me. His smile was back in place but there was a chilling look of distaste in his eyes.

'I apologise for that,' he said.

'Really, there's no need. I should have been happy to talk to her.'

'That really wouldn't have been wise. She's best kept quiet.'

'I'm sorry,' I said, inadequately.

'No, no. I'm the one who should be sorry.' He was all charm once more. 'I'm afraid you've had a wasted journey and learned nothing – except that there's nothing to be learned. At least I may have saved you a great deal of trouble. The book really does seem to be closed on Caroline Bethany.'

'Well, thank you for giving me your time.'

He could have phoned, I thought. Could have saved himself time and me that nightmare journey here and the equally nightmarish return trip. Why hadn't he?

He showed me out himself and stood, smiling faintly, as I belted myself in the car and started the engine, lifting his hand in farewell as I drove off. I was glad to leave – glad to be gone from that opulent house and the misery that I could sense there; glad to leave George Quigley and his phoney smiles.

I drove away from the house down a long country lane, but at the first opportunity I pulled off the road and sat staring straight ahead of me. I needed to think; needed to sort out my impressions.

George Quigley had sounded so sure, so

utterly convinced that Caroline was dead. The waters had closed over her head, he'd said. If she were still alive, the detective he had hired would have found her.

Did I believe him? Had he really hired a detective to find her? Or was he just trying to ensure that I would stop looking for her, stop trying to stir muddy waters?

Whatever his motives, I was glad now that I had made the journey and had seen him face to face, for I might have been more readily convinced of his good intentions had I only spoken to him over the phone. Now, having seen him, I found I distrusted him. More – I admitted to myself that I was frightened of him. Poor Rose, I thought again. What with George and Dora as joint minders, she might just as well be in prison. I thought of what Steve had said about the background of the Craven siblings: Rose, Rupert and Piers. Impossible not to wonder who or what had given them such a variety of hang-ups.

Just suppose, I said to myself, that George *had* hired a detective who had been unable to find Caroline. How did he know for certain that the story he had told Rose – that she had gone abroad – was untrue? Discount for the moment the possibility that he might know otherwise. Just assume he was telling the truth. Caroline could speak French and German fluently. She'd made a point of mentioning it in her letter. And hadn't Steve said she was of French extraction?

But George would have known that and would have explored that particular avenue as well as every other. It didn't, on reflection, seem much of a hope. If he were right and Caroline was dead, then it seemed logical to believe that Jamie was dead, too, and I felt hollow with grief at the mere possibility.

I sighed hopelessly, started the car and set out once more on my return journey. It was several traffic jams and numerous hair's-breadth escapes later that I found not only my driving skills had improved with practice but that my spirits had rallied a little. You may be right, Mr Quigley, I thought, somewhere between Henley and Heathrow, but the search goes on. No warning from you is going to stop me trying to find out the truth about Caroline.

Back at the hotel for a late lunch, I phoned the papers to see if there had been any answers to my ads. Only *The Times* could report any response so far. There were three replies, the girl at the other end of the phone told me. Did I want her to hold them or fax them to the hotel?

Fax them, I said, full of impatience; then I changed my mind and asked her to send them by the soonest possible post. Fax was

195

too open, I thought. Far better to keep the whole thing confidential. It was only after I had put the phone down that I wondered if I were getting paranoid about this whole business. Was I letting my imagination run away with me?

I phoned Steve, only to hear his answerphone message by way of reply. I tried his mobile, but that was switched off. It was then that I thought of the bank manager and remembered Steve had said that this afternoon would be his first chance to answer the summons. Maybe that's where he was, right this minute. I lay back on my bed and closed my eyes, thinking of him and sending all the positive vibes I could muster.

When the telephone rang I expected to hear his voice, but I found I was wrong. It was a woman who was at the other end of the line.

'Miss Crozier?' she said.

'Yes?'

'It's Caroline Bethany here. Caroline's aunt. I saw your advertisement in the *Daily Telegraph* yesterday.'

'Oh, hallo. Have you thought of something?' I was polite, but no more. This particular Caroline Bethany had not endeared herself to me the last time we spoke.

'It's simply that – well, I think we ought to meet after all. Have a talk. I wasn't entirely frank—'

'Oh, *please*!' I was all eagerness now, all memory of her former coldness gone. This, at least, was something positive, just when I was at a loss about where to turn next. 'I'd like that very much, Miss Bethany. Shall I come to Oxford?'

'No, no!' She vetoed that idea vehemently. 'Actually, I'm in London.'

'Then please, won't you come here? Come and have some tea.' (How Anglicised can you get? I thought.)

For a moment she hesitated.

'I don't honestly think that would be awfully wise,' she said after a moment. 'Do you know St James's Square? It's not far from your hotel.'

'I have a street map. I can look it up.'

'There's a garden in the centre of it, with seats. I'll be near to the statue in the middle.'

'It sounds very cloak and dagger!' I laughed, but there was no answering amusement in her voice.

'If I may make a suggestion,' she said, rather primly, 'go into the Piccadilly entrance of Fortnum and Mason and walk through the back entrance into Jermyn Street. Turn left and then right, and you'll find yourself in the square. One can't be too careful, you see.'

'You're serious, aren't you?' I said, after a shattered silence.

'Very. It may be only a small chance, but somebody could be following you. Can you come as soon as possible? I don't want to be too late getting back to Oxford.'

'I'll come right away,' I promised. But even so, having put the phone down I sat for a moment, incapable of movement, bug-eyed with astonishment. So there was, in Miss Bethany's view, something sinister going on; something so sinister that she considered it a possibility that both she and I might be tailed, our meeting spied upon. Maybe I wasn't paranoid after all.

It was a greyish sort of day, but dry. I had learnt how to get to Piccadilly by this time, but paused to enquire of Sue, my nice receptionist, whether I should turn left or right to find Fortnum and Mason. I then stepped out into the street – but not before I had stood for a moment on the steps of the hotel looking carefully in every direction. There was a uniformed doorman at the bottom of the steps, waving down a taxi for two elderly fellow Americans. There was a lady with a little dog on the sidewalk to my left. She passed the hotel and retreated down the street without a glance in my direction. A little further away, two girls in microscopic skirts walked along with their heads close together, deep in conversation. There was no one else, and none of the above were remotely threatening – unless you counted the dog, who looked the type of pooch that couldn't be trusted anywhere near a pair of ankles.

I found Fortnum and Mason without difficulty and recognised no one as I looked around, sniffing the aromas of all the luscious-looking foodstuffs that surrounded me. Might as well do the job properly, I thought, and went up the stairs to the second floor, coming down in the elevator almost immediately. Then, certain I hadn't been followed, I found the rear entrance that Miss Bethany had mentioned, turned left as she had instructed, and within five minutes found myself in St James's Square.

There were trees and daffodils in the square, and flocks of pigeons; and all around the old, gracious houses which everywhere are such an ornament to London. It didn't take much to imagine how it must have been when lords and ladies lived there with their hordes of servants and their carriages. Now cars were parked all round the perimeter of the square and the houses were offices and embassies.

A path went round the outer rim of the square and others crossed it to meet in the middle. I could see the seats and the statue. A woman was feeding the pigeons from a paper bag and assorted pedestrians were walking purposefully down the path that

199

crossed the square as if they were taking short cuts to somewhere else. As I drew closer to the centre, I became aware of a slight woman dressed in brown who appeared to be engaged in reading the plaque at the base of the statue. She turned and watched me as I approached her.

'Miss Crozier?' she asked quietly when I was close enough to hear her.

'Yes, I'm Holly. And you're Miss Bethany? I'm so glad to meet you.'

'Shall we walk? It's a little too cold to sit, I think.'

I glanced sideways at her as we strolled along, trying to assess her mood and her angle. And her age. She was, I thought, in her late sixties, but she looked younger, not only because of her slim build and upright carriage but also because her skin was so soft and unlined. Her clothes were neat, unremarkable; her greying hair, as Steve had said, was pulled back in a knot. On her arm was a red plastic shopping bag, full of books.

'I've been to the London Library,' she said, indicating them. 'It's one of my few extravagances – expensive, but so valuable to me. I still teach, you see. Just part time these days, which gives me time to write a little. Freelance, of course, but I hope to do more when I finally give up teaching next year—'

200

She broke off, realising that I had stopped walking.

'Please,' I said. 'Could we talk about Caroline?'

'Ah.' She looked around her then, and as if satisfied that there was no one able to overhear us, she took a step nearer to me. 'There is a question I should like to ask you,' she said. She had rather a precise, scholarly way of speaking; authoritative, too, as if she were not used to being disobeyed. Typical schoolmarm, I thought, still not disposed to like her very much. It seemed, at that moment, that my first impressions had been the right ones. She was cold and unfeeling.

'Ask away,' I said. My voice must have expressed a bewilderment tinged with annoyance. She appeared to melt a little.

'I'm sorry. This must seem most peculiar to you, but I feel it's necessary. I believe, when you were young, that Jim had a pet name for you. Would you be kind enough to tell me what it was?'

'Why in the world—?' I stared at her and with an air of polite enquiry she stared back. 'Well, sure,' I said, shrugging my shoulders. Might as well humour the woman, I thought. 'Jim used to call me Tommy. When I was a kid, I wanted to be a boy, you see, and people said I was a tomboy.'

Miss Bethany was smiling, and I had to admit that the change in her was quite remarkable. She looked warmer now, more approachable.

'Well, now, that's most satisfactory, Miss Crozier,' she said, as if I had passed some kind of test.

'Oh, Holly, please! What is all this?'

'Let's carry on walking.' We did so, and I caught her smiling at me sideways. 'You see, Holly, I had to be sure. I was convinced – well, almost convinced – when you telephoned me, but you're not the first person to question me about Caroline. Ten years ago I swore I'd never reveal where she'd gone and I never have done. Between us we devised this little test, just to ensure that you are who you say you are.'

'She's alive!' Joyously I seized her arm and pulled her to a halt once more. 'Where is she? Is she in London?'

'Oh, do lower your voice, my dear. One really can't be too careful.' She looked over her shoulder. 'You must promise to keep this to yourself.'

'Is she really in so much danger?'

'I think, perhaps, that we all are, you included. You see, others have died. It's Jamie that makes Caroline so fearful. I dare say if it weren't for him she would have gone on where your brother left off.' We had reached one of the seats, and she paused.

'Perhaps it's not too cold to sit for a few moments.'

I don't think I would have noticed if a blizzard had been raging, I was so thrilled to hear that Caroline wasn't dead after all. I sat down beside her.

'She phones me each week,' she went on. 'From different locations, of course. I told her about your call and she was very excited – but fearful, too, for those monsters have tried everything they know to find her. Even though it's been so long, she daren't trust they've forgotten her. They know, you see, that she knows.'

And Aunt Caroline seemed to be assuming that I knew, too. I didn't, not for sure, but it was beginning to make sense to me.

'It's all about forgeries, isn't it?' I said. *'That's* what Caroline knew!'

'Exactly. What else?' She looked at me severely once more. 'You must give me your word not to tell anyone of Caroline's whereabouts. That she's even alive—'

'But I must tell Steve,' I said. 'You've met Steve, Miss Bethany. He said he remembered you – remembered your ring. He was a friend of both Jim and Caroline. He's helped me, supported me—'

'And you're in love with him!' Her tone was dry, more than ever like a spinsterish schoolmarm. 'That always tends to addle the judgement, in my view.'

'But you've *met* him,' I said again, feeling mildly irritated that I'd given myself away so completely. 'He's utterly trustworthy, and very worried about Caroline.'

Frowning, she turned her gaze away from me and seemed to be concentrating on the distant statue, her lips pursed. For a long, suspense-filled moment I waited, feeling as if I were one of her pupils awaiting judgement on my latest assignment.

'I think,' she said at last, 'that I must wait for Caroline to confirm that you can reveal her whereabouts. However, I see no reason why you cannot explain why it was necessary for her to leave England so precipitately. I do remember,' she added, with a small smile in my direction, 'that the young man in question was quite charming. He was one of those most unusual young people who continue to treat those of us past middle age as if we retain the use of a few grey cells. Such people are quite rare, I find. And as I recall,' she went on, with another smile, 'he was very attractive.'

I was definitely warming towards her, I found, and smiled back in agreement.

'Please tell me about Caroline,' I begged. 'All I know is that she had the baby in Oxford.'

'Yes, at the Radcliffe. Before that there had been one attempt on her life that misfired. Someone tried to push her under a train in

204

the rush hour, but thank God she was saved by a man who was close by. He assumed it to be an accident. Heaven knows, those platforms are far too crowded; in fact, in my view it's a wonder such things don't happen more often. However, Caroline was certain it was no accident. She left Greenway there and then and came up to Oxford. She stayed with me a night or two, then rented a cottage in a tiny hamlet and hardly moved from there until Jamie was born. Her intention was to go back there, but I suppose since nothing more had happened we had both grown a little slack and complacent. She came to me direct from the hospital, so that I could help a little – cook for her and so on – and it worked so well that she stayed on.'

She paused for a second or two, her lip caught between her teeth, as if the memory of that time was still painful.

'Miss Crozier – Holly – I really can't express how it hurt me to utter the words I used the other day – that Caroline and I quarrelled and that I couldn't bear to have the baby in the house. Nothing could have been further from the truth! I *loved* having them; in fact, I look back on those days as a kind of golden time. I wanted them to stay, and begged Caroline to move in with me permanently. She wasn't at all averse to the idea – we always got on so well – but then one afternoon, when she was alone with Jamie, she left him in his Moses basket indoors while she went into the garden to hang out some washing, and when she got back she found Piers Craven – that filthy, foul, unshaven monster—' Her voice shook as she spoke these words and she had to pause a moment before she could continue. 'She found that horrible man sitting on the settee with the Moses basket beside him, holding a gun to Jamie's head.'

'My God!' Though I had never seen Caroline or Piers Craven, I could imagine the scene and it made my blood run cold. 'What happened? He didn't actually shoot?'

'No. He threatened. He said that they would be watching her – that if she had any crazy idea of going to the police, they would find her wherever she was and that her baby would be killed. He put it as bluntly as that. You see, Holly, he knew that Caroline knew.'

'Exactly what?' I asked.

'What Jim had found out, that there was a conspiracy at Lovells – had been one for years. That ghastly man Higginson was a key player, of course. Caroline had known that Jim was about to have sufficient documentation to prove it when he was killed. She was ninety-nine per cent sure that his death was no accident, and she tried to convince the police of it, but really there was no firm evidence and they wouldn't take it any further.'

'But surely when someone tried to push her under a train they took a different attitude?'

'There was no way she could prove that wasn't an accident, either. In the event, it didn't work, so she never even mentioned it to the police. She just took precautions.'

'I see,' I said. But I didn't really. All this murder and mayhem seemed a grossly exaggerated way to protect a little gentle art forgery.

'What Piers Craven's visit did,' Miss Bethany continued, 'apart from putting the fear of God into Caroline, was to prove to her that George Quigley was in the conspiracy up to his neck. You see, it was he who had bought the house in Wales for Craven. As his secretary, Caroline had known that, and had thought it very generous of him, but now the penny dropped and she realised that he must have recouped the price many times over by his share of the profits from the forged paintings. Craven actually mentioned it, assuming she knew.'

'So he – Piers Craven – is the actual forger.'

'He and his small team. Some years ago one of them died in a so-called road accident, just like Jim. Caroline and I assumed he had wanted out for some reason. Maybe he developed a conscience about it; we don't know. Anyway, he paid the price.'

'Steve told me about him.'

'They could never have simply allowed him to leave, you see. He would have known too much.' She reached out and touched my arm, seeing my distress. 'I'm so sorry, my dear. These are wicked men, there's no doubt about it.'

'It seems—' I hesitated. 'Out of proportion, somehow. I mean, what kind of money are we talking about?'

'Millions,' she said simply. 'And as I said, Higginson's role is all important. He's a clever man, is our Mr Higginson. A world authority, highly thought of.'

'Even so, it seems strange to me that his authority is never challenged.'

'I said he was clever. He seldom attempts to pass off a fake Rembrandt or Renoir or Monet – though, having said that, it was a Corot that attracted Jim's attention in the first place. Do you know that there are eight thousand Corots in galleries all over the world? Yet the artist never painted anything like that number. Van Dyck, too. It's generally reckoned he painted about seventy pictures, yet there are two thousand in existence!'

'You're not blaming Higginson for all of them, surely?'

'No, no, of course not. Caroline says that he sticks mostly to the middle-ranking people. Old Victorian artists who are enjoying a renaissance, and so on. He knows the trends, knows which obscure water-colourist is about to become fashionable, what part of the country they tended to paint. That, you see, is as much an artist's trademark as his signature. And they're clever, no doubt about it. Really talented artists. Such a pity that they have decided to go down this road. They might not always make a great deal of money in one fell swoop, but over the years they must have amassed an uncountable amount. Twenty thousand here, ten thousand there – plus forty or fifty thousand for the occasional important sale. Even more these days. Month by month, year by year. It all adds up. Jim rumbled him but apparently only by chance. He had his doubts about the Corot, as I mentioned, but it was an overheard telephone call that really aroused his suspicions and caused him to investigate further. And caused his death,' she added, sadly.

'So you are quite sure Jim was deliberately killed?'

'Quite, quite sure. Piers Craven admitted it. He assured Caroline that her baby would be as dead as his father if she ever mentioned a word about the paintings, and that they'd be watching her. He was, she told me, utterly convincing. She believed every word. By the time I got home she was quite distraught, and that night we sat up talking for hours and hours. She said she had no interest in the forgeries – that Jamie's life was worth more than every picture ever painted – and much as I love art, I have to say I agreed with her. But what frightened her almost as much as Craven's threats was the fact that someone else might get to know of the conspiracy and blow the whistle. What then? Could she be sure that she wouldn't get the blame? Oh, she longed to do something to avenge Jim's death, I promise you – she burned to bring the murderers to justice – but it was Jamie that mattered most, and by the time we went to bed we had come to only one conclusion. Somehow they would both have to be spirited away.'

'How did you plan to manage that?'

'The very next day I drove them down to Exeter and they flew from there to Jersey. We told no one, made no phone calls that could possibly be traced. We thought no one would think of Exeter. Gatwick or Heathrow, perhaps, even Stanstead or Luton, but not a little airport like that. From Jersey they went to France. We still have distant relations there, you see. She changed her name to Caroline Dufy – Dufy being the name of our forbears, who came from Grenoble – and years later she took out

French nationality. Jamie has grown up fluent in both French and English and is, I can assure you, a most delightful boy.'

'George Quigley tried to tell me she must be dead. How did Caroline stand him, by the way? He's a horrible man!'

'She knew that. Oh, at first she simply thought he was rather smarmy but quite harmless. Later she learned differently, but she put up with him for Rose's sake.'

'He said he'd hired a detective to find her because Rose was so upset when she disappeared. He drew a blank, he told me, but there's always the chance he was lying. Maybe he didn't look for her at all.'

'Oh, I think he did, but not for any altruistic reason. He simply wanted to silence her. Certainly it's what Caroline always feared – that's why she took great care to cover her tracks. Our relatives in Grenoble may be distant, but they proved very helpful. She didn't go to them directly – she was too afraid that Craven would know about them from Rose – so she went underground in Paris and contacted them through an intermediary. One of her relations – a second cousin of mine – had a close friend in Paris, quite high up in government service. Caroline confided in him and he passed her off as a niece who had been living in Martinique but had unfortunately had all her papers stolen.

Quite unethical, of course, but justifiable under the circumstances, I feel.'

'Doesn't she ever come back to England?'

'No. She won't risk it – not once in all the years she's been away has she ever come back. I go to see her every year, but circumspectly. We meet, quite often, in a third country – such a lovely holiday we had last year in Corsica!' She glanced at her watch. 'My goodness, the time has flown! I simply must go or I'll miss my train.'

'You haven't told me exactly where she is,' I said as we set off across the square in the general direction of Piccadilly. 'Or what she's doing now. I so much want to meet her. And Jamie, of course. I can easily go to France.'

'France? Oh, didn't I say? She's not there any more. She married two years ago – a delightful man, a widower. You mustn't mind, my dear,' she said, seeing the look of surprise on my face.

'I don't mind,' I said. 'Of course I don't! She mourned Jim for quite long enough, I'm sure. It's just that, for some strange reason, I've always imagined her coping alone. Is she happy?'

'Very! As I said, Paul is a most kind, cultivated man with an excellent career in the French foreign service. His wife died most tragically a few years ago, leaving him with two little girls – one no more than a

212

baby at the time. Jamie is absolutely delighted with his stepsisters.'

'I'm glad,' I said. 'Really, really glad. But wherever they are, I intend to go and see them. Young Jamie is my only living relative.'

'Really?' She looked at me with some amusement. 'Well, I don't think you'll have much difficulty in finding them. Caroline and Paul have been living in Washington for the past six months. Globally speaking, they're right on your doorstep.'

Perhaps it was hysteria. Perhaps it was the swing from the total hopelessness of this morning to the relief of knowing that Caroline was alive and well and living in the States. For whatever reason, after a moment's astonished silence, I burst out laughing. Eventually even Aunt Caroline was laughing with me. Then, just as suddenly, I fell silent, quite serious now.

'They shouldn't be allowed to get away with it,' I said. 'Those guys – those murderers – we can't let them go on.'

She looked at me fearfully.

'For God's sake, don't make me regret I've told you all of this.'

Slowly we continued our walk. I was conscious now of a fierce anger – of clenched fists and a singing in my ears.

'It won't do,' I said. 'They killed my brother, remember. And would have killed

Jamie. I can't forget that, and I don't intend to.'

With some surprise, I recognised my mother's voice – her harshness and singleness of purpose and determination.

'You're in danger too, you know,' Aunt Caroline said. 'They will assume that you know everything that Jim knew. He could have written to you.'

'I was a child!'

'They will think it's the reason for your journey.'

'Well, all the more reason to make sure they pay the price for what they did.'

'And all Caroline's been through to keep Jamie safe?' Aunt Caroline caught my arm and pulled me to a halt once more. 'Is that to go for nothing?'

I could feel some of the aggression draining out of me, but the determination remained.

'Someone's got to do something,' I said. 'Caroline needn't be involved. And I don't intend to spend my life running away from them.'

For a moment she looked at me without speaking. Then she sighed and nodded.

'I suppose it's time,' she said.

Ten

Aunt Caroline and I parted more amicably than I would earlier have believed possible, and I hurried back to Quentins – still un-followed, as far as I could tell – agog to impart to Steve what she had told me. Or part of it, at least. She had still insisted that I should not mention Caroline's exact location to anyone until her permission had been sought and given. I was inclined to think that she was being over-cautious, but I gave my promise readily, knowing that Steve would understand.

I was actually reaching for the phone in my room to call him when it rang. This time it *was* him, and before he could say a word – and certainly before I registered all the noise that was going on in the background – I was pouring out the news: Caroline and Jamie were alive and well.

He was as joyful as I had been to hear it. Even so, he cut me short.

'Listen, Holly, I have to go,' he said. 'I'm at the airport.'

'The airport?' My voice swooped with

215

astonishment. 'Why? Where are you going?'

'Scotland. I've decided to make a quick trip to see Andrew. I want his advice.'

'How did it go at the bank? Bad?'

'Couldn't be worse.'

'Oh, Steve – *please!* I wish you'd let me—'

'Holly, I'm going to talk to Andy. He'll know what to do – raise a loan or maybe take a partner. He's the business head in our family.'

'Taking a partner doesn't seem such a bad idea. Especially if she's young and enthusiastic and willing to learn.'

'Do I know someone like that?'

'You sure do! It'll bear talking about, Steve.'

'Well—' He laughed. 'Maybe you're right, but not here and now. Look, I really must go. I'll phone again.'

'How long will you be away?'

'A couple of nights, maybe. Back Friday, I should think – anyway, I'll call. Holly, it's great news about Caroline.'

'Isn't it, though?'

It was, of course, and my joy in it was undimmed; but still it seemed something of an anti-climax that for a while I wouldn't have Steve to celebrate with.

'I'll let you buy the champagne when I get back,' he said, as if divining my thoughts. 'Bye, now. Take care. Don't run any risks. Holly—' A small pause followed. I could

216

hear airport noises in the background. A tannoy, the babble of conversation, a child crying. 'Love you,' he said softly, before breaking the connection.

I sat for a moment in a kind of trance, until strange noises from the receiver made me replace it hastily. I went to the window, opened it wide and leaned out. Early greyness had given way to sunshine and scudding clouds; spring at its loveliest, full of easy promises – promises, I was well aware, that were not always kept. Still I was conscious of hope, of a sudden excitement that couldn't be denied. 'Love you', he'd said; and he hadn't absolutely vetoed my suggestion of a partnership. Surely it wasn't such a bad idea? I knew nothing now, but I could learn. I *wanted* to learn. I had felt, just as Steve felt, a dawning love for old things and good craftsmanship. It seemed to me that the entire world of art and antiques was waiting for me, offering me pleasures I had barely been aware of.

Meantime I had some thinking to do. Aunt Caroline's warning that I, too, could be on the gang's hit list had come as a shock. Such a thing had not occurred to me – but it did explain the interest that my arrival had caused. For a split second I wondered whether I was mad to stay here, especially with the knowledge I now had that Caroline and Jamie were in the States.

217

And what about having to watch my back for the next n years, never mind having to dismiss once and for all the thought of bringing Jim's killers to justice? I could just imagine what Mom would say about that. And what about Steve?

No, I said to myself. I wasn't about to go anywhere. Instead I concentrated on trying to think what steps I could take to make sure Higginson and his gang met their comeuppance, and it struck me that the first step would be to find some way of proving that there was in fact an illegal connection between Higginson and the rest of the gang.

But Higginson was above suspicion, well thought of by his peers, the last man anyone could imagine being crooked. He sat on committees, Steve had told me, appeared on TV panels as an art critic, wrote pieces for specialist magazines. It simply wouldn't be believed if wild accusations were to be levelled against him, and even if forgery were proved to have taken place he would find some way of shifting responsibility for it on to the shoulders of some unfortunate underling. That was the kind of thing he was good at, Steve said. And if even that proved to be impossible, he would pass it off as a genuine mistake, the sort that even an expert might make once in a while. He might, under those circumstances, be forced to eat a slice or two of humble pie, but still no one would believe he had been wilfully authenticating forgeries for years in order to line his own pockets.

There *had* to be a way to prove his involvement, and I thought long and hard to bring it to mind. There had to be some way of proving that he knew exactly what he was doing when he gave his seal of approval to paintings he knew full well weren't the real thing. I longed to be able to discuss it all with Steve, but in his absence I spent my solitary evening creating wild plots that would unmask Higginson as the villain of the piece, only to dismiss them as unworkable. I thought the matter over from every angle, but I was no nearer finding a sensible solution by the time sleep overtook me.

The following morning I received the answers to my ad in *The Times*. The first was from a detective agency, offering to be of assistance in return for a (so-called) reasonable fee. The second was from a woman in a place called Southport who said when she was a girl at high school in Oxford she had been taught English by a Miss Caroline Bethany, but had seen or heard nothing of her for the past fifteen years. (I was lucky, I realised, bearing in mind the girls that Miss Bethany senior must have had through her hands, not to have received hundreds of letters giving the same information.) The third was a great deal more interesting, though hardly shed any light on the Caroline question.

It was typed on heavy, cream-coloured paper of a very high quality, and bore the address 7, Horse Guards Court, Pierrepoint Gardens, London SW1. But what made me gasp with astonishment was the name that was engraved above the address. It was none other than that of Sir Timothy Crofthouse, Bt.

'Dear Miss Crozier,' it read.

I was interested to see your advertisement in today's *Times*. I am afraid I have no information regarding the person you are seeking, but I have reason to think you must be the daughter of the late Martha Crozier of New York. She and I were old friends, and if, indeed, you are her daughter, it would give me great pleasure to meet you while you are in London. Perhaps you might even spare the time to have dinner with me?

Do, please, give me a call on the above number.

He was, he said, sincerely mine, Timothy Crofthouse.

Equally sincerely intrigued, I read the letter over again. Crozier wasn't such a singular name. How come he'd been so sure that I was Martha's daughter? And how come he'd been such friends with Mom when all the world knew how little she liked Englishmen? She'd certainly never mentioned him as far as I could remember.

Should I ring him, as requested? What a question! I knew perfectly well that my curiosity wouldn't allow me to resist it, and as soon as I finished breakfast I went back to my room and dialled Sir Timothy's number.

I hardly expected to get through to him right away, but to my surprise he answered the phone himself.

'Crofthouse.' The voice was crisp and assured and very, very upper-crust English.

'This is Holly Crozier,' I said.

'Well, hal*lo*! How good of you to call.' That was better. Now, though still upper crust, he sounded warm and much more human. 'Where are you? In London?'

'Yes – at Quentins Hotel. But tell me, how did you guess I was Martha Crozier's daughter?'

'I recognised your brother's name. I never met him, but I heard your mother speak of him.'

'Oh!' I was silent, thinking this over. 'But – but when and where did you know her? I had no idea my mother had any English friends. She never came to England – at least, only once, and that was only for a couple of days.' I didn't elaborate on this. She had come to London to attend the inquest on Jim and to bring his body back to the States and to my certain knowledge she had been in no mood then to forge friendly relations.

'Ah, but you're wrong,' Sir Timothy told me. 'She came here in the summer of 1975.'

'She came here? To England?'

'She did indeed. She never mentioned it?'

'No. Never. But, of course, that was before I was born.'

'Yes, of course; I guessed that. She only ever spoke of her son. What happened to him, and why does his girlfriend need friendship and support?'

'He – he died. Nine years ago.'

'I'm so sorry.'

'You sent flowers to my mother's funeral. That was good of you.'

'I – thought a great deal of her. I never forgot her.'

'But how did you know about her death?'

'Lilian phoned me. Lilian Wheeler? You know her, of course. We kept in touch over the years – Christmas cards, and the odd dinner with her and Frank whenever they were in England or I was in New York. You do know them?' he added, when surprise kept me silent.

'Yes,' I said faintly, more and more bewildered. 'Yes, I know them well.'

Yet they'd never said a word about this English baronet, who was apparently so friendly with my mother. And if so friendly, why had he called on Lilian and Frank when he visited New York while, apparently, ignoring her? It didn't make sense. Why hadn't they, or Mom, ever mentioned him?

'Well, how are you fixed about having dinner?' he said. 'Is tonight too short notice? Tomorrow evening I have an engagement and the following day I must go down to Fincote – my country house. It's my wife's birthday and we're expecting a houseful of people.'

'Tonight would be fine,' I said.

'Then how about the Athenaeum at eight? It's a club, quite close to St James's Park.'

Where Steve had found a parking meter, I remembered, the time we went to the wine bar. It seemed about a hundred years ago.

'I'll be there,' I said.

'I shall look forward to it.'

Baronets are human, too, I reminded myself as I put the phone down – but even so, I found myself feeling just a little daunted at the thought of meeting this aristocratic mystery man.

What, I wondered, did one wear to have dinner with a titled gentleman at his club? Were trouser suits out? Was a long skirt necessary? Was this, maybe, an excuse for buying something new and gorgeous? An opportunity for a little retail therapy? It must be some kind of record that I hadn't engaged in it long before this, and an indication of how the problem of Caroline had occupied my mind. A lack of interest in shopping was never an accusation that could be levelled at me.

On the other hand, was there anything I ought to be doing this day to bring Higginson's comeuppance ever closer? Much as I tried, I couldn't think of anything. I didn't want to go anywhere near Lovells in case he saw me, which would only serve to warn him of my continued interest. It went against the grain merely to hang about waiting to ask Steve's advice, but he knew this world so much better than I that it seemed the most sensible option. So, taking one thing with another, I came to the conclusion that a day off might prove therapeutic.

'Knightsbridge, here I come,' I said out loud.

It was much, much later in the day when, bags with famous names suspended from several fingers, I managed to hail a taxi to take me back to the hotel. I subsided thankfully on its back seat with a sigh that was part weariness, part satisfaction.

An entirely successful expedition, I thought, leaning my head back and closing my eyes, picturing again the garments I'd bought; the lovely lines of the soft wool dress in that heavenly colour, half green, half blue. Such skill, I marvelled. How did they cut a length of material so that it hung like that?

Then there was the suit. Well, every girl should have a black suit, but not every girl was lucky enough to be able to be able to secure one like the little number I had swooped upon in that boutique in Beauchamp Place. And then, of course, I had to buy the top that went with it...

'Shocking, innit?' I opened my eyes to see the taxi driver grinning at me in the rear-view mirror. 'Wears you out, spending money.'

'But what a blissful way to go,' I said.

We were stuck in a traffic jam – hardly an unusual occurrence in London, I had found. It gave me time to look assessingly at the various other garments displayed in the shop windows along Knightsbridge, and I was gratified to see nothing that I would have dreamed of trading for the clothes in the bags that clustered round my feet.

We made a little progress before coming to a full stop again, and this time I found we were opposite a small boutique selling ethnic sculptures and primitive paintings.

'Provenance' was the name of the shop, the letters scrawled in black against a terra-cotta background. The sight of it dragged me back to the problems I had temporarily put out of my mind.

Provenance, I thought. Provenance. That was the key to everything. Paintings couldn't just appear in a saleroom from some anonymous donor and be sold for exorbitant prices. Their origins had to be known, their previous owners documented, which was, of course, where Higginson came in. Surely there had to be some way of proving that the provenance of Higginson-authenticated forgeries were as much a fake as the paintings themselves?

I needed to ask an expert. Steve himself was the first to say that this was not his field, not in the way that it had been for Jim. But there must be someone else—

Sir Timothy Crofthouse! A good chap, Steve had said, and involved in the arts, anxious to save the nation's treasures from being sold overseas. Of course, that might not necessarily mean he was an expert on paintings – the term 'arts' covered a multitude of different skills – but at least he would be concerned. And, in view of the fact that Jim's death might be involved, his regard for my mother would be an added incentive to help.

How much should I tell him? So much depended on him and how we got on together that I felt I could make no plans. I'd have to play it off the cuff.

I was aware, suddenly, that the taxi had come to a standstill and that the driver was looking over his shoulder at me, a big grin on his face.

'Penny for 'em?' he said.

I opened my purse and fumbled inside for the money.

'Oh, they're worth a great deal more than that, I promise you,' I said, casting a jaundiced eye at the meter. 'And so, I see, is my ride.'

He grinned again, pocketed the notes I handed over, picked up another couple who were just leaving the hotel, and disappeared in the direction of Piccadilly.

I wore the black silk suit to go to dinner with Sir Timothy even though I had a few misgivings about the brevity of the skirt.

A taxi dropped me at the door of the club just after eight. I went in and was greeted by some kind of attendant who, when told that I was a guest of Sir Timothy Crofthouse, pointed me in the direction of a tall, silvery-haired man standing at the foot of the stairs. I approached him, smiling a little tentatively, and for a moment I thought the attendant must have got it wrong and that this wasn't Sir Timothy after all, for there was no answering smile on the man's face – in fact, I had the impression that he was taken aback to see me walking towards him. Shocked, even. But then he appeared to take himself in hand and came to meet me

with a charming smile, his hand outstretched.

'Holly? How good of you to come! I'm
delighted to meet you.'

'I'm not late?' I said, thinking that perhaps
I had mistaken the time. I could think of no
other reason for that strange expression I
had noticed a moment before – unless my
skirt was, after all, too short for the Athenaeum.

'No – no, not at all. Shall we go and have
a drink before dinner?'

He shepherded me to the bar and we sat
sipping our Martinis, making polite but not
very easy conversation. From what Steve
had said, I had expected a man who was
worldly-wise and urbane, but instead he
seemed almost ill at ease. I felt that we were
both hesitant, summing each other up. He
was an elegant man, I saw, fastidious in his
dress, with an expensive-looking haircut and
manicured nails. A nice face, I had to give
him that, with a handsome, rather promi-
nent nose and deep brown eyes.

But an edgy man. Not the kind of man
one could relax with. It hardly seemed possible that such a man could be shy, but this
was the only conclusion I could draw from
his manner, and I began to think that Sir
Timothy, after all, was not a man I could
confide in.

But over dinner things improved a little.

Perhaps the pre-dinner drink had dispersed his inhibitions, or maybe it was the wine. For whatever reason, he seemed to relax and become the charming host I had expected. He began talking of the first time he had met my mother – in New York, it had been, at the home of Claude Reinberg, the big theatrical impresario.

'My father was alive then,' he told me, 'and he'd dispatched me to negotiate the sale of Crofts. There were two American firms interested at the time, but maybe I didn't do my job very well because they both pulled out. I don't think I was ever quite forgiven, even though sales picked up and we enjoyed years of highly successful trading. And when we did sell to a German company, we were able to get a far more advantageous price. At the time he was not at all pleased, and he didn't hesitate to let me know it! He said I hadn't concentrated on the job in hand. He hadn't sent me there to enjoy myself, he said. I'd allowed myself to be distracted.'

'And had you?'

'You could say so. I met your mother, didn't I?'

And had fallen in love with her, I realised, even though at that time she was still married. Well, a number of men had been attracted to her wit and sparkiness, as well as her appearance, but still I was a little surprised that she had been Sir Timothy's type. She had been younger then, I reminded myself. Softer, maybe, and less abrasive. I found myself warming towards him more and more.

'You said on the phone that my mother had been to England.'

'That's right. She came to stay at Fincote.'

'I still find it strange that she never spoke of it.'

'Well—' He hesitated, took a sip of wine. 'Maybe she wanted to forget it. I have to confess it wasn't a happy time – and then, of course, she became very successful in her own right. When I knew her she was just starting out. But tell me about you. What do you do with yourself? Have you followed in her footsteps?'

Maybe the wine had worked its magic on me, too, because I forgot my earlier reservations, finding that conversation between us seemed easy now. I had no hesitation in telling him about *Bower Street* and my strong feeling that this represented the beginning and end of my career as an actress, and how I was unsure now of what to do next. And I told him about the house at Corey Cove and my reluctance to sell it. I even told him about Jim, but still I said nothing regarding Lovells or the art scam that I felt sure was being operated by Higginson.

I had told him, in passing, that Jim had

worked at Lovells, and it was he who returned to this as we sat over coffee.

'I wish I'd known him,' he said. 'He sounds a young man after my own heart. I'm passionate about art myself and have managed to get together quite a collection at Fincote. I intend to leave them to the nation.'

'I hope your heirs don't mind.'

'My wife and I only have one child – a daughter, Davina – and I don't think she's much interested. Of course, she could change. She's only eighteen. She left school last summer.'

'What's she doing now?'

'Enjoying a gap year, travelling around the Far East. Youngsters these days are so independent. One has to let them go, but I admit we worry about her. I'll be relieved to see her back.'

'I'm sure you will.' I smiled at him. He was nice, I thought. A kind, loving sort of man. Davina Crofthouse was a lucky girl. And suddenly, not altogether logically, it was at that moment I decided to tell him what was on my mind.

'May I – may I confide in you?' I asked him a little hesitantly.

'Of course.' He looked concerned. 'Is something worrying you?'

'You could say so.' I took a breath. 'It's rather a long story, I'm afraid.'

'Fire away.'

I told him everything – well, everything except Caroline's whereabouts. It took quite a while, for he stopped me from time to time to take me back over various points or to ask questions, but right from the start I was impressed by the way he listened, fastening at once on the more important points in my narrative.

'I know Higginson,' he said, when I had finished. 'We were on a panel together for some Channel 4 TV programme. Can't stand the man.'

'Nor, apparently, could Jim. He was definitely on to something before he was killed.'

Sir Timothy seemed lost in thought.

'We can't possibly assume that all, or even the majority, of paintings Higginson authenticates are suspect,' he said at last. 'After all, he is a man of the highest reputation – which is, of course, the key to the whole operation. If he loses that, he loses everything.'

'What can we do? He and his cronies are ruthless murderers. We can't just let him go on.'

'No.' For a moment he said nothing, clearly lost in thought. 'There's an art sale at Lovells on Friday morning,' he went on at last. 'Viewing tomorrow. I'd intended to go and have a look at it anyway, so I'll go ahead and see if anything strikes me as being remotely suspect. But it's not going to be easy, I'm afraid. I know a fair bit about art, but I'd never describe myself as an expert and by their very nature the forgeries are going to be first class. Maybe I can recruit someone else, more knowledgeable than I.'

I suddenly remembered the journalist Steve had introduced to me at the sale in Surrey, the one who had spoken so kindly about Jim.

'What about Serena Newbold? She's a journalist.'

'Yes. I know her, too. She's a bright girl. Knows her subject.'

'Maybe together you could spot something.'

'Maybe. But Holly—' He reached out and put his hand over mine for a moment. It seemed a perfectly natural thing to do, more avuncular than predatory, and I didn't resent it at all. 'Don't get your hopes up too much. There may be nothing remotely suspicious about this auction. It can't happen every time.'

'I know that! But if there is—?'

'Then I shall buy it.'

'Whatever it costs?'

'Well, I'll do my best. It'll be worth a lot to bring this crowd to justice. I shall feel—' He stopped, hesitating for a second or two. 'I shall be doing it for Martha,' he said at last. 'Jim was her son, and if what you say is

233

right, he died so that these bastards could go on making money.'

'You loved her, didn't you?' I spoke softly, seeing the look on his face, and he smiled ruefully.

'Yes, I did,' he admitted. 'And I think she loved me. I *know* she did! I wanted her to end her sham of a marriage and marry me – and at first she said that she would. Then she came to Fincote and met my parents.' He stopped abruptly.

'What happened?' I asked. For a moment he said nothing, staring down at the table, his mouth twisted. Then he looked up at me.

'They treated her atrociously,' he said, bitterness in his voice. 'She wasn't at all what they wanted for me, you see. She was married already, and they hated the idea of the sacred name of Crofthouse being dragged through the divorce court. She wasn't, as they said, "our sort of person". I was ready to defy them – damn it all, neither of us were children! I was thirty-six at the time and she was a year or so younger. I tried to persuade her to go through with it, said I would leave England, settle in America, but she took fright – decided she wanted no part of it. And who could blame her? I certainly didn't.'

'So she went back to the States?'

'And would never see me again. Or speak

to me. She said it was the only way she could deal with it. For a while I hoped that maybe one day she would come round, but she never did. Lilian told me once that I'd broken her heart – which I thought was a bit hard, since I was under the impression she'd broken mine – but whatever the truth of it she steadfastly refused to have anything to do with me. It took me a long time to get over it – more so, I think, because I knew that nothing had really changed between us.' He paused a moment, then laughed ruefully. 'That doesn't really make sense, does it? I expect I'm kidding myself. If she'd continued to think anything of me, we could perhaps have met as friends.'

'She was a strong-willed woman,' I said. 'If she decided that not to see you at all was the only way she could deal with losing you, then that's what she would have stuck to, no matter how much she wished it otherwise. To me it seems right in character.'

'Does it?' He raised his eyebrows a little. 'Well, I told myself that too, until—'

He broke off and this time didn't continue. He signalled to the waiter, signed a chitty. The evening was over, I realised, leaving me with much to think about.

'I've enjoyed meeting you so much,' Sir Timothy said as we walked towards the door. 'Martha must have been very proud of you.'

'Well, I was proud of her,' I said. 'And I enjoyed meeting you, too. I feel I understand her more now. She – she didn't have much time for Brits, you know.'

He laughed at that.

'I'd heard. Well, I can understand that.'

'I'm sorry she broke your heart.'

'It mended. Eventually I met Marian, and she and I have been happy. We suit each other. She's a marvellous woman.'

But he didn't suggest that I should meet her, or visit Fincote, which I should dearly liked to have done. Well, if he co-operated over the art scam that was more than I had any right to expect, I told myself, as I thanked him once more for a wonderful dinner.

'I'll contact Serena and be in touch,' he said, as he put me into a cab. 'You'll still be at the hotel?'

'Oh yes,' I told him. 'I'll be there.'

In this, I wasn't like my mother. No one was making me rush back home in a hurry.

Eleven

I felt restless the following morning, impatient to hear what Sir Timothy thought of the pictures on view at Lovells and anxious to know if he had been able to recruit Serena Newbold to our side. However, there seemed nothing that I could usefully do about it, so I spent the morning with a party of American ladies from the hotel, rubbernecking on the river. They stayed at Greenwich to visit the Cutty Sark, but I returned to Westminster, suddenly determined to go to Lovells myself. What, after all, did it matter if Higginson saw me there? I'd be in a roomful of people and I had every right to view what was for sale, and even to put in a bid the following day if any picture caught my fancy.

As it happened, I didn't see Higginson or either of the two girls I had met on the first occasion; instead a different cast of employees altogether seemed to be staffing the place.

The paintings were a mixed bag from both the eighteenth and nineteenth centuries.

There were a number of seascapes, which my catalogue told me were the work of one John Lynn, 1832; some oils – flowers and a still life – by Valentine Bartholomew, 1834; a group of watercolours depicting scenes in British Guiana attributed to an artist called Charles Bentley. There they go again, I thought. There was something definitely equivocal about 'attributed'. I stared at the pictures for some time, thinking how marvellous it would be if I could spot some absolute proof that they were fakes – some piece of flora or fauna that absolutely, positively, categorically, did not belong in British Guiana. However, since my knowledge of the flora and fauna, or even the location, of British Guiana was non-existent, I merely sighed and moved on.

My spirits lightened a little when I looked at the next picture, for I was able – correctly, I found, when I looked at the catalogue – to identify it as a Zoffany. At least I had something to thank Mr Higginson for! He had added this small item to my pathetically limited artistic knowledge.

This picture was entitled *Sir Vaughan le Maire and family at Cottslow Barton*. Unlike the previous work I had seen, this one showed the family in their garden; Lady le Maire, looking rustic, clad in a sprigged muslin dress with a white fichu and a wide-brimmed straw hat decorated with flowers and tied under her chin with pink ribbons, looked rather like Marie Antoinette playing in her toy farm at the Petit Trianon. She sat beneath a tree with a blonde, angelic-looking child on her knee. Beside her, an equally blonde and angelic girl stood smiling, proffering a toy lamb to her small sister. On the arm of the seat, casual but proud, sat Sir Vaughan himself in wine-red breeches and surcoat, white-stockinged legs elegantly crossed, and beside him, on his left, stood a boy of nine or ten, head erect, his dress vaguely military in design. In the background, a more soberly dressed woman – governess or maiden aunt, perhaps – held another small child, sex indeterminate, who leaned from her arms towards its mother.

The family looked elegant and prosperous and very pleased with themselves, and once again I admired the meticulous accuracy of the painting, those lovely flesh tones and the differing expressions. I could feel the breeze that blew the leaves on the trees, and the texture of the hair of the little dog that sat, head on paws, before his mistress; though even as I did so, I began, dimly, to understand Higginson's objection to the style. Perhaps art should be more than a glorified reproduction of its subject?

But still I looked, beguiled and a little amused by the sight of so much perfection. My gaze travelled from one handsome face to another, finally alighting on the woman in the background, the sole exception to this array of beauty. An impoverished relation, I decided, seeing her clothes, which were plain and unadorned, in total contrast to the rest of the family. An orphaned niece, perhaps, with no hope of a dowry, thus rendering her unlikely to make a suitable marriage. A burden on her brothers, more than likely, her only option to be found a place in a more wealthy relative's establishment. As far as I could remember from my reading of Jane Austen and the Brontës, governesses frequently had this kind of background.

Surprising, I thought, my gaze homing in with more concentration to her face, that the artist hadn't used his skill to make her look a little happier with her position in life. You'd think Lady le Maire would object to seeing a member of her household looking so tragically miserable; it contrasted oddly with the sweetness and light generated by all the other subjects. This woman's eyes were full of pain, her mouth taut as if she were about to give a cry for help. A bit like Rose Quigley, I thought idly. And then my attentioned sharpened still further. This woman wasn't just *like* Rose, she *was* Rose! Why hadn't I noticed it before? I felt a sudden shiver of excitement that grew and grew until I could hardly catch my breath.

Was it obsession? Some form of madness that made me superimpose Rose's likeness on a totally dissimilar subject? I didn't think so, but I walked away from the picture, did my best to give my attention to others, wandered down the row and finally came up again, back to the Zoffany.

It was Rose. There could be no mistake. The face was small and thin, the eyes disproportionately big, the expression one of unhappiness and bewilderment.

Was that the kind of face the artist had thought suitable for this poor relation, so clearly of lesser importance than the family she served? Oh, surely I had to be mistaken – but how could I be, when I had seen this same face in the flesh only the day before yesterday? What astonished me now was why the likeness hadn't hit me forcibly between the eyes the moment I'd looked at the picture.

I found that my heart was pounding so hard that I could feel it fluttering in my throat. This has to be significant, I thought. It just has to be! There was nothing that could convince me that only by coincidence had the artist given his subject this particular face, that particular expression, and I looked round wildly, hoping against hope that I would see Serena or even Sir Timothy so that I could tell them that, consciously or unconsciously, the artist had used a living

241

model. Neither was present at that particular moment, and with one last, long look at the picture, I left the room and went out once more into the street.

I needed a telephone. Why, I asked myself, hadn't I brought my mobile with me from home, or furnished myself with one at the beginning of this visit? I would have given anything to have one in my purse right now. Still, the hotel wasn't far away and I proceeded towards it with all speed.

It was Sir Timothy's secretary who answered my call. He was at a meeting, she told me, but was expected back at any time.

'Could you get him to call me urgently?' I asked.

'Certainly. If you give me your name and number, I'll leave a note for him. I'm just on the point of leaving.'

I duly gave her the required information, begged her to underline the fact that the matter was urgent and put down the receiver, positively tingling with frustration. I contemplated calling Serena – almost any activity seemed better than nothing – but I thought better of it. It wasn't that I didn't trust her, simply that it seemed advisable to wait and see what reaction Sir Timothy had gotten from her before I contacted her myself.

I paced up and down a little, then opened the door of the minibar and gazed at its contents, sorely tempted to pour myself a drink to steady my nerves. I even reached for the little bottle of gin, but changed my mind at the last moment and took out some Coke instead. I felt I needed all my wits about me.

When at last the phone rang, I snatched at it instantly.

'Hallo?'

'Tim Crofthouse here. I had a message—'

'Yes! I've got to talk to you!' Even through my excitement I was aware that he'd called himself Tim. It seemed to mark a significant advance in our friendship and I sure liked it a whole heap better than Sir Timothy, which had from the beginning felt like a formal, prickly barrier between the two of us. 'I went to see the pictures at Lovells this afternoon, and I'm pretty sure one of them must be a fake. The Zoffany.'

'Really?' He sounded interested, but also surprised. 'You mean the le Maire family? I saw it myself this morning, but didn't spot anything amiss.'

'The governess, or aunt, or whatever – she had Rose Quigley's face. Can you believe that? I'd know it anywhere! Surely it couldn't be coincidence?'

'Are you sure?'

'Absolutely.'

He greeted this with silence, as if he were thinking over the implications.

'That's amazing,' he said at last, his voice so soft I could barely hear him. 'Amazing! I wonder what Serena will have to say to that?'

'Were you able to contact her?'

'She's coming round here at six thirty. I have a dinner engagement and she has to go to the opening of some gallery or other later on, but we thought there'd be time to meet. I was going to ring you anyway to suggest you came too, if you're free.'

'Yes – yes, of course I'll come. I have your address.'

'See you later, then.'

I looked at my watch. Half past four! Two whole hours to fill somehow. But how? Well – I picked up a comb and tidied my hair, for somehow in my excitement I had managed to turn myself into a fair replica of the wild woman of Borneo, and then – what else? – I went downstairs to the salon for tea. When in England, I said to myself.

Pierrepoint Gardens turned out to be somewhere behind Whitehall. It was quite a short street with government offices of some kind on the corner and a couple of large blocks of mansion flats further along, of which Horse Guards Court was one. The building was quite old – maybe Victorian, I guessed – with lofty ceilings and solid-looking doors. An elevator took me to the third floor where I discovered Apartment 7 and Tim, as I was trying to get used to thinking of him, opened the door to me. We went into quite a wide hall, furnished with a wonderfully carved table which I knew immediately Steve would approve of, and through arched doors into the sitting room where Serena was already waiting for me.

We greeted each other, said how good it was to see each other again, but wasted little time on these preliminaries.

'Sir Timothy tells me you've made a discovery,' she said.

Since speaking to Tim, I'd had plenty of time for doubts to creep in. Maybe it *was* just a coincidence, after all. Or maybe – and this really was far-fetched – maybe the woman in the picture was some long-dead ancestor of Rose's.

'I – I was pretty sure the woman had Rose Quigley's face,' I said, a little hesitantly, feeling less sure by the minute. 'I suppose it sounds crazy...'

Serena neither agreed or disagreed with this.

'The woman in the Zoffany. Sir Timothy told me.'

I was conscious of an impatient movement on his part.

'Oh, for God's sake call me Tim,' he said, including both of us in this. 'I can't bear all this formality.'

'Suits me,' I said, grinning at him. He was an OK guy, was Tim, and I could quite understand my mother falling for him twenty-odd years ago. He was still a handsome, distinguished-looking man. Back in the seventies he must have been a knockout.

'I saw the picture myself this morning,' Serena said. 'Do I take it you mean the woman in the background, holding the baby?'

'That's the one.'

'But she's nothing like Rose Quigley! I know Rose. She's quite a pretty little thing.'

'Maybe she was once,' I agreed, 'but she sure as hell isn't now. I saw her yesterday, remember. She showed me a photograph of herself and Caroline together, and believe me, I could barely recognise her. She's lost a lot of weight and her face is – well—' I shrugged, rather at a loss to describe it. 'Just like the woman in the picture. She looked almost anorexic. She's certainly one unhappy lady.'

'I imagine that picture will fetch at least a million,' Tim said. I was taken aback by this.

'That sounds an awful lot.'

'Zoffany's *Colmore Family* sold for well over that at Christie's last year,' Serena said. 'And prices haven't fallen, that I'm aware of.'

'I thought the gang almost always stuck to the lesser known, less expensive artists.'

'Well—' Serena shrugged her shoulders. 'I guess Zoffany asks for it, in a way. If you're right, that is.'

'Oh, I wish you could see Rose for yourself! I don't think you'd have any doubts then.'

'Surely we can take Holly's word for it, can't we?' Tim said, weighing in on my side. 'After all, she saw the woman only yesterday. And I have heard of this happening before. The artist does it instinctively, I understand, not realising he is giving himself away by painting a contemporary face, someone known to him.'

Serena nodded slowly, agreeing with him.

'Yes. It has been done, I know.'

'Suppose—' I began. Then shut up. The thought that had crossed my mind seemed so bizarre.

'Go on,' Tim said. 'Any suggestion might be helpful.'

'I doubt this one will. It just occurred to me that maybe whoever painted it might have *wanted* Rose to be recognised.' For a moment they both looked at me and said nothing. 'Does that sound totally ridiculous?' I added.

'Not entirely,' Serena said slowly. 'I mean, it's not altogether likely that Piers Craven paints every forgery himself, and it's therefore not outside the realms of possibility that he could have fallen out with one of the

247

artists. We know he has this kind of arty commune in Wales and it seems logical to suppose that if there's some kind of scam, then they're all at it.'

'Steve Maitland said that one of them – a young man – was killed up there some time ago. Maybe it was because he wanted out. So perhaps if another of them wanted the same thing—'

Serena had been looking down at the carpet, frowning as if it might give her inspiration if she looked at it long enough, but now she lifted her head slowly and looked at me.

'I remember,' she said. 'He was run over, wasn't he? Like Jim?'

'I'm told so.' I remembered, just in time, that I wasn't supposed to know what Aunt Caroline had told me. 'His girlfriend thought it was a suspicious death, Steve said, and tried to get the police interested, but they dismissed it as an accident.'

'So,' Serena said, 'maybe it's not easy to resign from Piers Craven's little band of brothers. Maybe whoever painted the le Maire family thought that if he subtly showed his hand by painting a contemporary face, one which someone in the art world might recognise, then the whole operation might be blown apart.'

'Which could land him in jail,' Tim pointed out.

'Maybe the lesser of two evils.'

'So what do we do?' I asked.

'I'll buy the Zoffany,' Tim said, and I felt bound to protest.

'No – it's too much—'

'I can insure against it being a fake,' Tim said. 'At least, I think I can. You can insure against most things, at a price.'

'The paper might be prepared to cover that,' Serena said. I still felt dubious.

'It's still a lot for Tim to find.' I was feeling responsible, besieged by fresh doubts.

'Well, I suppose there's a chance it might not reach a million. The *Colmore Family* picture is well known and excellent of its kind. This one isn't quite of the same standard, and it certainly isn't well known, if at all. It was said to have been discovered in France, in some remote chateau.'

'Isn't that a bit suspicious in itself?' I asked.

Serena shrugged her shoulders again.

'Not necessarily,' she said. 'That's the way things turn up.'

'I shall buy it anyway,' Tim said firmly. 'If it's genuine, I'll be glad to own it. And if it's not, and proves to be instrumental in exposing Higginson and his cronies, then it'll be worth it.'

'But what happens after you've bought it?' I asked. 'How do we prove it's a forgery?'

'There's a place in Cambridge where these

things are tested,' Serena said. 'It's horrendously expensive, but I feel pretty sure the paper will pay for that. After all, we pride ourselves on our investigative journalism.'

'And if it does prove to be a fake, then Higginson will have some explaining to do,' Tim said. 'We would have to make damned sure that the alleged Zoffany was proved to be the tip of the iceberg.' He beamed round at us, as if savouring this possibility. 'Well, now – everything seems to be tied up very nicely, then,' he concluded. 'I think a drink is called for, don't you?'

'Love one, but I must be off,' Serena said, gathering up her enormous bag and standing up to shrug herself into her cape. 'I'm a bit late as it is. Forgive me, Tim – I'll take you up on that drink some other time.'

'Get those villains behind bars, and it'll be champagne all round,' Tim promised.

She left us, and somewhere out of sight Tim poured our drinks, leaving me to look around the room. The chairs and sofa were modern enough, covered in a kind of faded chintz, but there were a few pieces of furniture that looked interesting – a chest of drawers, a bureau, an old carved chest under the windows. There were a couple of watercolours of rural scenes – but no photographs, I noticed. No picture of his wife or daughter. I was curious to know what they looked like and found this rather disappointing.

'When are you expecting your young man to come home?' Tim asked as he came back into the room, glasses on a small tray.

'Sunday, I think. He said he would phone—'

The front door bell shrilled, interrupting me, and I fell silent.

'Who the blazes—? Excuse me a minute. I wasn't expecting anyone.' Tim put his drink down and went to open the door, his voice reaching me from the hall. 'Probably Jehovah's Witnesses. Or a double-glazing salesman.'

But I could tell by his exclamation of surprise as he opened the door that neither of these guesses were right.

'Davina, my darling! You could have warned me! When on earth did you get in?'

'Two hours ago. Heathrow.'

'You should have said! I'd have met you.'

'It was a sudden decision. A couple of our lot got a bit too mixed up in Burmese politics and we felt we ought to leave before things turned ugly. Oh, Dad—' There was a short silence which I, listening from inside the room, interpreted as time for a quick hug. 'Dad, it's wonderful to see you – to be here.'

'It's lucky I *am* here – I could easily have been at Fincote, but there's a bit of business

251

I have to take care of. I was actually just in the middle – listen, love, why don't you take your stuff through to the spare bedroom, have a wash and brush-up, and by that time I'll be totally at your service.'

Not able to avoid eavesdropping from the inner room, I felt even more disappointed and also a little hurt that for some reason Tim seemed determined, not only to keep me away from Fincote but to prevent my meeting his daughter, too. What was wrong with me? Not good enough, after all?

'Oh, come on Dad, have a heart.' I heard thumps, as if a bag of some kind was being thrown down in the hall. 'Can't you give a poor girl a drink before we start on the washing and brushing-up?'

I couldn't see what was happening out there, but I sensed that she had stepped round her father and was coming nearer. Two steps and she was round the corner, through the door, and into the sitting room, where I was perched on the edge of the sofa, feeling unusually ill at ease.

I stood up as she came in, determined to show my readiness to leave, if that's what Tim wanted. She was wearing jeans, a T-shirt that had clearly seen a lot of travelling, and one of those Barbour jackets in much the same condition. Her hair was cut short and curled all over her head, but although I took in all these things in one swift glance, it was her face that made my jaw drop with astonishment.

I could have been looking into a mirror.

Twelve

Tim, coming into the room just behind her, stepped forward a little and put his arm round her shoulders.

'Davina,' he said. 'I want you to meet your half-sister, Holly Crozier. Holly, this is Davina.'

Neither of us spoke, but we continued to stare at each other in astonishment.

'Why – why didn't you say?' I managed to stammer at last. Then light slowly dawned and my astonishment turned to anger. 'You weren't going to tell me, were you?'

'Now come on – sit down, both of you. Have your drink, Holly—'

'That's your answer to everything, isn't it?' My bitterness surprised me and I made no move to do what he asked. 'Is that what you all do – push it under the carpet, cover up any unpleasantness, have a drink and forget it? We have to keep our British upper lips stiff at all costs, don't we?' I was shaking, I realised, as I bent to retrieve my purse so that I could storm out.

'It's not like that!' He left Davina and

254

came over to me. 'Holly – please listen and try to understand. I swear to you that until last evening I had absolutely no idea of your connection with me. Your mother never told me – never dropped the smallest hint! Do you think, if I'd known, I wouldn't have insisted on seeing her – seeing *you*? You must believe me. Please sit down and let's talk about this.'

But it was Davina who sat down, slumping wearily into one of the deep armchairs.

'I don't know that I can take this in,' she said. 'It's been the weirdest day. But I agree with Holly, Dad. You've got some explaining to do.'

'I know. And I'm trying to do it. Please sit down, Holly.'

I looked from one to the other, hesitated a moment more, then, slowly and reluctantly, did as he asked. I still felt hurt. It seemed quite obvious to me that without Davina's untimely arrival, he wouldn't have admitted to our relationship and would have allowed me to go back to the States quite unaware of my parentage.

'I'll get you a drink,' he muttered to Davina, and headed for the kitchen.

'Could it be coffee?' she called after him. 'I'm quite addicted to instant so don't go to any trouble.'

For a second, in his absence, there was silence between us. We looked at each other.

'Well!' she said. 'Quite a turn up for the books. Why is one surprised to learn that one's parents have pasts?'

'Doesn't it bother you?'

'It'll take a bit of getting used to, I'll admit that.' She studied me in silence for a moment, then grinned widely. 'He had no choice but to come clean, did he? No hope of keeping our relationship dark.'

'I see now why he didn't suggest I should visit Fincote.'

One trousered leg over the arm of her chair, Davina half turned as her father came into the room, coffee cup in hand.

'Thanks,' she said as she took it from him. 'Any more skeletons in your cupboard, mystery man? Can either of us expect the odd extra brother or sister to pop out of the woodwork any minute now?'

She was cool, I thought. Even this revelation, young as she was, didn't seem to have fazed her one bit. I saw them exchange smiles and suddenly I was conscious of the most unworthy feeling of jealousy. Davina was so secure in her father's love. She knew nothing would alter it; that the affection they shared would be compromised neither by time or circumstances.

Whereas I ... I caught myself up short, not wanting to go down that self-pitying road.

Tim came and sat down beside me, turning me round to face him. His expression was serious now. 'Holly, I swear to you I am telling the truth. When I saw you last night for the first time, it was like a kick in the solar plexus. I knew at once, of course, that I was your father. How could I doubt it? Not only were you the image of Davina, but you were the right age, too. From the first, I had absolutely no doubt that you were the result of the love affair between Martha and me.'

'But you didn't say—'

'I didn't know *what* to say! Put yourself in my place for a moment. I was totally shattered, could hardly string together enough words to say good evening, let alone find the right way to tell you I suspected I was your father! I needed time to think. Damn it, even now it's only been a matter of hours! I simply didn't know what to do. I wanted to tell you, but as I said, I've been in touch with Frank and Lilian over the years and never once have they mentioned you. Why, I asked myself – and I could only come up with one answer. Your mother hadn't wanted you to know, otherwise she would have told you. And she hadn't wanted me to know. That's why she would never have anything to do with me, not ever. It seemed to me at first that perhaps I should leave well alone. Respect her wishes. Maybe you'd been fond of your father – your supposed father – oh, I know he was a rogue, but even rogues can be lovable, and it occurred to me that it could be a terrible blow for you to find out that he wasn't your father after all. I felt I had to get to know you better so that I could sum up the situation.'

He paused, looking at me searchingly.

'One thing I have to tell you,' he went on, as I remained silent. 'I thought you were a marvellous girl, and that Martha had done brilliantly without any help from me. So brilliantly, that I wanted to tell you. Wanted to claim you.'

I looked at him, longing to believe him. My tone was still cynical, however.

'And not doing so had nothing to do with not wanting to rock the boat here, with your wife and daughter?'

He smiled a touch ruefully at that and lifted his shoulders.

'Well, it can't be the easiest thing in the world to tell a wife that you have a daughter from a previous relationship, but I have no reason to think that Marian wouldn't understand and accept you. After all, you were conceived well before I'd ever met her. Neither of us were what you could call young and innocent when we married.'

'I've always wanted a sister,' Davina said. I looked across at her. Now that I studied her more closely, I could see that she was several years younger than me and that there were other differences in our two so similar faces. Her nose was slightly retroussé, her eyes deeper set. There were other indefinable differences, too. There was a gentleness about her, a confidence that was in no way brash or bumptious but spoke instead of someone who was happy within her own skin. She might be a few years younger than I am, I thought, but it wouldn't surprise me if she could teach me a hell of a lot.

'So have I,' I said.

For a few moments we looked at each other assessingly, and then she smiled.

'I must tell you something about my dad,' she said. 'He's a good, kind, loving man and I trust him absolutely. He doesn't tell lies. If only a few of his genes have trickled their way down to me and lodged in my bones then I feel I've been blessed. You should feel the same way.'

I glanced at Tim and saw that he was moved by this. He reached out and touched Davina.

'Thanks, darling,' he said. He then stretched out his hand towards me and, unable to withstand him further, I reached out and clasped it. 'I would have told you,' he said gently. 'Believe me, I was so proud of you. Proud of you both. Did ever any man have two such beautiful daughters?'

Davina laughed.

'Improbable as it may seem at this moment, Holly, I do scrub up quite well.' A yawn seemed to catch her unawares. 'Oh, sorry! I didn't sleep a wink last night and very little the night before. It was all a bit hairy, getting to the airport before the security guards got to Jake – the guy who'd been spouting anti-government propaganda. I must say, all this coming on top of it, I feel a bit as if I've sleepwalked into a B-movie. How do I know this isn't a dream?'

'Because Holly will be around when you wake up,' Tim said.

'Well, I'm not going to bed yet! I want to know all about her.'

I knew – had known for some minutes – that Davina and I were likely to be friends. How lucky I was, I thought – how incredibly lucky, that having found a sister she should prove to be someone so immediately warm and likeable. And Tim, too. He, not that glowering, brutal-looking man in the photograph whom I had always unconsciously feared, was my father!

A small, glowing feeling of euphoria warmed me, and it was a glow that intensified as we sat and talked, the three of us, about the past and our lives and loves. I discovered that Davina felt about Fincote very much as I felt about the house at Corey Cove; that she, too, was at a kind of crossroads in her life where she had to make a decision about her future. Was she to go to university, as her parents wanted her to do?

Or follow a growing desire to go straight into a job in the fashion world and start learning her trade from the bottom up?

We'd been talking for some time when Tim suddenly leapt to his feet, having just remembered that he was due out to dinner.

'And I must go,' he said. 'Can't possibly cancel! I'm making the after-dinner speech. And I haven't even changed yet!'

He rushed off and I stood up, saying that I had to go so that Davina could get some sleep.

She stood up, too, and for a moment, side by side, we looked into the mirror in its heavy gilt frame that hung over the fireplace.

'We're not really alike,' she said. 'Look – eyes, nose, mouth. All different.'

'But put together in the same way,' I pointed out. 'Somehow the cumulative effect gives the impression we're identical.'

'We have the same chins.'

'So we have!'

'And cheekbones.'

'You're right.'

'I wish I had your hair! I loathe mine.'

'I don't believe it! I used to pray nightly for curls when I was a kid.'

'Well, aren't you glad now your prayers weren't answered?'

'D'you know,' I said, suddenly remembering the lady in the cafe where Steve and

I stopped for tea, 'I think I've already been mistaken for you. It was in a tea shop in a village called Something Cross, not far from Fincote.'

'Simmings Cross,' Davina said. 'Quite likely! I do meet a friend there sometimes. I say – we might be able to have quite a bit of fun between us ... Hey, do you know when you smile like that you look the image of Dad? Aren't likenesses odd?'

'Spooky,' I agreed. And I felt a small chill as I remembered how much hung on the likeness I thought I had detected between Rose Quigley and the woman in the picture. Suppose I was wrong?

I didn't want to think about it.

Steve called me that night, quite late.

'Where've you been?' he asked. 'I've been trying to get you all evening.'

'Steve, I've got so much news I don't know where to start,' I said. 'You're not going to believe it!'

'Try me!'

'Well—' I took a breath, daunted by all I had to tell him. 'I discovered today that Tim Crofthouse is my father! Yes, honestly – I know, it's fantastic, I had no idea, but he and my mother had an *affaire*. They were going to get married but she chickened out.'

I gave him a brief run-down of events and moved swiftly on to my recognition of Rose

Quigley and Tim's determination to secure the Zoffany for himself so that it could be tested under laboratory conditions.

'Well, I suppose that's good news,' he said, 'but I wish you hadn't gone to the viewing. These people are dangerous, we know that, and if they get the idea that you're involved, anything could happen.'

'Aunt Caroline said much the same, but I'm sure there's no need to worry. I didn't see a soul I recognised.'

'Well, keep away from the sale itself, Holly. Promise me? There's absolutely no point in running risks, and from what you say, Sir Timothy has it all in hand.'

'Don't worry! My part in the whole thing has finished now. I just hope I'm right and this really is a picture of Rose.'

'I've heard of it happening.'

'Steve – enough of that! What's your news? You sound remarkably cheerful.'

'I am! Cautiously cheerful, anyway, thanks to a fellow countryman of yours.'

'Who's that?'

'One Adam Voss. Heard of him?'

'I don't think so.'

'Well, he's not of your world. He's an oilman. A very well-heeled oilman who can afford to indulge his fantasies – his latest, apparently, being to buy a castle in Scotland, complete with battlements and moat. Andy's met him in the way of business and took me along to see him this morning, because – guess what? – he wants to furnish the place with real, genu-wine antiques.'

'Which is where you come in.'

'You bet your sweet life I do! I visited the castle with him today and made suggestions about what he should buy to go where. He was employing an interior decorator, but sacked the guy because he found he was taking too many kickbacks from various dealers. Rich Voss may be, but he's careful, too. His girlfriend can do all the designer decorating stuff, he says. What he needs is someone to steer him round antiques.'

'Sounds as if it could be tricky.'

'Actually we hit it off quite well. One or two of the major items I can supply; they're already in the warehouse. The rest I shall have to scout around for. Fortunately he knows and trusts good old Andy, and therefore he trusts me by association. And to think I only came up here to ask Andy where he thought I could raise a loan! As it is, I think Mr Voss might well have saved my bacon.'

'Oh, Steve, I'm so glad,' I said. 'So very, very glad! And I love Mr Adam Voss.'

I heard Steve give a kind of grunt.

'Never mind him,' Steve said. 'What about me?'

'That depends,' I said, greatly daring. 'What about the partnership?'

'I've been thinking about that.'

'And—?'

'We'll talk about it.'

'Come back soon,' I said softly. 'I'll be waiting.'

He'd be back Friday afternoon, he said, and we arranged that I should go to his flat about five. I couldn't sleep for thinking about him and about my new family and the future and the marvellous fact that Caroline and Jamie were still alive. Life suddenly seemed painted in brighter colours than I had known it for ages, full of promise. If a chorus of angels had suddenly broken into a spirited rendition of 'Happy Days Are Here Again' it wouldn't have surprised me in the least. I was even too happy to stay angry for long with Frank and Lilian Wheeler, who had known that I had a father in England but who had chosen to keep me in the dark. They'd done it, of course, to keep faith with my mother, who had wanted it that way. Even so, you'd think that with her gone, they'd maybe have second thoughts—

But then again, I thought, struggling for understanding, she was a strong woman who dominated them in life. Was it so strange that she had the same ability, even after she had gone? And then I took to wondering what she would have been like if she'd married Tim after all. Would it have lasted? Maybe not. On the other hand, it was possible that if she'd put her mind to it she could have got the better of his disapproving parents in no time flat. And it was on the wings of a fantasy concerning growing up at Fincote that I finally drifted off to sleep, full of eagerness to see what the following day would bring.

Thirteen

Next morning it took very little time for my euphoric glow to be replaced by a feeling of nervousness and foreboding. This was such an important day; the day of the sale, the day when events would unfold at my instigation, events that were supposed to prove the guilt of Higginson and his gang. I felt an enormous responsibility for the outcome. Suppose I was wrong and the likeness to Rose was no more than a coincidence, or no more than a result of my overheated imagination? And suppose that Higginson and his cronies had already decided I was a danger to them? I couldn't imagine now why I had so casually dismissed Aunt Caroline's warning and Steve's fears for me, for today I didn't feel at all brave and confident. These were ruthless men, already guilty of murder. How could I have been so arrogant as to think I was any kind of a match for them, even with powerful friends?

The stakes in this game were considerable, and after all, what hard evidence did we have? Even if I were proved right about the picture, even if we went on to prove that there was a conspiracy to defraud the public not only with this particular painting but with many others, how could we possibly prove that Piers Craven had admitted to Jim's murder and threatened Caroline's baby? Even if Caroline could be persuaded to testify, there were no other witnesses, not one thing that would stand up in court. Her word against his. Nothing more.

All the happiness of the previous day seemed a distant memory as I faced the fact that after all my promises not to put Caroline and Jamie in danger, this was precisely what I might have done, putting myself in danger at the same time. And for what? Merely to prove that not all paintings sold by Lovells were what they were claimed to be.

Well, Serena and Tim were fully in the picture, I reminded myself. I simply had to trust them to do what was best. After all, Serena had the power of the *Sunday Chronicle* behind her, and journalists and reporters knew how to dig for facts where others did not. All we could do now was go ahead with the plan as it stood. Tim would buy the picture and we'd take it from there.

Keep away from the sale room, Steve had told me; so while I was agog to know what was going on there, I looked around for some other activity that would occupy my attention.

And that was easier said than done, for really I could think of nothing else. A woman I had spoken to on the river trip the previous day asked me to join her on another excursion to the Tower of London, but though I thanked her for the offer I told her I'd been there and didn't really want to go again. But when I saw her taxi leaving the hotel I regretted the decision. I should have gone, I thought. It would at least have occupied the time. Now I had several hours to kill on my own. It occurred to me to phone Davina to see if we could spend some time together, but then I remembered the poor girl's exhaustion of the night before. It was my guess she would still be sleeping.

Where could I go? Well, why not an art gallery? It somehow seemed the logical thing to do, and if I failed to give Turner the attention he deserved, I saw enough at the Tate that morning to be dazzled by his brilliance. I would go back there, I decided, when I was in a calmer, more receptive mood.

I was back in the hotel by midday, but it was well after one o'clock before Tim's phone call came to put me out of my misery. All was well, he reported. Bidding had stopped short of a million and a quarter and the picture was his.

'I'm taking it down to Fincote with me tonight for safe keeping,' he said. 'Then first thing on Monday I'll go and deliver it myself to the Institute in Cambridge – I've already made arrangements. Then there's nothing we can do but wait for the verdict. Once we know for sure that it's a fake, then we can swing into action. Serena has it all in hand – she's well in with the Fine Arts lot at Scotland Yard. Now Davina and I are hightailing it for Fincote and Marian's birthday party. Davina, by the way, is absolutely delighted with her new sister! I'd have asked you to come too, but I suspect you want to stay in London to welcome your Steve home.'

'You guessed right,' I told him. 'And maybe your wife wouldn't welcome the shock of my appearance. Not on her birthday.'

'I shall tell her, though. So maybe next weekend—?'

Next weekend! I felt I had lived several lifetimes since last weekend and couldn't begin to contemplate what yet another week would bring.

'See how she feels,' I said cautiously. 'You know I'd love to come.'

'Well, I'll be in touch when I get back from Cambridge on Monday. I hope you and Steve have a great time.'

Not long now, I thought, looking at my watch. Maybe even as I sat there in my room, he was on his way to the airport to catch the plane to London. I leaned back and closed my eyes, picturing him, imagining being in his arms again, recapturing the feel and the thrill of it, astonished all over again that here, when I least expected it, I should have met someone like Steve. I knew exactly what others would think; that I hadn't known him nearly long enough to feel this way about him. Well, phooey to them! I knew how I felt – how I had felt from the moment I saw him, though I still found the overwhelming attraction hard to define or explain. Maybe it never could be. Maybe it was enough to put it down to chemistry, though I felt sure that this was only part of the story.

It is said that girls tend to fall in love with men who resemble their fathers. Well, the opposite was true in my case. My father – my alleged father, I remembered, with some satisfaction – had been selfish, brutal, untrustworthy and unreliable. Steve was the direct opposite of all these things.

Was I searching for some kind of security, then? Could be, I acknowledged. But if that were all, wouldn't I have looked around for someone with a little more cash at his disposal? Some friendly neighbourhood millionaire to take me under his wing?

I didn't want a millionaire. I wanted sweet, sexy, penniless Steve. Maybe love at first sight sounds not only unlikely but positively corny, Hollywood at its worst, but take it from me, it exists all right.

The shrill bleep of the telephone interrupted my reveries and I snatched at it, sure it would be Steve, hoping that he would be telling me he was about to leave Scotland. The alternative – that his departure had been delayed – was not to be contemplated!

But it wasn't Steve.

'Holly Crozier? Is that Holly?' The voice was tremulous and hurried, hardly more than a whisper, the words tripping over each other. 'Holly, this is Rose. You've got to help me. Please, please will you help me? There's no one else I can turn to.'

'Rose! What's happened? You sound terrible.'

'I'm desperate, Holly. *Desperate*! You must help me.'

'What's wrong? What can I do?'

'Listen—' Rose lowered her voice a little. 'I haven't got long. I was so sorry yesterday not to talk. I wasn't myself. They give me things, you see. Medication, injections – oh, I need help, I know that, but all they do is stuff me full of tranquillisers so that I don't know what I'm doing or saying. I'm not as bad as that, honestly! Some days I feel almost normal. I'm normal now. I may not sound it, but truly I am.'

'But why—'

'Because I know too much.' She gave a

272

laugh that ended on a sob. 'I know how your brother died, how that young man in Wales died. I have to talk to someone! Please come and take me away.'

'Yes – yes, of course I'll come. Tell me where to meet you.'

'There's no one else but you, no one I can turn to. No friends any more. And I'm so afraid! I think Piers killed Caroline. Piers or one of the others. Maybe it was George, and one day he'll kill me, too. You must come.'

'Rose,' I said, trying to put more authority in my voice in order to stem this tide. 'I'll come. Tell me when and where.'

'I don't know—' She broke off suddenly and was silent a moment.

'Rose?'

'Dora's coming,' she whispered, even more urgently. 'I'll be in the garden—'

And that was it. The phone went dead and I was left holding my end of it, anxious but impotent, full of questions that could not now be answered. Questions such as *when* would she be in the garden? And if she were in the garden, where would Dora be? Still more important, where would George be? I felt distinctly unenthusiastic about the whole enterprise.

But no one, hearing Rose's voice, could fail to be moved by her desperation. I couldn't see how I could possibly ignore her; besides, wouldn't she provide the conclusive testimony we so badly needed? She knew how Jim had died, she'd said. If that truly were so, then for our sake as well as hers we had to rescue her.

We? It was down to me, I realised all too soon. Tim and Davina were on their way down to Fincote. Steve was miles away. I tried phoning Serena at the *Sunday Chronicle* but she wasn't at her desk, and though I tried her mobile it was impossible to raise her. Even though Rose hadn't given me any specific time to pick her up, I felt I had to go as soon as possible.

Which meant there wasn't any time to waste. I'd have to hire a car once more. Well, I'd driven to Henley before and I could do it again, even if I didn't particularly relish the idea. The garage was only just around the corner and they seemed to have several models on offer when I phoned to ask them. Still I stood irresolute, wishing there was some other solution.

I felt bad about it, but I just plain didn't want to leave London right then, partly because the thought of Dora and George put the fear of God into me and partly because I wasn't sure I'd be able to make Steve's flat by five o'clock as we had arranged. And I'd been counting the minutes! I wondered whether to call Steve on his mobile, but I could guess all too readily what he would have to say. I could hear his voice now urging me not to go to the saleroom. How much more insistently would he tell me to keep away from the Quigley ménage! I decided to leave a message on his answerphone at the flat. Rose had called, I told him, and had been frightened, desperate to leave Willow Cottage. She had made it clear she had information that would give us all the evidence we needed, so I was going to get her. I'd see him just as soon as I possibly could.

'Love you,' I said, as a kind of postscript.

Well, now there was nothing for it but to go. Maybe I was being rash and foolish – in fact, I knew quite well that this was the case – but I couldn't think of any alternative. And I was, now I thought about it, looking forward to telling Rose that Caroline was alive and happy.

The traffic was as awful as ever – worse, if anything. But at least I knew the way now and was able to drive to Willow Cottage with confidence, out of London, along the freeway, through Henley and out the other side.

The clocks of Henley were pointing to three thirty as I drove through the town. Rose could hardly accuse me of wasting any time, I thought, and I hoped that she had been able to station herself somewhere easily accessible. I planned to reverse into the drive and keep the engine running while she leapt in and we made a swift getaway. 'In the garden' seemed an awfully vague description of her location, given the size of it, but hopefully she would be up near the road, keeping a lookout for me. What would she be doing – picking flowers? Walking the dog? Hiding herself behind a convenient bush? Heaven alone knew! I wondered how much freedom she was allowed, how she passed her time on the good days, why she couldn't contrive to give her wardress the slip without involving me. I knew the answer as soon as I asked it. In her present state, organising anything so complex was quite beyond her. Poor Rose, as Rupert had said.

Willow Cottage was set in a leafy lane parallel to the river, a lane that was bordered on both sides by woodland which thinned as I approached the opulent, widely separated houses. I drove past the gate a yard or two, then reversed into the drive as planned, holding the door as I half stepped out of the car to look around for Rose, the engine ticking over.

I could see no sign of her. No sign of anyone. The door of the house was closed, the windows looking blindly into the garden under the wavy line of thatch. For a moment I hesitated, feeling exposed and vulnerable as frantically I looked this way and that, wondering what I should do, how long I should wait here. My heart was pounding with nervousness and I was about to leave, thinking I would drive away from the house and conceal the car somewhere before coming back to scout round on foot, when suddenly the heavy front door opened and Rose slipped out of it, anxiously glancing around her. She was dressed in the same boiler suit she had worn before; no coat, no bag. Her hair flapped round her face, blown by the wind, and she looked as insubstantial as a child as she began to run towards me.

'Get in, get in,' I urged her and, her breath sobbing in her throat, she did so. I slammed the car into gear and gunned the engine, already moving by the time she was beside me, but even so, I was not quick enough. A muscular, greasy-looking man built like a barn door was already bolting the gates to prevent our exit, and as he turned round to face us, he was smiling as he raised a gun and pointed it directly at me.

I stalled the engine, paralysed with shock. He seemed to have come out of nowhere. He swaggered over to my side of the car and opened the door, leering at me.

'I don't think so, sweetheart,' he said.

For a moment nobody spoke or moved, though I could hear Rose making a strange, mewing noise rather like a frightened kitten. I gathered together my shattered wits.

'You have absolutely no right—'

'He's got every right,' said another, more cultured voice somewhere beyond my right shoulder. I turned my head to see that George Quigley, dressed in country tweeds with a shotgun over his arm, had approached from somewhere unseen. He ignored me and looked across me to address Rose.

'What do you think you're doing, darling?' he asked. He smiled as he asked the question, but there was a steely, menacing edge to his voice and Rose's panic seemed to increase. 'Come along. Get out of the car. Both of you,' he added in my direction, hefting his gun as if to remind me of its presence.

I had decided that my only hope was to appear both innocent and annoyed.

'There's no need for that,' I said. 'Rose said she wanted to see me, just to talk about Caroline. I couldn't see why—'

He interrupted me.

'Get into the house,' he said, then turned to his trained gorilla, who was still menacing me with his own gun. 'Joe, come and get her, will you? I'll take care of Rose.'

Protestations would get me nowhere, I realised. Joe yanked me out of the car and, gripping my arm like a vice with one hand, the other holding the gun in the small of my back, he marched me up the drive with George and Rose a few paces behind. I heard Rose give a yelp of pain and tried to twist round to see what was going on, but Joe put a stop to that. Rose was crying now, entreating George to let her go, not to hurt her any more.

'You bastard,' I shouted. 'Leave her alone.'

'Shut it,' Joe said menacingly, pushing me so hard that I staggered and almost fell.

'Careful,' George warned, using his pleasant voice again. 'We shall want Miss Crozier in one piece.' We had reached the house by this time and I saw that Dora had also materialised and was standing on the threshold, ready to give Joe a helping hand by reaching out and pulling me inside. 'Well, here we are, Miss Crozier,' George said. 'Welcome once more to my humble abode.'

Later, locked into a small attic room, I had time for regrets. I should never have come alone, I realised that now. Had always realised it, really. Why the hell hadn't I waited until after Steve had come home? Had I, in my arrogance, really thought I was a match for this evil bunch of men? I could only plead that like so many disastrous decisions, it had seemed the right thing to do at the time.

I suppose the bottom line was that I hadn't taken Rose seriously enough. I'd underestimated George Quigley's violence and had paid the price, though in fact it was

Dora who'd seemed to take great pleasure in manhandling me into the sitting room and administering a stinging slap to my face when I continued to protest.

Desperate as I was at my own plight, I couldn't help worrying about Rose. She was still uttering those strange, mewing cries as, having dealt with me, Dora hurried her away upstairs.

'Why don't you let her go?' I demanded of George. I had been thrust into the depths of one of the large armchairs in the sitting room and he was perched on the arm of the one that was nearest to me. He had parked his rifle in the hall, but still looked menacing. 'She's no threat to you. She only wanted to talk about Caroline. I thought it would be some kind of therapy for her.'

'She has all the therapy she needs,' he said harshly. 'Keep your nose out of it. It's none of your business.'

It occurred to me that I would only make matters worse by being aggressive and I moderated my tone accordingly.

'I guess you're right,' I said after a moment. 'Maybe I owe you an apology. I just wanted to help, that's all. There's really no need for these strong-arm tactics.' I smiled at him placatingly, feeling a bit of a traitor but sure that at some later date it would be possible to get Rose away from him. With my hands on the arms of the chair

I pushed myself up, still smiling. 'Well, I can see she's in good hands, so I'll be getting back—'

George leaned across and shoved me back into the depths of the chair again.

'No, Miss Crozier. You're not leaving. I think you and I should have a little talk, if you would be so kind.'

'Do I have a choice?' I was doing my best to keep cool, but my voice sounded strange and high in my ears.

He smiled at me thinly.

'Not really. You see—' He got to his feet and, with his hands in his pockets, came and stood close in front of me so that I was forced to strain to look up at him. 'I happen to know that the reason you came here had nothing to do with helping Rose. You thought she had information. No—' He lifted his hand to as if to prevent me denying this. 'There's no point in protesting your innocence. You see, I happened to lift the extension in my study just as you answered her phone call, so I heard every word.' He laughed, dismissively. 'Poor Rose! She's so terribly naive.'

So he knew; knew that I knew how Jim, and the other young man, had died. Knew that Rose was prepared to give evidence against him. Knew that he and his cronies were about to be exposed. I remembered what Aunt Caroline had said – that they

281

might assume that Jim had confided in me before he died and that I could be in danger, too. Why hadn't I taken her more seriously? All my bravado left me and I felt hollow with fear.

'There's another thing,' he said, taking a few steps away from me, then returning to look down on me again. 'I didn't know you were an art collector, Miss Crozier.'

I was a little bit disconcerted by this sudden change of tack and had to collect my thoughts.

'I'm not! Well, I'm interested in art, of course.'

'But you only collect certain paintings, yes? Or are you just a mercenary little bitch who's out for anything she can get?'

'What?' Genuinely puzzled and outraged, I stared at him. 'That's a very offensive thing to say!'

'As I said before, don't play the innocent, Miss Crozier! We all know you're not that.'

I took a deep breath, fighting my rising panic.

'I'm not with you, I'm afraid. What are you talking about?'

'A certain Zoffany painting? The le Maire family?'

'What's that got to do with me?'

Exasperately he flung himself down in a chair and glared at me.

'Don't play games, Miss Crozier. You were

282

seen at Lovells this morning.'

'Lovells?' I gave a short laugh. 'You couldn't be more wrong. I went to the Tate.'

He totally ignored me.

'Where is that picture, Miss Crozier?'

'I don't know what you're talking about. I have no picture.'

'Oh yes, of course—' He smiled as if he had just remembered the truth. 'It was Sir Timothy Crofthouse who was doing the bidding, wasn't it? But you were there, weren't you, hanging on his arm, clearly delighted when it was knocked down to him. It didn't take a great leap of the imagination to see that he was buying it for you. And was rewarded by a kiss! It didn't take you long, did it, to find a friend in high places?'

'You're wrong!'

'Why did you want that particular painting, Miss Crozier? And, more importantly, what have you done with it and what have you told Crofthouse? Is he party to all your wild suspicions or just a poor, gullible sap you've managed to twist round your little finger?'

My fear increased, intensified now by the sudden knowledge that I had not only put myself in danger, but also Tim and Davina. God, how I'd mucked everything up, put everything and everyone in jeopardy. It was clear that Davina had gone to the sale with her father and had been mistaken for me by someone who knew me only a little and Davina not at all. It was, after all, understandable. Hadn't the lady in the tea shop been similarly confused?

'He knows nothing,' I said. The words emerged as a croak and I had to clear my throat before I could say anything more. 'He and I – we sort of became friends a few nights ago. He wanted to give me a present and I saw the paintings that were in the sale and rather fell for the Zoffany. So I asked him for that.'

'And he happily shelled out a million and a quarter pounds? Really, Miss Crozier, I don't doubt that a few nights with you would prove a rewarding experience, but this seems excessive even for someone as generous as Crofthouse.'

'He's a very generous man.' I attempted a laugh. 'He didn't admire my taste in art much—'

'So where is it now? *The picture!*' He had suddenly leant over me and at these words he brought both his hands down violently on the arms of the chair, one on each side of me, his face thrust into mine, so close that I shrunk away from him. 'You'll tell me eventually,' he said menacingly. 'I want it and I intend to get it, so tell me where it is now and save us all a lot of grief.'

'I – I don't know where it is.'

'I don't believe you!'

'It's true. It went to be packed up.' I was improvising wildly, sure of only one thing – that I had to direct these men away from Fincote and the Crofthouse family.

'You're lying. You and Crofthouse took it somewhere in the back of his Roller. You were seen. Is it at your hotel?'

'We took it to be packed.'

'Where?'

'I don't know. I don't know the name of the firm or where we went. It was some-where—' I hesitated, my thoughts racing. 'Near the river, I think. I don't know London very well. Anyway, what does it matter to you? Why are you so keen to get hold of it?'

He didn't answer, and of course I didn't need him to. The picture was evidence. I knew it and he knew it, no matter how I strung him along.

'You're lying,' he said again. Then, as if losing patience with me, he went to the door of the room and shouted for Dora.

'Take her to the top room,' he said when Dora appeared. 'Keep her quiet. I need time to think what to do.'

Dora took my other arm in a grip like iron and together they manhandled me towards the stairs.

I struggled, but didn't speak, for I knew now that all protestations, all pretence of innocence, would count for nothing. I was mad at myself for getting into this situation. I'd said the wrong thing, I felt sure. I'd done the wrong thing, should never have embarked on this crazy mission to rescue Rose. Who did I think I was? Superwoman?

For a while I was on my own in that top room, left to my thoughts and to the contemplation of my prison. It was, in fact, quite a pleasant bedroom, with a sloping ceiling and two small dormer windows overlooking the front drive. There were pretty green and white drapes and a matching bedcover, and a connecting green and white bathroom. A guest room, I imagined. Not much used and just as impersonal as the rest of the house.

I peered out of the window. I could see the sweep of the drive ahead of me and my hired car still parked halfway down it. Even as I watched, the greasy man who Quigley had referred to as Joe walked towards it and got into the driving seat. I saw him slam the door but could not hear it. The windows were clearly double-glazed and soundproof; I was insulated from the world here in this cosy little prison.

Joe backed the car up towards the house and round somewhere to the left, out of my sight. Somehow this made me more frightened than almost anything else that had happened. There seemed a finality about it, as if they were wiping away all trace of my presence here. I ran back to the door and rattled the handle, knowing it was pointless, knowing it was locked.

I contemplated the lock for some time. In films, people opened locked doors so easily with a credit card or a nail file. I doubted I could be so successful, but anyway I couldn't even try. My purse had come off my shoulder during my journey up the stairs and Dora had prevented me from picking it up so that I had no possessions with me at all, except my jacket and my watch. I opened the drawers in the little chest, but they were all empty.

Frustrated, I sat down on the bed and stared at nothing. It was almost five. I wondered if Steve were already in his flat, if he'd heard my message, what he'd be thinking. What a crazy airhead I was, most likely, and he'd be right.

After a while I heard the sound of the key turning in the lock. It was Dora and the greasy man.

'You'd better go in first, Joe,' she said. 'Hold her down.'

I looked beyond him to Dora and saw to my horror that she had a hypodermic syringe in her hands.

'Come along now,' she said briskly. 'I don't want any hysterics.'

'Don't touch me!' I shouted, shrinking

287

away, but, as instructed, Joe was there, reaching to hold me so tight that I couldn't move. I kicked out at him but that only made him hold me tighter still.

'I've got 'er,' he said.

I struggled, but it was useless. I had kept my jacket on as if in denial that I was there for any length of time but now it was forcibly pulled off me and my shirt sleeve was wrenched upwards. I felt the prick of the needle, heard Dora's satisfied grunt as it went home. And that was it. I felt suddenly as if I were at the end of a long tunnel, everything spiralling away from me.

Fourteen

When I regained consciousness, I sensed I had been moved to a different place. Not that I could see anything of my surroundings. The dark pressed down on me, evil and almost tangible, but the room smelled different, felt different.

I was cold and desperately thirsty, but it was the dark that was my undoing, and in those first minutes I was more frightened than I had ever been in my life before. I tried to sit up, but my head swam and I felt so sick that I let it drop back again. For a moment I lay still, sinking back into the kind of mindless desperation that had me whimpering like a child. I think I even called for my mother – and perhaps it was the thought of what she would have to say if she could hear me that enabled me to will myself back to some degree of composure. Panicking wildly would achieve nothing. I needed to be calm and strong and determined if I were to get through this in one piece, not revert to helpless childhood.

Wherever they'd taken me, it was deathly

quiet. As I tried to calm myself I saw that there was, after all, a small amount of light in the room – not light that allowed me to see anything much, but a kind of greyness coming from high up on the wall to my left. It was in the form of a narrow, horizontal strip.

I swung my legs to the ground and stood up, staggering a little at first. What had that horrible woman given me? It could have been anything, but I hoped and prayed it was nothing addictive. It was probably something intended to put me out long enough for them to move me easily from Henley to wherever I was now without having to deal with my struggles, and that, of course, was what worried me most of all. Where *had* they brought me? And how how would anyone know where to find me? There seemed only one answer to that. They wouldn't.

As my eyes became used to the dark, I could see that the walls were light in colour, with a dark-painted door in the corner of the same wall as the strip of grey. I blunder-ed over to it, knocking against a chair and sending something metallic crashing to the ground as I did so. In the blanketing silence it seemed as loud as the combined per-cussion sections of several orchestras, and having almost jumped out of my skin I waited a moment or two to see if it would cause any reaction from outside the room. There was nothing. The silence continued as before.

I found the door and tried to open it, but of course it was locked – and bolted, I decided, seeing the way it seemed to be held top and bottom as well as in the middle. But at least, feeling round the door with my fingers, I was able to locate the light switch and dispel the dark.

My prison, I now saw, was a small, windowless room, roughly six feet wide and not much more in length. The light was coming from a line of frosted glass set in the wall about two feet or so from the ceiling. This was obviously some kind of storeroom, for there were two large cans of what looked like oil of some kind as well as two large wooden crates, banded with a criss-cross metal strip. I squatted down to read the label on the cans and saw that it was turpentine.

Of course! The whole place reeked of the stuff. I'd been aware of it all along but hadn't gotten around to identifying it. Now that I had, it occurred to me that I had probably landed up at the heart of this operation – in Wales, at Piers Craven's commune. So what was in the crates? Paintings? Artefacts of some kind? They, too, had labels on and I saw that one was addressed to a firm called Mycroft Antiques in

Chicago and the other to the New York branch of Lovells.

It was hardly surprising, now I thought about it, that this racket reached across the Atlantic. The market in the States for European art and artefacts was virtually limitless, and it made sense to think that something more must be involved than simply a handful of greedy men in London creaming off the odd million for an occasional forgery in Lovells' London auction. A few fake old masters, even if those little words 'attributed to' had to be added to their description in an auctioneer's catalogue, would no doubt make a sizeable amount in New York or Chicago.

My watch told me that the time was eleven twenty; over six hours since I'd been in Henley. Which, I guessed, could mean my captors would have had ample time to take me almost anywhere in the British Isles – or out of it, come to that. Six hours was a hell of a lot of travelling time and I could be quite wrong about my location; still, it seemed to me that Wales was the most likely place.

I surveyed my prison once more. It wasn't at all how I had imagined the commune when Steve had spoken of it. I had envisaged a collection of attractively rustic farm buildings, but this room looked neither attractive nor particularly rustic.

Everything was dirty, in need both of cleaning and of a coat of paint. The ceiling had several huge brown stains on it and the corners were festooned with cobwebs. The mattress I had been lying on was covered with a thin blue blanket, ragged at the edges, with parts of it so worn that it was practically transparent. The pillow was minus a pillowcase so that its stained cover was on view, and it made me shudder to think how long I must have been resting my head on it.

In the opposite wall there was another door, but any hope that this might lead outside was dashed immediately. It opened into a washroom; just a basin and a lavatory. These weren't clean, either, but were at least better than nothing. I couldn't imagine who would ever want to sleep here. Maybe it was simply kept for emergency occupation of some kind; certainly it looked as if no one had been there for a long time.

I could see immediately what had caused that loud metallic noise when I had knocked into the chair. It was a can of orange soda that had fallen to the floor, and lying beside it was a plastic packet containing a couple of sandwiches. At least they didn't intend me to starve. Not yet, anyway. My thirst was so desperate that I opened the can immediately and took a few sips. Never has a can of orange soda tasted so good!

I felt marginally less despairing after I'd had a drink and eaten the sandwiches. They gave me the energy to do a bit of banging on the door and shouting for help – both activities proving quite useless, as I think I knew they would be from the start. The silence was almost uncanny, making me feel that I was alone in the world.

Alone and very cold. Shivering, I sat down on the edge of the bed with my arms wrapped round me, facing the thought that George Quigley and his helpers might be busy at this moment devising some amusing little accident that could befall me so that I'd be out of their hair for good. For a moment that awful, mindless panic swept over me again, but then it occurred to me that they wanted the incriminating picture and I was supposed to know its location. Perhaps killing me was, at the moment anyway, not an option. Torture seemed more likely; and at this thought the panic returned and only a great effort of will restored my thought processes.

Whatever they had in mind, I sure hoped they weren't intending to leave me here too long. I'd always suffered from mild claustro-phobia. I hated elevators even though I forced myself to use them, and I had never been able to nerve myself to take a rush-hour tube anywhere in London – or the subway in New York, come to that. I made myself breathe slow and easy and tried not to think of the four walls that enclosed me, but something told me that as time went on this wouldn't be so simple.

I stood again and moved to stare up at that line of frosted glass. It actually consisted of small windows, I realised. There were four of them, each measuring roughly a foot high and a little over a foot wide. All were closed, but they looked to me on more prolonged inspection as if they were ventilators that were meant to open. Even so, whoever had brought me here had thought they pre-sented no opportunity for escape and, looking at them, I felt I had to agree. Even if I were able to move those crates—

But I had the chair, too, I remembered. I could stand the chair on the crates. The only problem, I found, was that I couldn't move the crates one single inch. I spent far too much energy trying and failing, and as for heaving one on top of another, the idea was laughable.

That just left the bed. Maybe I could stand the chair on the bed and climb up on that. At least I could try. It was better than sitting and getting more and more fright-ened and depressed.

Moving the bed against the wall was easy enough, but climbing up on the chair was a different matter, mainly because the chair wobbled wildly on the mattress with its sagging bedsprings; however, I managed to balance precariously on it in the end. Now I could reach the windows, but though I saw they were designed to open up and out, I couldn't shift any of them, as the paint of years had cemented them firmly in place. I pushed and shoved, but it was a totally useless exercise. They were stuck fast.

For a moment I leant against the wall and closed my eyes, weak with frustration. But – what shifted paint? Turpentine, of course! How kind of them to leave me some! Only thing was, I couldn't open the darn cans. They were sealed and wired up, totally impenetrable.

Defeated, I looked up at the windows again. I needed some kind of sharp instrument, a knife or a chisel, but of course I had nothing of the kind. Even a nail file might have done, but my purse hadn't been restored to me and was still back in Henley, as far as I knew. It was quite some time later that, slumped despondently on the side of the bed once more, my eye fell on the plastic package that had held the sandwiches. The edge of it was hard, I remembered. And quite sharp. I'd nearly cut my thumb on it when I'd tried to extract the sandwiches. Maybe there was a chance it would do.

It took a long time. I selected one of the windows and patiently I scraped and thumped, thumped and scraped, all the time having to shift my weight to keep balanced on the chair. It was a surprisingly exhausting exercise. Twice I fell off, once bumping my head quite hard on the wall to the point where I saw stars, but no real damage was done and I clambered up again and started scraping once more.

When finally the window moved and I was able to push it open I sagged against the wall, swamped with relief as if my troubles were over. Little did I know they were just beginning!

Full of curiosity, I looked through to see what was on the other side of the wall. To my disappointment, I saw that the window opened not to the outside world but only to another room – a vast, quite cavernous place which, I could see in the limited light from my side of the wall, had two huge skylights in the soaring roof as well as what looked like an array of lighting equipment. These were all close to me. The further part of the room was lost in shadow, though I could see various shapes. I guessed that it was once a barn but had now been adapted to office and studio use. It seemed very much the kind of place I had expected since I had first heard of Piers Craven's rural hideaway.

There was no window apart from the skylights, as far as I could see. No means of getting out of the room other than through the door, which I felt pretty sure would be locked. By craning my neck I could see that right underneath me was a table of the kind that architects use, complete with drawing board, and beside it was a desk with a computer and – of more immediate interest to me – a telephone. Hungrily I gazed down on it. It seemed the answer to everything, the solution to all my problems. Somehow I had to squeeze through that window and get down there.

Which was a lot easier said than done. I could kill myself if I went down head first – but I could see no other way. I needed a ladder – a rope – anything that could help me climb up above the window on this side so that I could somehow get through feet first. Even that appeared pretty hazardous, I thought, as I looked at the drop below me.

But I hadn't got so far only to give up now. I surveyed my small, bare prison. No sheets to tear up, but there was that old, threadbare blanket which I felt sure would be just as easy. I tore it into three strips, knotted them together at one end and and plaited them tightly into a rope, half of me amazed at myself for doing something so utterly and ludicrously melodramatic. I felt as if I were starring in some banal TV show of the kind I wouldn't put beyond the scope of the committee that wrote the script of *Bower Street*! How, I wondered, would Mary Lou McAllister cope with this? I couldn't even begin to think.

But however melodramatic, I thought my scheme just might work. I clambered up on the chair again and tied the makeshift rope around the entire window, slotting it through the gap that had appeared at the top when I opened it outwards so that it dangled down nearly as far as the bed.

At least I could move that unstable chair out of the way, and I was thankful for that, but the window creaked ominously as I shinned with great difficulty up the rope. To my relief, it held, and I was able to pull myself up. That was the easy part! It was then that I somehow had to find a way of manoeuvring myself through the gap without hurtling to the ground on the other side of the wall, or falling back on the bed.

I'd never been much of a gymnast, but at least I'd kept myself in pretty good shape, which was as well since I needed all the agility I could muster. I'd removed my boots before I started all this climbing about, and gone halfway up my makeshift rope before tipping them up and over into the next room. I'd heard them thump as they landed next door. Then I'd continued up the rope and scrabbled with my feet against the wall, managing to get them through the window. It was the rest of me that presented the problem and for a moment I froze, unable to move. It was impossible, I told myself. I couldn't do it. I was at quite the wrong angle. If I let go the blanket rope, I would fall, but I couldn't get my body through the gap without letting go at some stage. At least I wasn't cold any more. I could feel the sweat running down my face, whether from fear or exertion I wasn't sure.

You've *got* to, I told myself. And, gritting my teeth, I strained and wriggled, still clutching the rope, until half of me was through. I then found that if I continued to cling to the rope with my left hand, it ought to be possible to grasp the bottom of the window frame with my right, which would enable me to lower myself as far as possible into the next room. I can't do it, I thought. I can't. I *can't*! But then I felt an ominous jolt and realised that the window, now supporting all my weight, was coming loose from its hinges.

I realised I'd run out of options so, quickly, before I could think about it any more, I twisted round and somehow managed in one movement to change my grip so that first one then both of my hands were holding the edge of the window frame, with my face pressed against the wall of the next-door room, my legs dangling over a drop of about six feet. Maybe it doesn't sound much, but it sure looked a long way down to me.

I dropped to the floor, twisting my ankle a

little as I landed. It was mildly painful, but I rubbed and flexed it and I soon realised I'd done no serious damage. In any case, it was a small price to pay under the circumstances. In fact, as I looked up at the tiny window above me, my exit from it seemed like a miracle. I think it was at that moment that I began to think that I really might make it. It was an outcome that had seemed most unlikely only a few minutes before.

I sat and recovered for a bit, then reached for my boots and put them on. Very cautiously, I stood up and, in the light shining through from the other side of the wall, I squinted at my watch. It was a few minutes to four, and already the skylights showed that the night was becoming perceptibly lighter.

My first instinct was to use the telephone, but it occurred to me that I ought to try the door first, just in case it was open. I did so, only to confirm what I'd expected all along. The door was securely locked. I therefore wasted no more time and went as quickly as I could back to the phone, where I dialled Steve's number, my hand trembling in my eagerness. I prayed that he would be at home and not scouring the country for me, and I was in luck. He answered before the phone had rung twice.

'Yes?'

'Steve, it's Holly.'

'*Holly!* Where the hell are you? I've been—'

'Steve, I don't know where I am. I went to Henley, but I was drugged and taken some place else – I've no idea where, but I think it might be Piers Craven's place in Wales. They've locked me up but I managed to get to a phone—'

'Is the number on it?'

'What?' I was confused, not thinking straight.

'The telephone. Is there a number on the telephone?'

I peered at it closely.

'Not that I can see. The light's not good.'

'Holly, phone this number – 0181 300 9120. It's the police – a sergeant called Hillstead. I've spoken to him already and he knows all about you. Tell him you're being held against your will. He'll be able to trace the call and find out where you are. Have you got that number?'

'Tell me again.'

He did so and I repeated it back to him.

'Holly,' he said, his voice suddenly softer and almost as shaky as mine. 'Are you all right? They didn't hurt you?'

'I'm fine. Just frightened.'

'Hold on. You'll be home in no time. Hang up now and dial that number. I'll see you soon.'

I hung up and dialled the number. In a

few seconds I was speaking to Sergeant Hillstead, who sounded both efficient and reassuring.

'Wherever you are, we'll get on to the local police station,' he said. 'Just sit tight.'

'I'm not going any place,' I said. 'Just get them to come quickly.'

My fear, of course, was that Quigley or Craven would come before the police did and that they would see me and the phone. Then they would know that I must have called for help and that the police would be on their way.

It could happen, I thought. They'd be back at some time, I was sure of that, but there wasn't a damned thing I could do about it. I sank down on the floor behind the computer desk hugging my knees, making myself as small as possible in the hope that if they did come, they wouldn't see me – which was, it soon dawned on me, a totally ridiculous aspiration. Of course they would see me the moment they put the light on. And if the police didn't hurry up, morning would be here and there would be no need for artificial light at all. I could feel myself shaking uncontrollably.

At some point it occurred to me that if Quigley and his friends did come, I'd have a better chance of a swift getaway if I hid behind the door so that I was concealed when they opened it.

That's sensible, I said to myself, out loud; but it still took a few more minutes to summon the energy to move. It was as if the effort I had made to get through that window had drained me, both physically and mentally, and I didn't give much for my chances of being able to make a successful run for it, even if I had the opportunity.

Still, I had to try, so I got to my feet and went towards the door. It was during this journey, from one end of the barn to the other, that I realised there were no less than five easels between me and the door, plus three stands – heaven knows their proper name – on which sculptors place their work in progress. They, together with the crates, all seemed to bear out my previous suspicion – that this, in its way, was a small factory. Who was it who had said that the Zoffany painting represented the tip of the iceberg? I was convinced now that they were right. This was big business.

I stationed myself close to the door and waited some more. The silence was absolute. After a while, I pressed my ear to the door itself. Still I could hear nothing. Where were the police? I couldn't imagine what was keeping them. I seemed to have been waiting for ever.

Suddenly, I heard the muffled sound of a car and the faint slam of a door, then another door. Someone had arrived –

surely, surely this had to be the police? I felt a great surge of relief which was all too quickly dispelled when I heard a key being inserted in the lock.

Not the police, then, but the thing I had dreaded from the moment I had opened my eyes in that horrible little room. This had to be the return of the men who were implicated in the murder of my brother, coming now to deal with me.

I could barely breathe as I pressed myself flat against the wall, waiting for the door to open as I knew it must. I was afraid they would hear me long before they saw me, my heart was knocking so thunderously against my ribs, but they were talking as they came in and in the first few seconds seemed to notice nothing amiss, even though one of them flipped a switch and flooded the room with light.

'...got to get her out before the van comes for the crates,' one was saying to the other. It was a low, cultured voice, one I didn't recognise. Definitely not Quigley. Piers Craven, perhaps?

There was a grunt in reply, the sound of boots on a bare floor, then a sudden exclamation.

''Ere – boss, look. The little cow's climbed out!' That voice I knew at once. How could I forget Joe?

'Don't be a fool, man. How could she?'

305

The footsteps advanced further into the room. 'My God, so she has!'

I didn't wait to hear more, but darted round the door and outside into what I now saw was a kind of yard with another derelict-looking building opposite. I heard a shout behind me. There was no time to size up the situation or see in which direction I should run; I simply fled across the yard and round the back of the old barn opposite.

Immediately behind it was an area liberally strewn with rubbish of one kind or another – a broken sink, piles of bricks, sodden sacks – but beyond was an open field. Dawn was definitely breaking now, but a misty rain was falling and it was impossible to see more than a few yards in any direction, so that although I could make out a broken-down rail fence a short distance away, whatever was beyond it was totally obscured. I figured that my only hope of escape was to put as much distance between me and my pursuers as possible in the hope that the mist would hide me. Without pausing for more than a split second to review the territory, I dodged round all the debris and ran like crazy for the fence, hurled myself over it and kept on running, tripping over tussocks of grass, slipping on cow pats and patches of mud – running, running until suddenly there was nothing in front of me, just some kind of pit or quarry that fell steeply away to unseen depths, so that I had to skid to a halt and steady myself.

I had, from the first, known that one or both the men were coming after me. Now I glanced behind and saw to my horror that Joe was closer than I had imagined. My efforts to melt into the mist had been useless. Wildly I looked around and, with my breath sobbing in my throat, started to run again, skirting the quarry, making for some trees that had now come into view, kidding myself that somewhere over there I would find a place to hide.

I suppose I should have known it was hopeless. The trees were silver birches, their trunks thin and straight, incapable of hiding anything. Worse, I found that I had taken a path through them that led only to a high, mossy stone wall, dripping with moisture, part of some ancient building. I leant against it for a moment, panting for breath, then turned to find, as expected, that Joe had caught up with me. There was nowhere to run. The chase was over.

For a moment we faced each other without moving, the only sound the rasp of our breathing. Then his unpleasant face creased into a grin.

'Gotcha, you bitch,' he said softly, levelling the gun that I could now see was in his hand.

He reached out and roughly pulled me round so that once again I was in the position of feeling the gun in my back as, with both my wrists held in his left hand, I was frogmarched back over that soaking wet field.

'You won't shoot me,' I flung at him over my shoulder.

'Wanna bet?'

'Quigley wants me alive.'

'For the moment.'

Yes, I thought as I stumbled over the tussocky grass, skirting the quarry. Yes, I'd kind of figured that out. He'd hope to get information out of me, and then—

'So what kind of accident have you got worked out for me?' I taunted him.

Joe laughed.

'We'll think of something.' He gave me another push. 'Keep moving.'

'Like you thought of something for my brother?' He didn't answer and suddenly, disregarding the gun, I came to a halt and twisted to face him. 'Was it you?' I spat at him. 'Did you drive the car that killed Jim?'

He let go of me long enough to slap me across the face, so hard that I fell to my knees; then he hauled me up and slapped me again.

'Get walking, you little cow,' he shouted. 'I obey orders, that's what I do. Go on – get going.'

I turned and stumbled on, my face stinging with the force of his blows. I'd made him angry; not, perhaps the wisest thing under the circumstances, but at least I felt I knew for sure now what had happened to Jim, and who had been driving the car. I had no doubt that it was Joe. I was so angry, so full of loathing for this man, that any pain I felt seemed unimportant.

The journey back seemed to go on for ever. I hadn't realised I'd run so far, but eventually I could see the old derelict barn looming out of the mist, the one across the yard from the larger place where I had been imprisoned.

We were just about to emerge from behind it when Joe came to a halt once more as we both heard the sound of vehicles turning into the yard. My heart gave a great leap of hope; this, surely, had to be the police.

Joe pulled me back behind the barn and slammed me against the wall.

'Keep still and keep your bleeding mouth shut,' he hissed in my ear. 'Put your hands flat on the wall and keep them there. I'll shoot if I have to.'

This time I felt less sure that he wouldn't carry out his threat. He was tough and brutal and had virtually admitted back there in the field that he had killed once and would cheerfully do so again. I therefore did as I was told, but I couldn't help thinking of the blanket tied to the window, evidence of my escape from that little room. If the police went inside the barn, as I assumed they would, they would surely see it. Or had Craven, or whoever the other man had been, have had time to get rid of it? He might have done. Would almost certainly have done, I concluded despondently. He would have known that with a telephone so conveniently at hand I would have called for help and would be expecting the police.

And here they were. I could hear voices calling to each other, the sound of an intercom, car doors slamming, someone hammering on the barn door. And here I was, so close and yet so helpless, with my hands on the wall at shoulder level and the gun held firmly in my back.

'They'll find—' I began.

'Shut it!' Joe pushed the gun against me even harder and with his other hand slammed my face into the wall, so forcibly that I gasped with the pain of it. 'Keep shtum, or you'll get worse than that!'

The pressure of the gun eased a little and I realised he was looking, with great caution, round the side of the building to see what was happening in the yard. It took him less than a second and I had no chance to take advantage of it by making any move to escape from him; however, I did manage to ease my position a little and in doing so I saw that, directly below me on the ground at my feet, there was a half-brick. If I could pick it up, I thought, it would make a weapon—

But there was to be no time, for whatever he had seen had made him decide to move away from the yard again. I wasn't surprised. It seemed logical to think that the police would make a search of the area if they were unable to find me inside the barn. Somehow I had to do something to stop him taking me far.

'Move,' he breathed in my ear, jabbing me again with the gun. I groaned and sagged against him, buckling a little at the knees. He attempted to haul me up with his left hand, but I was too heavy for him and he couldn't prevent me slowly subsiding to the ground as if in a dead faint.

The brick had to be within my reach. Joe was swearing under his breath, pulling at me, bending over to try to lift me. I groaned again and shifted my position, opening my eyes just enough to see the brick right there. I was almost touching it.

Now, I thought; and while he was lulled into ignoring the danger, distracted by trying to move me, I grabbed the brick, half rose and smashed it with all my strength against the hand that, loosely now, was holding the gun.

I heard his gasp of pain, but it meant

nothing to me. All I cared about was that he had dropped the gun. I grabbed at it, snatching it a split second before he was able to reach it with a hand that I was delighted to see was already bleeding profusely. Shakily I pointed it at him as I scrambled to my feet and backed away from him a little.

'Don't try anything,' I warned him. 'Believe me, I'd be happy to put a bullet through you.'

Without taking my eyes off him I backed still further so that I was clear of the building and in full view of the men in the yard.

'Help!' I screamed, still with the gun trained on him. 'I'm over here. Help me.'

I couldn't see them but I knew they were running towards me – two policemen just as tough-looking as Joe himself, I saw when they arrived. Unlike him, however, they were on my side.

'Take it,' I said, handing the gun to them. 'You can take over now.'

Five weeks later, I stood at the long windows at Fincote, looking out on the park that surrounded it as I waited for Steve to come and take me to Heathrow. Tim was in London, attending some important directors' meeting; Marian was in a nearby village, giving a talk on the subject of miniatures to the Women's Institute. I'd said my goodbyes, tried to express the extent of my gratitude. My bags were packed and standing in the hall. Soon I'd be winging my way across the Atlantic to tie up various things there. I would be visiting Caroline in Washington – a meeting I hoped would be the first of many, for we had spoken several times on the phone and had already established a good rapport. But there was also the sale of the New York apartment to arrange and the packing up of my belongings. For I was coming back to England. Had there really been any doubt that I would?

The daffodils were over now, but there were magnificent rhododendrons on each side of the drive that led up to the gates, and splashes of colour nearer the house from tulips and forget-me-nots and bright pink azaleas. Easy to wonder how my mother could have walked away from all of this.

Five weeks, and it seemed as if I'd always known Fincote. Tim had said that of course I must stay with them. I needed cosseting, he said, and Marian had agreed and welcomed me here as warmly as anyone could have wished. Davina had been here too, and we had become friends. Suddenly, unexpectedly, I'd found a wonderfully supportive family.

'You will be back, won't you?' Davina said

now, coming into the room and joining me at the window.

'You'd better believe it!'

'And you're really feeling OK? No more horrors?'

For there had been horrors. I'd suffered from nightmares for a while, but was calm again now, simply thankful that my un-looked-for adventure had ended happily.

'I'm fine,' I said. 'Thanks to all of you. And especially now I know that Rose is being looked after properly. I was worried about her.'

'No need to be. Dad will make sure she's all right.'

'He's a good man.'

'I told you!'

'My mother wouldn't have been right for him, you know. I was just thinking about her and wondering how she could have borne to leave this place, but I'm sure she did the right thing. She was lively and amusing and very attractive, but she was just too restless to settle here. Country life would have killed her.'

'My mother loves it. Can't stand London.'

'Well, there you are,' I said vaguely, turning to the window again. 'I guess life has a way of working itself out.'

I hoped I was right. My thoughts turned to Quigley and the Cravens and Higginson and Joe, hoping they would all get their just

314

deserts. I had enough faith in British justice to think that they would, for they were on remand and eventually they would be standing trial not only for fraud and kidnapping, but murder as well. And there was talk of money laundering, too, in their dealings with America. Tim assured me that they were likely to be put away for a long time.

'Here comes Steve,' Davina said, as the battered old station wagon came into view. She laughed, but with affection. 'You're going to have to do something about that car.'

How little she knew him!

'He likes it,' I said.

I went to meet him. Davina, as always, was the soul of tact and lingered somewhere in the hall as I stood on the top step waiting for him to get out of the car and come up to me. He was smiling as he bent and kissed me.

'All set?' he asked.

'Just about. My bags are inside.'

'I'll put them in the car. We'd better get a move on, sweetheart. I was held up on the motorway.'

Neither of us moved, though. We just stood there – his hands on my shoulders, my arms around his waist, looking at each other as if we wanted to learn each other by heart before we were separated – as if we hadn't done so already! I noted the shape of his

315

face, those winging brows over the clear grey eyes, his mouth, his smile.

'I approve of that,' I said.

He laughed.

'Approve of what?'

I could have said 'of the way you look', but knew it would embarrass him.

'Of being your sweetheart.'

He bent his head and kissed me again.

'I'm glad,' he said. 'Because if I have my way, you'll be filling the role for a long, long time.'

Still I didn't move. I was wondering what my mother would have said about having an Englishman as my partner. In every sense of the word. Would she have accepted that I had to go my own way? That whatever prejudices she had cherished, whatever memories of past wrongs, I belonged to another time and another generation? Would she forgive me for finding so much happiness in the country she had firmly turned her back on?

Yes, I thought. I think she'd understand and accept. She would expect me to forge my own road in life and stand by my own opinion, for after all, I was her daughter, wasn't I?

'We really must go,' Steve said, gently and with love. Davina joined us in the hall as he picked up my bags, and we said goodbye, hugging each other with genuine affection.

'Come back soon,' she said, and I swore that I would.

I took one last look at the lovely old house, and followed Steve down the steps to the car. And as I did so, I could swear I heard one small, indomitable, intolerant Yankee ghost give a sigh of resignation.